The Place of the Herons

The Place of the Herons

... *a story of taboo obsession*

Patricia Herington

authorHOUSE®

AuthorHouse™ UK Ltd.
1663 Liberty Drive
Bloomington, IN 47403 USA
www.authorhouse.co.uk
Phone: 0800.197.4150

Published by AuthorHouse   03/12/2014

ISBN: 978-1-4817-8724-6 (sc)
ISBN: 978-1-4817-8725-3 (hc)
ISBN: 978-1-4817-8726-0 (e)

Library of Congress Control Number: 2014902670

Acknowledgements

I would like to thank Alan Burnell, Post Adoption Centre; Mary McLaughlin, Ealing Hospital Maternity Unit. and Christina Tom-Johnson, S.A.N.D.S. who kindly gave me help with my research. My gratitude also to Pauline Callow for invaluable advice and to daughter Barbara Kevan, Suzette Stratton and Christopher Haken for their assistance in producing this book.

For Mike.

Celebrations

Earthquakes demolish with no warning.

Chris raises his glass to Verina and freezes. His happy anniversary speech flies out of his mind. She looks unfamiliar, her face is distorted somehow, as if she's very tense—*is it the lighting in this place?* "What's the matter?"

She shakes her head.

"Have I done something? Or not done something? Tell me what's upset you. Wait a minute! That phone call, just as the cab arrived, who was it? Not that customer again?"

Staring past him she sighs, "It was my son."

"What? Something to do with Greg?"

"Not Greg. Another son . . . One I haven't told you about."

"I'm not with you. I don't understand what you're saying."

"Of course you don't. I'm sorry. This is going to spoil our special evening."

He can't see her face, she's rubbing her brow with her fingers.

"Please explain Vee, I'm floundering here."

"I'll try and tell it quickly to get it over with. I had a baby when I was a schoolgirl and they made me have him adopted. And now he's found me. That was him on the phone."

"Christ! . . . Why've you never told me? I thought we didn't have secrets."

"I'm sorry Chris, I wish I had told you. I always meant to eventually. At first, I was frightened you might not believe me—how it happened, I mean. I had a best friend at school, Jane, and she invited me to a party at her house. The other people there were all older than us, friends of her brothers from

1

University. There was a lot of drinking going on and we were not supposed to have any alcohol. Being daft girls, we dared each other to try a little wine. It made me woozy and I had to ask for some water. Someone gave me orange-juice. The next thing I knew I was waking up in bed in the spare room. All I could remember about the night before, was feeling sleepy, after dancing madly with Jane, curling up in an armchair and resting my head in a cushion. I assumed I had fallen asleep and that Jane must have looked after me. Sometime after that, I found I was pregnant."

"How old were you?"

"Not quite fifteen."

"Oh God. And you had no idea who . . .? She shook her head. "Was there any attempt to discover the culprit?"

"Not really. It would have been very difficult."

"It was obviously somebody who knew the house. Maybe one of your friend's brothers?"

"Chris, my parents asked these same questions. They were impossible to answer. I was in such a turmoil of terror and shame, anger and powerlessness. My mother wanted it all hushed-up anyway in case people thought I'd brought it on myself. But I hadn't been messing about or flirting with anyone. At that age I was much too shy. I think whoever gave me the spiked orange-juice knew what he was about; created an opportunity and made the most of it. I couldn't believe what had happened to me or why."

"What did you do?"

"I obeyed my mother. I had no choice. I didn't want to have a baby. I was sent away from home to stay with a dear aunt until the birth . . . He was a perfectly beautiful child and I fell in love with him but was made to give him up straight away for adoption. Which was of course, the best thing to do in the circumstances. I had to accept that I would never see him again."

She falls silent. Chris is thoughtful.

"I'm glad you know now. I've always had a guilt about not telling you but it never seemed the right moment. In the beginning, I didn't want to spoil things. Didn't want to risk losing you. I know now you would have believed me and would have been kind. Even so, I was afraid the truth might hurt you. I hope I haven't lost your trust, telling you so late?"

"You know what? I think we'd better start this evening over again," Chris raises his glass "Happy anniversary anyway."

"Thank you Chris, Happy anniversary."

"How did the lad trace you?"

"He didn't tell me."

"Now he wants to see you?"

"Yes."

"Only natural I suppose." He pushes his fork into his plate, the scallops taste like soda. "How do you feel about meeting him?"

"Terrified. Excited. Unprepared. He probably thinks I abandoned him. Rejected him."

"You were just a kid. You can explain you didn't have any choice . . . You don't have to see him if you don't want to."

"I do and I don't. I'm in shock. But I suppose I owe him something. You can't say no to your own child, can you?"

"What does he sound like?"

"Well-educated. Polite. His adoptive parents have obviously done their best for him. He tells me he's married and his wife's expecting a baby." She looks as if she's about to cry. "Oh Chris. I never foresaw this—that he would trace me and want to come and see me. I sometimes wondered if we might meet by accident."

"Did you? You still think of him then although we've got Cass and Nan and Greg?"

"Because we've got Cass and Nan and Greg. Occasionally, I'll catch sight of a young man at the bus-stop or in the library and fantasise about him being my son and knowing who he is, without him knowing who I am. But the last thing I want is to have anything or anyone causing ripples for you and me or the children."

"How did you leave things with him?"

"I said I'd have to talk to you and I'd ring him tomorrow. What I really need is time to take it in."

The waiter realises they have lost interest in their seafood, quietly removes their plates and pours more Champagne.

"No wonder you're in a state. Are you going to tell the children?"

"I have to, don't I?"

"How much will you tell them?"

3

"As much as I think they need to know. The truth always protects. Better they hear it from me. Oh God! Cass is not much older than I was then . . . Chris . . . this hasn't changed things between us, has it?"

"I have to confess that I'm as much in shock now as you are but we'll cope. We always do."

The waiter brings their next course.

She puts out her hand and Chris holds it tight. "Come on, give your old man a smile and try to eat your dinner."

—

It's quiet in the kitchen now the children have gone out. Chris passes his cup to Verina for more coffee. "So what have you arranged?"

"Monday. He's taking the day off and we're going to meet in the foyer of the Shaw Theatre."

"Why there?"

"Well, he said he'd be coming into Kings Cross. I didn't feel like meeting him on a station platform so somewhere on Euston Road seemed a good idea. I thought it wouldn't be too crowded and we'd be able to find each other easily. I can just stroll down from Warren Street . . . Why're you looking like that? You do see I have to go by myself, don't you?"

"Won't you need my moral support?"

"I hope not. He is my son. Besides, it's going to be an ordeal for him to meet his mother, it might be a bit much to have his stepfather there as well."

"I'd have thought my presence would help both of you. The whole thing could prove embarrassing."

She drinks her coffee and puts down her cup with a sigh. "I want to say something but it's difficult . . . You mention embarrassment and I am very shy about this meeting. If you came too, I'd be doubly uncomfortable. I can't explain why."

He makes himself smile at her "As long as you don't get upset. You will ring me if you need me, won't you? You could always jump in a taxi and come to the office."

"Of course. Thank you for understanding."

Cassie has just been reading her essay to him. "Mum's going to meet whatsisname on Monday, right?"

4

"Yes."

"Daddy, I'm the eldest. I've always been the eldest."

He swings his chair round and opens his arms to her "You're getting almost too big to sit on my lap nowadays."

She speaks into his neck "I know but I need a cug."

"Listen sweetheart, new situations aren't necessarily threatening. Let's not start worrying until we've got something to worry about. Mummy is a wise person, I think we can trust her to handle things carefully."

Verina calls them all for tea. She's buttering toasted tea-cakes when Nan sits down with a clatter and asks "Mum, who were you married to before you married dad?"

"I wasn't married."

"But you said you had a baby."

Verina shoots a glance at Chris who nods.

"I'll try and explain. I went to a party at a school friend's house. Her brothers were at university so everyone was older than us. The parents weren't there and there was a lot of drinking going on, which we weren't used to. We did have some wine though and I began to feel woozy and asked for water. Someone gave me orange juice but there must have been something in it because it knocked me out cold and I don't remember anything else about the party."

"What do you mean mummy, drugs?"

"Or alcohol. I don't know Cass. I had a vague memory of resting my head on a cushion and the next thing I knew, it was morning and I was in the spare room. I thought I had somehow put myself to bed. I didn't think about it again. Then after some weeks had gone by, I found I was going to have a baby. I knew it wasn't possible, that I hadn't done anything . . . so I couldn't understand. Then I thought about the party and decided something must have happened to me there and I told granny and granpa."

"And grandpa's a Vicar! Oh poor mummy. You must have been frightened to death."

"I was. And horrified and angry and ashamed."

Chris leans over to help himself to more toasted bun, "You didn't have anything to be ashamed about. Some bastard took advantage of you."

"What did granny say?"

5

"Granny was grim. It was as much a shock for her as for me. She didn't really know quite what to do."

Nan moves her chair nearer to Verina and links arms with her. "It must have been awful. Did they find out who did it?"

"No. There was an upset between the two families. I lost my friend and granny and grandpa couldn't have anyone in the parish knowing about it, so they sent me away to stay with an aunt." She shares out the last of the buns onto the children's plates.

"Then when the baby came someone bought it for adoption?"

"Yes Greg, he was adopted."

"Hey, this means I'm not your only son."

"But you are my special one."

Greg hurries round to squeeze her neck and kiss her "And you're my special mum."

"He's grown up now and married and his wife's expecting a baby."

"Will that baby be one of our relations?"

"Of course silly-billy, it'll be mummy's grand-child."

"You don't know everything Nan. What will it be to us then Cass?"

"A niece or nephew. We're going to be aunts and uncles."

"What did he have to ring up for?"

"You've had your father and mother all your life. Imagine knowing you had a parent somewhere you'd never seen, don't you think you'd want to see them? Wouldn't you want to see the person you really belong to? He's not going to upset our lives. He's got his own."

"Will he be coming here though?"

"I don't know yet. It depends how things turn out. He might not like me. I might not like him."

"He'll love you to bits mum. I've always been your only son. I expect he'll try and take you away from us."

"No he won't Greg. No-one could ever take me away from all of you."

"When I grow up, if I ever find that bastard, I'll kill him."

"Nan!" Everybody laughs.

Verina is not in the studio. Chris finds her still in the kitchen quietly weeping. "Oh don't Vee. You were very brave"

"I didn't enjoy telling them. They'll never see me in the same way again."

"Of course they will. It's like a story out of history to them. It's too remote for them to really be able to connect it all with you."

"Do you think so? Even for Cassie? I hope it's not going to make them feel insecure."

"I don't see why it should."

"Perhaps it's because I feel so wobbly myself."

"Well, you don't know what to expect. Neither does your son. He's in for a wonderful surprise. He won't believe it when he sees what a beautiful mother he's got and when he finds out what a special person she is."

"You're biased. Unhand me, I must do another hour's work before I start on supper."

—

Chris looks at his watch. Ten o'clock—*Vee will be coming out of the tube now, crossing over to Euston Road—walking along the pavement to find him—the bombshell—and she's shut me out—gone off to start a new phase in her life that's nothing to do with me—just as well she didn't let me go with her—you can never tell how things will turn out—if I don't like the boy, or the children don't, it'll cause problems—I already don't like him—don't want to meet him—don't want him anywhere near my life—anywhere near my children—far as I'm concerned, he's surplus to requirements—an intrusion—let's open the window, get some air in here.*

In the courtyard below, the sun picks out points of glitter in the grey flagstones, white and bronze chrysanthemums overflow their pots, the office cat, stretched along the ivy-padded wall, is fast asleep.

She'll probably ring me at lunch-time—I won't go out, someone's sure to be going for sandwiches—will she bring Alex home with her?—got to get used to using his name—accepting his reality—suppose she doesn't like him?—there's no chance he won't like her he'll take one look at her and . . . Christ! he might get a crush on her, like that apprentice she took on—what a performance!—the love letters—the tears—I know she never did anything to encourage him but it was disquieting—perhaps I'm too possessive—must try and be pleased for Vee.—hope things are going well for her this

7

morning—wish she'd ring, if only to tell me they've met up and she's happy—funny, I would never have guessed she had any secrets in her past—I suppose we all keep some things hidden from each other— hope she's not disappointed now she's got him back—at least this meeting should give her the opportunity to explain herself—why were there no adults there keeping an eye out at that bloody party?—catch us leaving our lot unprotected with drinking going on—we don't want any babies—Vee never thought hers would be any problem, it was just a painful shadow in the past—now it's become substance in the present—she'll probably be all right with it but to me, it's a threat—I'm going to have to prove how big a man I really am—can't visualise what to expect—will we have to spread out to make space for the newcomer—newcomers?—Alex's wife as well?—wonder what she's like?—he'll probably be all right—Verina is his mother even if she hasn't brought him up—should be making notes for tomorrow's meeting—do I care if we're promoting yet another beauty product for the older woman?—no I don't—everyone wants it to be yesterday—including me.

———

As he puts his key in the lock, a Cabbage White flutters past his eyes. In the house, he calls out "Vee?" but it's Chloé in the kitchen and a smell of burning toast. He pushes the lever up to release the blackened bread. "It doesn't pop up any more, I'm afraid."

"So I see now," Chloé smiles. "Sorry to invade your kitchen Chris but Vee asked me to. She's on her way home but she remembered that Cassie has a net-ball practice so she rang and asked me to give Greg and Nan some tea. You're early, aren't you?"

"Yes. I've brought some work home. I couldn't settle in the office today." He's immediately irritated for giving himself away and more so because Verina's not home yet.

"I've made some supper."

"This is kind of you Chloé."

"Oh it's nothing. It is a special day after all."

"Ah. Verina's told you."

"Yes. It's exciting, isn't it?"

"Yes." He sighs, "I suppose it is."

"You're not worried, are you? You've got nothing to worry about."

"Of course not. I know. I wish Vee would come home that's all. Did she say how long she is going to be? I mean, they've been together since ten thirty this morning."

Chloé puts a cup of tea in front of him, touches his shoulder and sits facing him. "They've got a lot to catch up on. She'll be home soon and you'll hear all about it."

"I am happy for her Chlo."

"I'm sure you are."

Nan comes rushing in. "Dad, look at Greg's hands, he says he's washed them."

"I have. Nan doesn't realise my skin is getting darker."

Chloé exchanges a grin with Chris and steers Greg to the sink and puts soap in his hands, "You can wash them again here."

Chris absent-mindedly eats as much marmite toast as the children.

Before going home, Chloé lifts the lid from a saucepan to show him steaming meat-balls.

"Chloé you're an angel. They smell delicious—all that lovely garlic."

"Vee won't want to cook when she gets in. There's rice in the pressure—cooker and there's some salad." She makes a charming little gesture with her spread fingers, "It's all just fill-belly but I hope it tastes good." She kisses his cheek and hurries off.

In his study, he unpacks his brief-case and settles down to try and do some work. Nan and Greg are playing in the garden. He listens to them, marvelling at how Nan can be fourteen with Cassie and nine with Greg. They are totally absorbed in their game. He wishes he could concentrate on something but he can't *shall I have a drink?—bit early and work'll go out the window—Vee might have phoned—where can they be?—what have they been doing all day?—Vee will be asking millions of questions— she'll want to know all about him—her face is so animated when she's interested in what you're saying—if she shares your thought, she interrupts to agree and the dark eyes keep changing expression—still fascinates me after all these years—her smiles, her attention will be for her son today—mustn't begrudge the boy—she'll come home brimming with her story.* The phone rings. He rushes to answer

It's Cassie. "Dad, can I stay and have supper with Gemma? Here's her mum."

"Ah Chris, you're home". Angela always speaks slowly as though she spends her life calming people down. "The girls are starving after their net-ball and I've made macaroni cheese for Africa. Cass can eat here if it's all right with you? I'll sit them straight down to their homework afterwards and Don will walk Cassie home no later than nine. All right?"

"Yes of course. Thank you Angela."

He looks at his watch, six thirty on what is beginning to seem the longest day of his life *even Cassie has forgotten—or has she?—perhaps she's staying out of the house on purpose* He wanders into the kitchen again and looks out of the window. Greg is sitting on a branch of the apple tree, the leaves are just turning yellow. Nan is standing by one of the cages cuddling her guinea pig. Does he want another cup of tea? He lifts the lid of the saucepan to smell the meat-balls again.

Greg comes in and helps himself to two bananas, "One's for Nan."

"Okay."

"You all right dad?"

"Sure."

Greg pats him on the leg.

The steamer is making a faint bubbling and there's a quiet hum from the electric clock on the wall. He hears the tick of a taxi and the slam of its door. No time to get back in his study and pretend to be working. He stays by the kitchen table listening to himself blowing out breath.

Verina at last. "Hallo. 'Sorry I've been so long." She kisses him and throws her jacket over a chair. Her cheeks are flushed.

"You've been drinking."

"Of course I have. I've been celebrating. And I mean to do some more celebrating now with you." She rattles through bottles in the pantry and emerges with a Gewurztraminer, "Into the fridge with you. Ooh. What's that lovely smell?"

"Chloé's made supper, meat-balls and rice and so on."

"She's a star."

"So? What's he like?"

"Oh Chris. He's wonderful. Wait 'til you see him. If you and I had drawn a blue-print of the kind of son we'd like, he'd be it."

"More than our Greg you mean?"

"Don't be silly."

She starts taking plates out of the cupboard.

"So it all went well."

"So well, I can't quite believe it. I'll have to try and get my thoughts in some sort of order so that I can tell you all about him."

"I was worried for you."

"Were you? Well, you needn't have been."

He goes off to his study for a Vodka. *She looks so happy—no use kidding myself I'm going to get any work done tonight.* He can hear the clatter in the kitchen and Greg and Nan asking eager questions. When he walks back in, the children are laying the table, Verina is serving the rice and the windows are steamed up as always. Verina comes round the table to him "I've so much to tell you. Where's Cass?"

He hugs her. "Don's bringing her back later. She's had supper with Gemma."

"Mum can we have supper now, I'm starving."

"Of course, Greg."

"And I want to hear about our big brother."

"Do you Nan? Perhaps I ought to wait for Cassie so as not to have to say everything all over again."

The children won't let her and Chris can see she's dying to talk about Alex in any case.

Nan wants to know what he looks like.

"He's tall—almost as tall as daddy. And the complete opposite of me, he's blond with greenish eyes and he's very handsome."

"As handsome as dad?"

"No, of course not. And not quite as good-looking as you either Greg."

Nan snorts but Greg is pleased.

"He's nice. He likes to laugh. It's quite difficult describing people really, you need to see them. Which reminds me," she gets up to find her bag "I told him you would all want to know what he looks like and I dragged him in to one of those passport-photo booths. Look" she hands the strip of photos to Chris. Shining hair, good teeth. In the last snap, Verina is laughing over Alex's shoulder, her cheek against his. It's like a sharp kick in the stomach—*teenagers on a day out.*

11

"Let's see dad" the children grab the snaps and are delighted with their new brother. "When's he coming to see us mum?"

"On Sunday. All right Chris?"

He feels sick. "Of course. Is he bringing his wife?"

"Oh yes."

"What does he do for a living?"

"He's in computers, I don't really understand what he does exactly but he seems to earn a lot of money. Faith's a lecturer. His wife," she explains to the children. Before their bed-time, Verina tries to supply all the information she has gathered during the day. When Cassie gets home, much of it is repeated by Nan and Greg and confirmed or amended by Verina. The two younger children go off to bed excited and making up a song about finding a long, lost brother who will do all their homework and fight any bullies. Cassie, by contrast, seems subdued.

"Anything wrong sweetie?"

"No mum. I'm just a bit tired. I had an essay to write tonight. I've done it."

She doesn't mention the 'quiet word' Angela had with her while they waited for Don to finish talking on the phone to a patient. She hadn't quite understood what Angela was talking about and partly resented her saying anything at all about their private family business.

"This sort of thing can be a bit traumatic Cass—a bit upsetting. It depends how things are handled of course and on the personalities of the people concerned. Yours is a stable family, I'm sure everything will be fine. But if you're ever worried about anything dear and need a friend to talk to, don't hesitate to come to us."

Cassie was so surprised she didn't know how to reply but Don came out of his surgery at that moment to walk her home.

—

Chris and Verina finally have the sitting room to themselves.

"You've had a momentous day."

"Yes I have. And a very happy one. I was very nervous at first and then delightfully surprised. I think he's as pleased with me as I am with him."

"I'm sure he is. I'm glad for you. The one thing I feared was that he might be a disappointment."

"Well he certainly isn't that."

From the dreamy look on her face, Chris knows she's reliving the day. He makes desultory notes in a pad on his knee, now and then glancing at Verina. He doesn't want to spoil her mood but he can't wait any longer.

"So how did you actually spend your day? You didn't tell us what it was like meeting Alex and so on."

"It's odd but I knew him immediately, the mother—rabbit thing I suppose. I saw this young man looking at photographs of actors. He had his back to me, I went up to him and said 'Alex?' and it was him."

"Had he described himself and told you what he'd be wearing?"

"Vaguely but the other youngsters standing round were in jeans and sweatshirts too. I think he expected me to be pudding-shaped with grey hair and sensible shoes."

"What did you do then?"

"Let me think, we walked up Euston Road, down Tottenham Court Road and into Soho talking all the time. We found somewhere in Old Compton Street to have some coffee and we just talked and talked and stared at each other. I'm sure if people noticed us, some would have thought he was my toy-boy. We had no trouble communicating, it was as if we'd always known each other. It was lovely. No shyness really. The waiters began to look at us a bit menacingly and we realised we'd been there for ages so we ordered some lunch and that satisfied them. After lunch we wandered around a bit until we found a nice little pub and sat in there for a while. When it began to fill up and get smoky, we went to find a cup of tea. I rang Chloé and soon after that I came home. It's been an unreal day, all a bit of a blur. I expect it is for him too. Although it's all marvellous, it is a bit of a strain. It'll be interesting to see how it all shakes down tomorrow. I need to go to bed. You ready?"

"Sure am."

They look in on the children and once their bedroom door is closed, he takes her in his arms to reclaim her.

"Will you still love me when I'm a grandmother?"

"When is it?"

"Sometime in spring."

"I may have to trade you in. I think I'm too young to be a grandfather."

They fall asleep with her head on his chest as usual.

—

The whole family comes out on to the steps as Verina opens the door. In something of a muddle, they all get themselves back in to the house with their visitors. Alex gives Verina an enormous bouquet, pink and orange Gerberas, large white daisies and several kinds of greenery. He introduces Faith. She is slender and pale, not yet showing the bloom of pregnancy. She smiles at Verina and hands her a bag, "We've brought you some wine and some goodies for the children. Hope they're allowed."

Verina, clasps her flowers and the bag and kisses Faith's cheek. "Thank you. I'll go and put these in water."

Alex, flashes a smile at the children "So these are my sisters and brother. I hope you don't mind suddenly having a new grown-up brother. It's great for me. I've always been an only child—like Faith. We'd have liked brothers and sisters, wouldn't we Faith?"

"Yes."

Verina has arranged the flowers in a tall vase on a table in the window and sits down to admire them

"We're only half-sisters and half-brother really." Nan is solemn.

Greg stands by Verina's chair gazing at Alex "We've all got the same mother though, that's what counts."

Chris examines him too *so here he is, the found who was lost—can see why Verina is so pleased with him—straight off a magazine cover—fitness magazine—shining with health—good-looking—no slouch in the charm department either, look at Verina's face!*

Alex has just complimented Verina on the speed and success of her flower arranging. "It's the shape of the vase, it does it for you." She's as radiant as if he's just given her a prize.

To make Faith feel comfortable, Chris asks her if she would like some tea or coffee. "Thank you. Tea would be nice." A faint flush comes to her face as she meets his eyes. *A natural girl, my mother would have called her. A delicately pretty, natural girl.*

The children stare at her and Alex, fascinated. Chris goes off to make tea.

Cassie gets fruit juice for Nan and Greg. The business of sorting out how people like their tea, passing round sugar and milk breaks down the slight stiffness between them all.

Nan and Greg both talk at once to Alex who laughingly tries to divide his attention fairly between them.

Faith has been answering Verina's questions to do with the baby. She stands up. "Please excuse me. I need to stretch my back."

Chris offers to show her the garden. Greg dashes after them, calling back to Alex "You come and see our animals."

"Right."

Nan jumps up and follows the others. "Don't disturb my guinea pig—she's pregnant like Faith."

Verina catches Cassie's eye and laughs softly.

"Wow mum! Wait til Gemma sees him!"

"Won't do her any good. She's too young and besides, he's married."

"Yes . . . They don't really go together though mum, do they? Do you think they do?"

"How do you mean?"

"They don't sort of . . . match."

"You've only spent about five minutes with them."

"I know. You and dad do . . . look right together I mean. They don't seem to . . . to me."

Chris and Faith are back.

"I must go and do something about lunch" Verina says as Chris comes back in and Faith offers to help. "You can come and do the beans if you like."

Chris picks up the paper. Cassie starts clearing cups and plates on to a tray.

"How do you like your big brother Cass?"

"Don't know yet. He's smashing looking."

He slips a Weber Clarinet Concerto into the player—*let's have optimistic music—now the lad's actually here, everything seems almost as usual—suppose there was nothing to worry about really— pleasant enough—though an air about him that suggests he's used to being indulged—probably his adoptive parents over-compensated—he*

15

and Faith seem to have slotted in—the children have accepted them apparently—in any case, they don't live round the corner so they're not likely to be coming in and out every five minutes.

—

Cassie and Gemma are on their way to school.

"I'll tell you why I'm fed up Gem. Saturday, right? I'm in the kitchen with dad and mum and Nan brings the letters in. Mum opens hers and says 'What fun! Just for filling in that questionnaire Chris, I've won a trip for two on The Orient Express.' I thought she was kidding at first. Then my mind goes lickety-spit, dad won't be able to go—he's always too busy—she'll take me. But oh no, she straightaway says 'I'll take Alex.' She didn't even ask us. I looked at dad and he had that shut-in expression he gets."

"D'you mean they're going abroad, to the Far East and all that?"

"Don't be daft. It's only a day trip—in England. You go into the country, that's all. But the food is supposed to be smashing and the train itself is all done up like the original Orient Express. Mum says that's an experience in itself."

"Perhaps Alex won't be able to go. He might have to work. He might get ill or something. In any case, if it's only a day out . . . ."

"That's not the point."

"Yeah. I suppose my mum wouldn't want to go without dad."

"Exactly."

"Would your dad like to have gone?"

"He wasn't invited. Neither was I and I'd have loved it."

—

"Faith? Hallo, it's me, Verina. How are you?"

"Fine thanks. And you?"

"Yes. Look, I'm ringing to say that although I murmured something about this week-end, actually, we won't be around. We're going down to visit my parents. I haven't told them yet about Alex and you. It's not something I want to tell them on the telephone."

"They're going to be very surprised. They'll be pleased for you—about Alex I mean. And Verina, you musn't feel you've got to have us every week-end. You need a break from us now and then."

"Oh, we love to have you as often as possible. I only wish you lived nearer. Is Alex there?"

"He's gone to the gym. Shall I get him to call you back?"

"No, don't bother. I'll catch him on his mobile. We'll probably all get together the week-end after next, if you're free. Give him my love and explain about the parents."

Alarms

They are having a chat in the conservatory, crisp curls of dry leaves around their feet. "I repeat I'm most dismayed" the old man says. "I'm sorry Verina but it strikes me as a situation fraught with danger,"

"What on earth do you mean?"

"You may be taking a viper to your bosom."

"Alex is not a viper."

"What I mean is, you know nothing about him. You can't possibly know what goes on in his head, how he grew up, what tendencies he revealed. Your relationship can only be a sham."

"Father!"

"Listen, you call him son and he calls you mother, they're just words. They don't mean what those words usually mean. They can't. You are not his mother, except in the sense that you gave birth to him—or rather, the child you were did. Now you are somebody completely different. You are two strangers who happen to share blood, that's all. I've been a priest long enough to know that blood ties can mean absolutely nothing. You can never be mother and son, you've missed out on that. You have to face up to the fact and accept it."

"You always say it's never too late. He and I already operate as mother and son. It's as if we've always been together. He and Faith, his wife, have become part of the family quite naturally."

"One day, he'll turn on you and accuse you of abandoning him."

"Father, I can't understand why you're so angry. I suppose it's because you're anxious but you've no need to be, honestly."

"This is going to be a blow to your mother."

"She ought to be happy for me. Alex is a splendid young man. She'll love him."

"You don't know what she went through, goes through . . . I know you suffered my dear."

The smell of geraniums is overpowering. She pushes the door open to let in sweet air from the garden and sinks back into the old wicker chair. As a child, she spent happy hours reading in this very chair which creaked delightfully as she snuggled down among the safety of its cushions.

"I don't want your mother upset. She hasn't been well."

"What's been wrong? Anything serious? How do you know my news won't cheer her up—make her feel things turned out all right after all? Surely I have to tell her? I want to tell her."

He sighs. "Of course she must be told but with your permission, I should like to be the one to tell her. There's nothing seriously the matter, it's mainly that she's worn out from helping me and parishioners' problems get her down"

"All right then, you tell her when you think the moment is right. But I can't see why you attach so much importance to . . . ."

"Don't you?"

"Of course I do. It is important to me. My son has been given back to me. Someone who has been missing from my life all these years. It's a cause for celebration not doom and gloom."

"Go carefully. You may be wrong."

"Why? This is all very depressing."

He's looking out onto the garden, apparently trying to sort out what he wants to say. A wasp buzzes around as Verina waits for him to continue.

"Your mother was waiting up for me that night. A parishioner, a dear friend, was dying. I sat with him and his family until the end. I had the car of course. I seem to think no clear arrangement had been made about whether or not you'd be staying at Jenny's—you so often did. Anyway, your mother felt concerned for some reason and when I got back, she decided to take the car and go to collect you. By the time she got there, the house was in darkness, everybody had gone to bed. She has never forgiven herself for being lackadaisical and just assuming you would be properly looked after. She still has bad dreams. Your marriage to Chris made her happy, especially

19

when the beloved grand-children came along. Yet in spite of all that and after all this time, she often says she should have given in to her instinct that something was wrong that night and gone much earlier to get you in a taxi and prevented what she calls 'all that beastliness for Verina.' It lives with her all the time."

"It wasn't her fault."

"She feels she didn't take proper care of you."

"She can forget all about that now. She'll feel differently when I bring Alex down to see her."

"No!"

His growl frightens her.

"You can't do that to her. I won't allow it."

"I don't understand father. Why not? Once you've explained to her. I'm sorry but you're really not making much sense."

"I expect, over the years, you've been able to push all the sorry business to the back of your mind?"

"I had to."

"I'm not reproaching you dear girl. Of course you had to. You may find this hard to believe, but your poor mother has never been able to do that—push it to the back of her mind. That's what I'm trying to make you realise. She remembers every day. If you like, it has stained her whole life."

"Stained? D'you mean it's become a neurosis?"

"Guilt can do that to someone with an over-scrupulous conscience. I've done everything in my power to release her from it. I even arranged for her to receive some counselling some years back, please don't ever tell her I told you. It wasn't much use, she hasn't been able to arrive at self-forgiveness. You are her only—beloved—child and she failed you, she thinks, by being too trusting. Making you go through with the adoption compounded her sin."

"You didn't tell her that, did you?"

"No. But I did want you to stay with us in your own home to be cared for and loved, with the child."

Verina touches his hand, "Thanks dad. It would have made things awkward for you both if I had. Mother sent me away for my sake. She was trying to salvage my life."

"It was partly for her sake too, she admits she couldn't bear to have a child around who would be a living reproach."

"You've given me a bit of a shock father. Mother always seems happy, especially when we're all together."

"Oh she is but deep down inside, she feels the relationship she has with you and her grand-children is a blessing she doesn't deserve."

"This is dreadful. I had no idea poor mum had these negative feelings. It's hard on you I expect. But think for a minute, isn't this all the more reason for her to meet her new grand-son and see that, after all, something very good has come out of it?"

"I'm not sure that she would regard your son as something good that has come out of it."

"Well, she hasn't met him yet."

"You know, your mother has some funny ideas. She believes, for instance, that the way in which a child is conceived will affect its character . . . This will be painful for you but your mother was relieved when the baby was adopted, she was expecting it to grow up into someone nasty."

His words tie them both into stillness and silence. The afternoon sun burns down on them through the glass. The wasp is still frantically managing to miss the open door.

Verina says quietly "Alex is not someone nasty. Chris accepts him."

"Does he have any choice?"

"That's not fair. He likes him. So do the children. I'm completely thrown by what you've told me about mother. I'm also bitterly disappointed. I come flying down here to share my wonderful news with you and you chuck cold water over me."

"I'm sorry my dear. But as I say, let me be the one to tell your mother. We have to go gently with these things. That means you too. No-one can foretell consequences. I hope for your sake, that your son will prove to be everything you say he is but give yourself time to get to know him gradually and truly. You will want and expect him to be wonderful so you may impose an image on him that isn't real. You'll find he's only human like the rest of us. Your Chris is a fine man. You've got a good, stable marriage and those three adorable children."

"Four!"

"Your mother and I would never want to see anything threaten your family's happiness. I know I'm not saying what you wish to hear today but I must tell you that I fear for you, I really do. And I'll pray. I've seen so many strange and unforeseen tragic happenings in my life and work."

"Forgive me father but do you think you sometimes let yourself be influenced by mother's . . . I don't know what to call it . . . pessimism? Superstition? I don't see why, given that we do have this good stable marriage, we shouldn't be able to accommodate one more family member."

He stares into her face without speaking.

"You'll tell mother anyway and let me know how she takes it?"

"I may not do so until after you've gone home."

"Whatever you think's best."

"You have understood, haven't you, that she may not be able to bring herself to meet your boy? Hers has been a long private struggle and she's getting on in years. We both are. As you get older and your bones stiffen up, something similar can happen to your thinking."

Verina watches her mother at the table. She looks relaxed as she pours tea. Her greying hair is drawn back in a knot but soft tendrils have come loose to frame her fresh, unlined face. Chatting and laughing with the children, she doesn't look as if she's getting on in years. However, when they leave, both parents stand at the doorway and Verina notices how tightly they grip hands.

—

Chris and Verina are getting ready for bed. "Are we taking Alex and Faith next time we go down?"

"I'm not sure that's going to happen for a while."

"Why not?"

"Well, the reason I asked you and the children not to say anything about Alex yet is because I haven't told mother. Dad wouldn't let me. He wants to tell her gently he says. It wouldn't surprise me if he decides not to tell her at all. We had a most peculiar conversation. It seems that mother has grieved all these years about what happened to me and blames herself."

"Not surprising."

"Apparently, she makes herself ill over it. I had no idea. So now he doesn't want her reminded and upset by being made to meet Alex. I ask you! I tried to tell him it might help her—you know, to see how well things have turned out after all—but he won't hear of it at present. I can't worry about it. They seem to live in their own weird little world, feeding each other's eccentricities. It was very disappointing but I'm not going to let anyone spoil things. They're both going a bit batty if you ask me.

—

They have almost finished supper when Chris arrives.

"We didn't wait for you. The children were starving as usual." Verina gets up and takes his plate of food from the oven.

Chris sits at the table "Fancy coming to Copenhagen with me Vee—just a couple of days?"

"When?"

"What about us?" Nan wants to know.

Cassie answers her "Chloé."

"Oh yeah. Good"

Chris takes out his pocket diary, "Early next month, the fourth to the seventh."

"Oh I can't. Don't you remember? I'm taking Alex on the Orient Express on the sixth. I'd love to have come otherwise. I've always wanted to see Copenhagen."

"Give the tickets to Alex then. Let him take Faith."

Verina is pulling the corners of her mouth down like a child, her head on one side.

"You'd rather go on a train ride with Alex than come to Copenhagen with me?"

"It's not that. He's looking forward to it—you know, a treat, a day out with his mum. You do see, don't you?"

—

Alex moves the television into the bedroom where Faith's resting. He switches it on but leaves the sound turned down while they wait for the film to start.

"You all right? Comfortable?"

"Yes thanks."

"Enough pillows?"

23

"Yes." She smiles at him "You are taking care of me."

"Well I don't want you squawking that you've got cramp in the middle of the film."

"You happy Alex?"

"Of course."

"I'm sorry to be a bit of a drag at times but with the pressure of work, I'm worn out in the evenings."

"Perhaps you should pack it in earlier?"

"Perhaps I should. My students have already asked me what they should do in an emergency. I think they're frightened by the size of my tummy and the baby's not due for weeks."

"After it's born, will your stomach go flat again?" He's adjusting the indoor aerial to get a better picture. "It will, won't it? I mean perhaps not straight away but you won't stay as you are now, will you?"

"Obviously not . . . do I look that awful?"

He's still busy with the aerial "Not awful . . . just a bit . . . clumsy, I suppose." He checks the time of the film. When he hears her murmur "Thanks", he turns round to look at her.

"Don't start, I probably don't mean 'clumsy'. You know I don't have your way with words. The film's starting in a minute. Let's enjoy it." He settles himself on the floor leaning against the end of the bed.

"This is the one Verina said we must be sure to see?"

"Yes."

"Which reminds me," she speaks to the back of his head, "have we got to go to the family again this week-end?" Bad move. She can tell from his back that he's annoyed.

"Got to? Nobody's got to go anywhere. I enjoy going. I thought you did."

"I do but I'd like it better if it was not taken for granted that we go every week-end. I don't like being tied down to the same thing all the time. It's different for you. The circumstances are special. But we shouldn't neglect Lilian and Phil and my parents. Also, you seem to forget that the week-end is the only time I have to do anything."

"Like what?"

"Like cleaning the flat, doing the laundry and so on."

"God Faith, you're so suburban. Is that really how you want to spend Saturday and Sunday?"

"No, of course not but while I'm still working . . . And I would like some time with you occasionally."

"At the family's," he's exasperated, "we're together for the whole week-end."

"We don't have any time by ourselves actually—I mean, just you and me."

"The film's going to start."

"I'm with the children all day and with Chris most evenings."

"The children love you."

"And I love them that's not what I'm complaining about. I think you ought to spend more time with them, you are supposed to be their brother."

"Do you want to see this film or not?"

"In the evenings you always go off to the studio with Verina, leaving Chris to look after me. It's a bit embarrassing actually. You want to watch he doesn't get fed up with you monopolising his wife."

He groans, "I don't monopolise her. If she has a job to finish, I like to keep her company while she's working. It gives us a chance to get to know each other without boring everyone else. I'm sure Chris understands that, if you don't."

He turns on the sound and music thunders over the film's title.

Faith gives up but things she still has to say clamour in her head *when did we last have a week-end at home?—I can hardly remember what we used to do—how we used to be—we seem to have lost our closeness somehow—no that's silly—what do I mean?—we've lost something . . . at the moment—special times?—yes, I think that's it—we don't have our special times any more—you're charming with Verina—but then I suppose she's more interesting than I am—the only time I get any charm is when you want me to cook something you like for dinner—I'm not your mother—Verina is—do you have to have two mothers?—actually, you've got three—Lilian couldn't be a better mother, adoptive or otherwise—we all look after you, how do you get us to do that?—you're a spoiled brat—will you grow up a bit when the baby's born?—God help us if there's anything wrong with it—if it isn't good-looking or something—you don't talk to me these days—no idea what you're thinking—if I want to discuss anything with you, you turn the telly on 'wait til the programme's over—by then, I've lost the impetus or I'm too tired—does pregnancy usually create distance between people?—dismal thought—that unattractive way of shrugging when I say things to you—you seem to find me stupid these days—keep telling me I'm getting whiney—don't think I am, it's just that you're impatient—'clumsy'! I know what that means—you think I'm graceless—well I didn't make this baby on my own—though I'm beginning to think I'll have to bring it up on my own for all the interest you show—you don't seem to care anymore what I'm feeling or thinking—watch it Faith!—mustn't let yourself get weepy—he'll lose his temper if he thinks you're working yourself up—as he puts it—surely it'll be better once the baby's here? you'll love your own child I hope—we'll have to grow up—be a proper family—you'll come back to me—our baby will distract you from Verina—create a balance—the beautiful Verina will be a granny then—that'll calm her down a bit—might make her behave more appropriately—she flirts with you and you flirt with her—Chris and I might just as well not be there half the time—I suppose you don't realise, the pair of you, how embarrassing and silly you look at times—always touching each other, holding hands, stroking each other's hair—it's nauseating, unhealthy—I suppose you'll get over all that eventually—I wish you'd talk to me about your feelings for Verina then perhaps I could help you adjust to this new relationship— give you some support at least—though I don't know what I could actually do, I'm inexperienced and ignorant here—as we all are—very strange and worrying—Chris feels as much at a loss as I do—doesn't give away much but I sense he's troubled—theirs was a great life til we came along—oh Alex, will you ever be able to accept that normal life means being here with me, your wife, and soon our baby?—it won't be so easy in future to drop everything and go bowling over to Verina's all the time—we'll lose some sleep to begin with and life is going to have to revolve around the baby's needs—you won't like that—it'll be a huge change for us but I'm looking forward to it, I love this little person already—wish I felt you did—we should be together in this—I intend to be a wonderful mother but I shan't neglect you in any way however much time and attention the babe demands—we'll be like we used to be again—please God—what's this film about? I'll try and get into it—might relax me—I don't want to spoil anything for you—want you to be happy—that's why I've been indulging you over Verina although—can't help it—she does make me jealous—still, once we've got the baby, she'll be the one on the outside.*

Some action in the film makes Alex chuckle.

Faith experiences a sudden flutter in her womb and wants to tell Alex but he is engrossed *I must stay serene—you're right Alex, I do have a tendency to brood and build things up—but do you still love me?—you never say so—if I ask you, you say of course, we are one—but we're not—I'm lonely.*

—

Verina and Cassie are clearing the breakfast dishes. Chris is finishing his coffee. "Have you told Cass about the trip?"

"What's this mum?"

"Alex can't come on the Orient Express after all. He's got an important meeting in Dusseldorf. I'm hoping you'll come instead."

Cassie has her back to them, still loading the dish-washer. "What about dad?"

"He'll be away. Do come Cass, it'll be fun."

"Thanks mum but they don't like it if you take time off from school, unless it's really important."

"Shall I write a note to Miss Barber?"

"No mum. Please don't."

"Wouldn't you like to come?"

Cassie closes the door of the machine and staightens up. Her face is pink and she doesn't look at Verina. "It's not really my sort of thing thank you mum. I'm off now, Gem and I have got to go to the library. Bye."

"That's put me in my place. Teenagers, God! She usually jumps at a chance to spend time with me."

"Unfortunately, she knows she was not your first choice."

"Oh hell! I wouldn't hurt my little Cass for anything. I suppose I was a bit insensitive the other day. I'm beginning to see what you mean Chris, it's not all that easy joining another person onto the family. I need to be tactful. I'll give the bloody tickets away, I don't want to go either now."

He's tempted to say it's a pity about Copenhagen but she's miserable. "Give them to Chloé and Joe."

—

It's become a tradition that the fifth of November is celebrated with Joe and Chloé in their garden. Joe is like a schoolboy about fireworks.

Faith and Cassie don't like the bangs so they watch the fireworks inside the part-conservatory-part-kitchen. Joe is sublimely happy. In spite of the fine rain, he manages to light the carefully arranged rockets and bangers so that explosions of colour and sound follow one after the other. Tonight, Chris lets Alex takes his place as Joe's assistant. Greg is dodging around, getting in the way, hoping to be allowed to strike a match. Irritated, Alex hisses at him to go away and he shoots into the house to squeeze up beside Cassie.

"Why aren't you outside?"

"Alex told me to go away."

Faith quickly assures him "That's only because fireworks can be very dangerous."

"I know that. I never do anything stupid."

Chloé gives them each a mug of home-made soup and a chunk of bread.

Alex is in the doorway. "Greg? You want to do the Catherine wheels? Your dad says you always do them."

"No thanks. You can do them."

Alex smiles persuasively, "I don't know how to. Please, you come and show me." Greg allows himself to be taken by the hand into the garden. His discomfiture forgotten, he makes Alex hold a Catherine wheel against a post while he hammers a nail through its centre. They light three at a time with spectacular effect.

Chris, Verina and Nan are watching and they cheer and clap hands. Chloé calls them in for soup too, to warm them up. "We'll have more fireworks afterwards."

Carrying jacket potatoes and sausages everyone soon wanders back outside again into the dark, drawn by the smells of wet cardboard, damp leaves and the whiff of cordite.

Chris sees Alex take a photograph of Verina holding up two sparklers. She's laughing and looks lovely. He goes inside to find another sausage and stands with Faith and Cassie as they watch Joe setting up another display. Verina is talking to him cradling her cup with both hands. Chris can see Alex standing behind her with his arms around her waist, his stomach contracts. Alex pushes his head down over Verina's shoulder and holds his cheek against hers. Chris glances instinctively at Faith but she's talking to Cassie. Joe always keeps something tremendous until the very last. This year he's been to Chinatown and found a rainbow fountain rocket. It lives up to its name, exploding three times high over the houses, showering colours over a wide area while everyone cries out "Aah!", "Fantastic!", "Lovely!". Joe is as pleased as if he'd made the rocket himself.

It's raining heavily now and they all move indoors. Alex has his arm around Verina. "My first fireworks-night with my own mother." He rubs noses with her "Your little nose is cold." He notices Faith watching "Hi pudd'n. Enjoy the fireworks?"

"Yes"

"That last rocket made the baby jump though" Cassie is concerned.

Faith strokes her stomach, "Yes it did but I expect he knows he's quite safe in here."

Chris thinks it's time to go. "Come on then. Thanks for a great evening Joe."

Verina kisses Chloé "Thanks for feeding the five thousand."

—

"Read this." Verina passes a letter over to Chris." Dad says we can't go down for Christmas."

"What?" He reads with a piece of toast in one hand. "From the sound of it, we can't go down ever again. The kids will be disappointed, they've been in the country for Christmas with granny and granpa since they were born."

"I don't know how I'm going to explain this to them."

"From what your dad says, your mum seems to have had some sort of nervous collapse."

"Yes—just because he told her about Alex. It's all so stupid and unnecessary. I think she's play-acting."

Chris pictures the beautiful old Rectory. The family treasures always come out at Christmas—Venetian glass baubles on the mantlepieces, a hand-made crib that the children are allowed to assemble. Candlelight and open fires to welcome them when they arrive, the mistily decorated Christmas tree standing in the hall and recordings of carols resounding through the house. "I'll be disappointed."

Verina has taken the letter back to re-read it. "It's not clear what's wrong with mother. Perhaps she's showing early signs of Alzheimer's. That's what I'll tell Alex. I've been making excuses for not introducing him to his grandparents but I did think we'd all be down there for Christmas."

"Did you?"

"I know what you mean. Because that's what I wanted to happen, I made myself believe it was going to." She pours more coffee for them both. "So okay then, we'll have Christmas in London and Alex and Faith can come here."

"Well Faith's parents or Alex's other ones might be expecting them to be with them."

"Not for our first Christmas? No. They must come to us."

Depression wraps itself around Chris like a damp quilt.

Cassie appears. "You two look sunny, what's up?"

"Granny's not well and Grandpa says we can't go down for Christmas."

"Yeah. yeah. . . . Mum, no. You're not serious? You are just teasing?"

"I wish I was."

"But we always go for Christmas, it's so special. It'll be awful if we don't."

"I know," she waved the letter, "but Grandpa says we can't this year because of Granny."

"If she's that ill, shouldn't we go down and look after her?"

"It's not that simple."

"I mean, we could do the tree and everything. You and I did the cooking last year, we could do it again. Granny needn't do anything."

"Put some toast in for yourself and I'll try and explain. You're old enough now to understand things. Grandpa has finally told her about Alex and she's got into a state about it all."

"Why?"

"Well it's a long rigmarole. She doesn't like being reminded about what happened to me and although I told Grandpa to explain that everything has turned out for the best, she's determined not to believe it. I think it's fear really. Grandpa knows that we all think Alex is great and that he and Faith have become part of the family but Granny still insists they'll cause upset in the family."

"So what you're saying is, she doesn't want to see Alex and so she won't see us either. Doesn't she love us anymore?"

"It's not that darling. I'm sure she does."

"She doesn't have to see Alex if she doesn't want to but she can't want to cut us off."

"I told you it wasn't simple. Grandpa doesn't want to impose silence on you children and he feels you're bound to mention Alex and he thinks that would be enough to upset her again."

"Sorry Mum, I don't get it. It all sounds weird to me. How long is it gonna go on for"

"Who knows?"

"So, the reason we can't have our normal Christmas—which we all love so much—is down to Alex. Something else for him to spoil. Granny's not wrong, there already is upset in the family. As far as I'm concerned, if it's a toss-up between having my grandparents and our special Christmas and having an extra brother, sorry Mum, I know which I choose."

"That's not fair. It's not Alex's fault."

"Do you want me to tell Nan and Greg?"

Verina is sitting with her head bowed.

"Mum?"

"Somebody has to."

Cass runs out banging the door.

The next minute, Nan rushes in to throw herself sobbing onto Chris. "It's not true Daddy, is it?"

Greg follows her. "Mum, it doesn't seem right that five people should have a miserable Christmas because of one new person in the family."

"We're not going to have a miserable Christmas, just a different one."

"Well I don't think it's fair."

"Life often isn't fair, you'll have to get used to that. Where's Cass?"

"She's on the phone talking to Chloé. Can we have Christmas at Chloé and Joe's if we can't go to Granny?"

Nan looks up, "That would be good."

"No we can't. Too many of us. Alex and Faith will be here. I know you're very disappointed but we can have a good time at home you know . . . Cheer up. I expect Chloé and Joe will come round . . . Look, Daddy and I are depressed about it too but Granny can't help being ill and we mustn't be selfish. You can come with me to buy decorations for the tree if you like and you can decorate it. What do you think? Nan?"

"Don't care."

Verina sighs. "Greg?"

"It's made me go off Alex a bit you know."

"Oh God."

"He doesn't really mean it Mum. Don't be upset."

"Can we have a tree as big as Granny's?"

"You'll have to ask Daddy."

"I suppose we'll just have to make the best of it."

"Yes Nan, I'm afraid we will."

—

She has brought mugs of tea into the bedroom. Alex props himself up to take his and Faith heaves herself up on to the end of the bed facing him. "Hey you, when was it arranged that we'd spend Christmas at Verina's?"

He gulps his tea. "Ah . . . I'm really thirsty. You were there. The children were talking about Christmas and they wanted us to go and you said 'yes'."

"I don't remember any talk about Christmas."

"You were definitely there. I expect you were tired and not paying attention."

"No Alex. You're making it up. You've just gone ahead and made plans without consulting me."

He grins "Course I have, it was to be a surprise. Remember last year? You went to all the trouble of cooking Christmas dinner, we sat down to eat it and ended up feeling a bit lonely with just the two of us."

"I do remember that but I also remember feeling guilty, we had let both sets of parents down because you didn't want to be bored to death."

"We're not going to have last year's row all over again, are we?"

"No we're not. I would like to go home this Christmas though and be with my mum and dad."

"I've already told Phil and Lilian that the baby could come any time about then so it's better if you stay near the hospital. I assumed you'd told your parents the same. Look, next year we'll have the house and they can all come to us.—And mind the baby!"

"We could get to the hospital from my parents' if I went into labour early."

"Causing a lot of anxiety for all the rest of us. No I don't think so Faith. I'd like some more tea please." He held out his mug, "I'd. have thought you'd be pleased, not having to do any cooking."

"I like cooking and it's better for me to keep busy. I don't mind visiting over the twelve days but I'd much rather we had Christmas by ourselves."

"I can't think why. We didn't enjoy it much last year. Too late to change now in any case, it's all settled."

"Not by me it isn't"

"You can't disappoint the kids, they're looking forward to having us. If you decide you'd rather not go, it'll be awkward trying to explain."

"I don't see why."

"Look, I'm sorry, I should have cleared it with you first but I honestly thought you'd be pleased. You don't really mean you don't want to go, do you? What you're mad about is that I went ahead."

"You shouldn't make plans without telling me. Besides being your wife, I do exist as a person in my own right."

"The kids will be delighted."

"You keep talking about the kids but what you mean is you'll be delighted. Instead of being stuck here with a nauseous wife, you'll be spoiled and drooled over by your mother."

"As is my due. Should be good though, there'll be a lot going on and we'll be included. You like their friends, don't you?"

"I feel like an intruder at times. I'm sure we occasionally upset their routine."

"For an intelligent girl, you do talk tripe sometimes. Verina's always saying how well we fit in. They all love you. You'll enjoy yourself. You know you will. We're going and that's that!"

Alex jumps out of bed and runs off to shower. While she's making toast and more tea, he reappears and starts shadow-boxing round the kitchen, grunting and roaring. He pretends he's about to plant a punch on her chin and Faith ducks away. "Calm down Alex." He takes no notice and continues to dance about and aim punches into the air around her.

"Leave me alone."

"I feel so good—so full of energy."

"I'm glad you do. There's your breakfast. Now let me go and wash."

"Are you going to be long?"

"Why? Do you need the bathroom again?"

"No. I just want to get going."

"I've got a few things to do before we leave."

"Really Faith, you don't seem able to organise yourself. You've got nothing to do all day now you're not working. Why can't you just shower, dress and go?"

She stands sipping her tea and regarding him over her mug.

"Is there anything you want me to do?"

"Not really."

"All right then, I'll push off down the gym for an hour shall I? Leave you in peace to sort yourself out. Then when I get back, we can go. Right?

The flat door closes after him.

He wears me out. He's like a big puppy around the place, creating mess, making demands, never still.

—

Chris is late getting home because of the usual Christmas drinks in the office. Using the excuse that the children were waiting for him, he escaped before things turned silly and arrives, feeling relief and pleasure, at his own front door hung with its festive wreath. The house is unexpectedly quiet. Someone is listening to Schubert. He puts down his brief case to push open the sitting room door.

No lamps on, just light from the fire and the gleam of the Christmas tree. Verina is in her chair with Alex near her, on a low stool. "You two look peaceful." He keeps his voice low against the music and closes his inner ear to the alarm which has started up at the back of his mind.

"Hallo Chris. It won't be peaceful for long. The children are on a high."

"Well it is Christmas Eve." He sinks into a chair. "Where are they all?"

"Faith's helping them to get ready to go out. Nan's changed her outfit three times. Would you like Alex to fix you a drink?"

"No thanks. I won't have any more just yet."

Alex wanders over to the door, "I'll go and see if they're ready shall I?"

"Please."

Chris and Verina sit in silence as the sonata comes to an end. He senses he has spoiled a tranquil moment for her and Alex "When are we due at Joe and Chloé's?"

"Oh, any time. We've been waiting for you."

—

They haven't far to walk. Nan and Greg run ahead.

Lighted candles welcome from every window and the front door stands open. Joe is on duty behind a snowy table at the foot of the stairs, ladling hot punch into glasses as people walk in.

The decorations in the drawing room glow magically in the candlelight. People are talking quietly.

Solicitous Chloé greets Chris, "You sit in Joe's chair, before someone else does, I can see you're tired." She settles Faith too, into an upright chair, a cushion behind her back and a plate of savouries at her elbow.

"She's lovely, that Chloé isn't she?" Don has come over. "But then so's Verina and so's my Angie. We're three lucky men."

"Yes." Chris looks to see where Verina is. She's talking to an elderly neighbour. He likes her in that brown silk, it shows off her slenderness and her dark eyes. The old woman she's talking to is boring yet Verina is listening to her patiently. He wants to go over and give her a squeeze. Just to be in the same room with her has always made him feel at peace. He decides to have some punch after all. "Strong stuff Joe." "Yeah. Recipe's a family secret. Guaranteed to start your Christmas off properly."

The hall is full of people, some leaving for drinks or dinner elsewhere. Chloé persuades those who are left to huddle round the fire. Verina chooses a sofa and Alex joins her holding her hand and watching her talk and laugh with a proud smile on his face.

Vlady, an artist neighbour, whom Chris can't stand, has thrown himself cross-legged down on the floor nearby and is working swiftly on a drawing of them. After a while, he shoves

35

the sketch at Chris with a nod towards them, "It's like young love, isn't it?"

Faith hears him and Chris catches sight of her stricken face as she jumps up and hurries from the room.

He passes the sketch back without a word. The candle-light is wavery, unstable, deceptive. He shouldn't be drinking on an empty stomach but here's Greg and Nan offering him sausage rolls and anchovy toast. He takes some of each and stuffs his mouth.

Vlady suggests to Verina that she should sit for him.

"You're a landscape painter."

"Mostly, yes but when my eyes are given feast of beautiful woman, I want to be portrait painter. Your mother should be painted, no?"

Alex's lets go of Verina's hand.

"You must get your husband to commission me. I charge not much because of pleasure it will give me." He rolls his hands about in the air and smiles at her with his mouth open. "For ages, you know, I want paint you" he leans towards Alex "and not only paint. You understand?"

Alex scowls at him and turns away.

Joe comes in, supporting Faith and settles her back in her chair. "Just imagine, this time next year, there'll be a baby crawling round, tearing up parcels and pulling the tree to bits. Staggering thought, isn't it?"

For a few minutes, Faith becomes the centre of interest until Verina sees that she's finding it uncomfortable and diverts attention by asking the others about their plans for Christmas.

Chris sits back in the shadows and observes Faith *poor kid, she's been crying—what are we going to do about Alex and Verina— they're completely unaware of how they look to other people—that little shit Vlady!—God, if only it wasn't Christmas.*

—

In his dream, he and Verina are in the Champs Elysees. He loses sight of her in one of the caves. She's somewhere in the basement but the basements stretch away . . . away . . . under pavements. He can't find a way out. He groans and wakes himself up.

36

Verina throws an arm across him, "Alex . . . darling . . . what's wrong?"

He shoots out of bed and stands absolutely still in the dark waiting to be sure that she has not really woken up. He's now wide awake, controlling his breathing so as not to rouse her. He creeps to the door, fumbles for his dressing gown, pulls it on and leaves the bedroom. He's suffocating. Downstairs, he rummages in the hall cupboard, manoeuvres damp socks over his feet, tugs his boots on quickly and lets himself out. *I need to breathe.*

There's been a heavy fall of snow but there's no wind and it seems almost warm. He sets off into the silence. The unfamiliar scene could be an extension of his dream. Between the street lamps, surreal trees sculpted by snow, lean over a wide terrain of unsullied white. He takes great gulps of the snow-freshened air and tries to feel anchored to the world by the crunch of his steps. He mutters to himself *it doesn't mean anything—it's natural—she was probably dreaming about him—he is her son—I dream about the kids—she's been drinking too—so have I—probably not thinking straight—she wasn't awake so she didn't know what she was saying—it's not just that his name is uppermost in her mind—she sounded so concerned—hasn't shown much concern for me lately—not even noticed I'm fed up—perhaps not her fault though—I've been so intent on showing how generous, how big-hearted I can be—how is she supposed to guess I feel marginalised?—usually she doesn't need to have things spelled out to her—she doesn't know I'm putting on an act—never had to do that before—what else can I do?—can hardly say to her I'm being eaten alive with jealousy watching you and your son growing more and more infatuated with each other—thought I was handling it all rather well—too easy-going?—it's all getting too intense—thought it was simply a matter of adjustment—none of us has had time to properly adjust—will we ever?—what's going to happen to poor little Faith?—rotten timing, being pregnant now—a few more weeks and things might have eased into a more normal situation—alone out here in the middle of the night can be honest with myself—I live from day to day denying what's before my eyes—afraid to look ahead.*

Two figures are coming towards him. Aware of his dressing-gown and his nakedness underneath, he turns back but someone is calling his name, it's Chloé. She and Joe run up to him and link arms. "We've been to midnight Mass." "Come

37

and have hot rum and lemon, it's traditional on Christmas night. You're obviously not ready for bed," Joe pauses "well you are . . . ." They all start laughing.

Chris knows he doesn't have to offer any explanations. However, as they walk on together kicking up the powdery snow, he's afraid he might blurt out all kinds of confessions and indiscretions to these good friends. It will be difficult to say nothing. He has never before put up a barrier against these two.

In their warm room, Joe stokes up the fire and Chloé re-lights the candles.

They know something's wrong but they won't ask me questions. I want to get things clear in my mind before I say anything. It might sound as if I'm criticising Verina. Thank God for their kindness and understanding though it makes me want to bellow.

Chloé's eyes are shining and her cheeks rosy. She's pulling off her big woollen scarf which she's wearing over one of Joe's old sweaters. "I love Christmas, don't you Chris? Joe pretends he doesn't, he says it's for children."

"It is." He puts a plate of mince pies on a low table "It's for children and you, my little snow-fairy." He lifts a handful of her shining, blonde hair and lets it flow through his fingers.

"It is mainly for children of course, which is why we're looking forward to our first Christmas with all of you. I can't wait to see their faces as they open their presents."

Joe has given him hot rum which is helping him control his welling anguish.

"Vee and I are so glad you're going to be with us. This is the first Christmas we will not be with Vee's parents. Your coming will make up to the kids for their disappointment. With Vee's mother being unwell . . ."

Chloé touches his hand, "Vee explained. It's sad for the children to have such a drastic change. It's usually the adults who seem to suffer disappointment."

Joe is immediately protective "What do you mean Angel?"

"It's as if people bring the memories of all their other Christmases—which they look back on as being special—and . . . ."

"Wonder why they're not any more" laughs Joe.

"I suppose it's the child in us."

She's looking at Chris so he feels he should respond. "It is a funny time, it seems to make people think of their hidden sorrows."

"P'raps it's a reaction to a lot of false Christmas jollity. Have you noticed, there's often a row at Christmas?"

"That's because people drink too much" Chloé sits gazing into the fire. "It's strange how the old ones often die at Christmas."

"There you are, can't take the disappointment. They wait years and years for it to be like when they were kids, it never is, so eventually they die of disgust." Joe tops up their glasses.

Chloé is only half listening. "Perhaps we all look for perfection in life because we're born with an idea of it. Maybe it's a memory tucked away inside us." She looks at the two men "Don't laugh at me. I think we sometimes get a flash which we half recognise . . . you know . . . . falling in love, new baby . . . Christmas. It's what gives us hope, some meaning to life."

Chris studies her affectionately. "You may be right."

"Talking of babies, I do like Faith. She's a sweet girl."

"She is. She gets on like a house on fire with the children."

"And Alex? How do you get on with him?"

Chris hesitates, "I don't really know him all that well yet. I suspect he's still a bit on his guard with me. He's much more relaxed with Vee of course."

"You're very tolerant Chris. I'll be honest, I'm selfish. I couldn't take it if Chloé had a son who suddenly turned up and started trying to appropriate her."

"Oh he can't quite do that, Vee does have the rest of the family to look after."

"Sure" Joe persists "but you both work hard and your free time is precious. The lad must take up some of your private space?"

Joe's reading my mind. "It's early days. He and Vee are still getting to know each other. I can't begrudge any of that. Vee is so happy."

"I'm sure she is but you don't look so good, if you don't mind me saying. Just watch that it doesn't all get a bit out of hand mate. You and Faith mustn't be left out of the picture."

"Joe!" Chloé warns.

"Chris knows what I mean. People can slip into habits. Things can get spoiled. I'm only saying Chris, be a bit selfish. Have another drink?"

"No thanks. I'd better be going. Heavy day tomorrow."

They go with him to the door. Joe flings an arm across his shoulder, "Keep swatting the flies mate."

Chloé hugs him hard "Have a really happy Christmas. See you in the morning."

He makes his way carefully down the snow-covered steps and trudges home feeling he's received a benediction.

—

In the morning, Chris opens the door to a Joe and Chloé with armfuls of presents. He winks at them so they won't mention his midnight prowling. Verina hadn't even noticed his absence from bed.

Alex wants to give out the presents. He's kneeling by the Christmas tree, squeezing each parcel and giving it a little shake before passing it on. Verina's cheeks are flushed, perhaps from the champagne. She gives Alex a push "Stop being naughty. You're keeping everyone waiting." He rolls over on the floor and they both giggle.

He chooses a few more presents. Everyone is busily tearing off paper.

"Nothing for me."

"There are things for you. Don't be silly."

Alex looks up at her, smiling, "Anyway, I've got my best present." She bends across and kisses him on the mouth.

Joe interrupts, "Okay. Break it up you two. There's a job to be done."

"Aye, aye sir." Alex gives out the rest of the parcels. Chris sees Joe raise his eye-brows at Chloé who makes a resigned little moue.

—

After the magnificent dinner, it is decided that they will watch the DVD of 'Casablanca' which Alex has bought for Verina.

Faith goes upstairs to have a sleep but is down again in minutes with a parcel which she hands to Verina, who quickly gives it to Chris. "You haven't had your present from me Chris, sorry." She's already wearing the Italian brooch he bought for her but she forgot all about him this morning. He doesn't want anything now, it's too late. He wants to sulk and kick the furniture *too much trouble for her even to wrap it up, she asked Faith.* Unwillingly, he tugs at the sellotape and reveals a camera *thanks!—the last thing I need—she knows perfectly well I have access to all kinds of cameras at work—I actually told her about particular CDs and books I would like—she'll have been shopping somewhere with Alex—buying God knows what for him—suddenly remembering 'Oh dear, must get something for Chris' and picking up the first thing she saw—I'd like to throw this out of the window— through the glass!* It's an effort to thank her.

"It's supposed to be dead simple. You just look through there, line up the picture you want and press the button." *She's telling me how to use a camera now!*

"Take a photo of me and Alex on our first Christmas." She snuggles up to Alex, rests her head against his shoulder and smiles. Obediently, Chris raises the camera, gets them in focus and presses the button.

"We can run that off on the computer later. Let's settle down now and watch the film."

Alex is sprawled in the chair Chris likes to sit in, so he takes another.

"You're a bit far away over there, aren't you dad?"

"No no Cass, I'm fine here. I've seen it lots of times anyway." He doesn't care if he sounds grumpy.

Nan attacks Greg "Aren't you a bit big to be sitting on mummy's lap?"

"I'm sharing her chair actually."

"Be quiet now. Let's watch the film."

Chloé and Joe are on the sofa. He has her hand clasped tightly in his and resting on his knee.

Chris sighs. Chloé is Joe's life and he is hers. That's how it should be.

—

He goes to bed soon after Faith, leaving the rest of the family to a noisy game of monopoly. He had little sleep last night and soon slips thankfully into oblivion. Thirst wakes him up again. He doesn't know what time it is. Verina's lamp is still on for her but she isn't there. While he looks for his watch, there are murmurings on the landing and he hears Verina

41

laugh. Instantly alert, he strains to catch what's being said. He has to force himself to stay put, willing Verina to come to bed.

More subdued laughter and he can't keep still any longer. He gets up, wraps himself in his dressing gown and opens the bedroom door. Alex and Verina are sitting side by side on the stairs whispering and giggling.

"I need some soda-water" he says and goes downstairs *they're like children, and as innocent as children.* He pushes away the shadow growing across his mind *you can bring something into existence by imagining it hard enough.* He carries his glass back upstairs and says firmly "Goodnight Alex."

It's another ten minutes before Verina joins him—an unfamiliar Verina. Over the years, they have established slow, delicate rituals in their love-making but tonight Verina dispenses with all that and surprises him by her urgency. Relief floods through him and he responds to her with all the gratitude of a man with everything restored to him.

—

A smell of garlic and wine from the kitchen. Chris wanders in to investigate and finds Verina watching from the window as Alex and Greg build a snow-man. He slips his arms round her waist but she disentangles herself, "I've got to check the oven Chris."

He helps himself to some coffee. "Anything I can do?"

"No thanks, it's almost ready."

He sits at the table wanting her to meet his eye and give some sign that their night is still with her. Moving from cooker to table, she continually glances out of the window. When she finally turns to ask him to find the girls for lunch, she looks at him as if he's a stranger.

He starts up the stairs *she's just preoccupied—stage-managing all these meals and activities is not easy—the sense of distance between us is coming out of my poisoned imagination—there was no distance between us in the night—on the contrary.*

—

42

It's decided a stroll by the river would be good. During the walk, Verina had Greg and Nan holding her hands all the time with either Cassie or Alex trying to get a word in across them.

Back in the house, Chris escapes to his study. Verina's letters are kept in a special drawer in his desk. Pushing his hands down among the loose sheets, he fishes out pages at random, as he enjoys doing. Lines from an early note sing up at him. *Your face is imprinted behind my eyes, I wonder if others see you looking out through them? . . . . I could fly off and circle the moon without a space-suit.* Her idiosyncratic writing covers the lined paper on which she pretended to be making notes at a lecture; *I was like a genii in an oriental fairy story, all squashed down inside until you lifted out the stopper and released the enormous ME that has grown huge with all this love. Now I can flow all around you and luxuriate in our loving.* Like she did last night. He knows he's indulging in this secret habit, reliving the past, in an attempt to push away fear. There was a strange element in last night's passion. That's why Verina is avoiding him today.

He rejoins the others. Alex has given him a biography of Laker, soon they are deep in discussion about the great men in cricket.

—

It's late. The children are happy and sleepy and ready for bed. Verina and Alex announce that they need fresh air and are going out for a walk in the snow.

"Can I come?" Cassie asks.

"No I don't think so darling, you're up late as it is."

"Mum. I'm nearly sixteen!" She flounces across the room. "Goodnight Faith and Bump. Goodnight Dad."

"Goodnight Mum?" But she's gone.

Chris smiles ruefully, "I'm baby-sitting, am I?"

"Oh Chris, do you want to come? I thought. there's Faith and . . . ."

"Quite right. I'll look after Faith."

"There's no need Chris, thanks. I'm going to bed myself now."

The other two are hurriedly buttoning up coats and winding scarves round their necks, already halfway out of the door.

"I don't want to go out. I'm going to read my Laker by the fire. Off you go you two."

He and Faith can hear Alex and Verina laughing as they try to get down the steps without slipping.

"I'll have to clear those steps tomorrow" Chris smiles at her, "we can't risk you having an accident at this stage."

—

He is in bed with his book open but all the time waiting for Verina and Alex to come in. He hears the front door close at last but they stay downstairs for what seems a long time *it's pathetic to keep looking at my watch, they're probably just having a hot drink—very quiet—have they have come upstairs yet?* He's annoyed *she's been giving great chunks of herself to everyone else all day—especially Alex—now she should give some time to me—what is she doing?* His heart is banging away in his chest. He gets out of bed and opens the door. The landing is in darkness but the light from the room behind him shows Alex, leaning over the banister holding Verina's hand. They blink in the sudden light and unclasp their fingers.

"Did we wake you?"

"No. I was reading."

Alex says "Goodnight" and hurries up the stairs.

Chris gets back into bed and picks up his book again. Verina undresses and slides in beside him "Are you going to read long?"

He suddenly has to get out of the room. "Actually no. I've just had an idea that I think I should go down and make a note of. Put your light out. I won't be long."

Down in his study he tries to sort out his thoughts. He doesn't want a repetition of last night but his brain refuses to examine the reason *what were Verina and Alex doing on the landing in the dark?* His rational mind says nothing much *but holding hands?—whispering?—like lovers—mother and son, was that in order?—outside my bedroom door too—as though I don't matter—I'm going to have to say something—Faith's probably been waiting for Alex the way I've been waiting for Vee—poor kid— thank God they're going home tomorrow.*

—

Greg and Nan are setting the table.

Cassie is making salad dressing. "Gemma's mum says you look far too young to have a son as old as Alex, mum."

"Really?"

"Yes and Gemma thinks you can't ever go out together—everyone will think he's your young lover."

"Cass!"

"Well that's what she said. She fancies him like mad. She thinks he's good looking enough to be a model."

"God forbid!".

"Faith's going to choose a name for the baby from the list I wrote out for her" says Nan.

"I helped" Greg reminds her "and she said if it's a boy she hopes he will be like me. Mum. Why don't they come and live here with us now?"

Cass tosses the salad, "They practically do already."

"We've got enough room. And they are, sort of, your children too. The baby could share my room. We wouldn't be jealous, would we?" he appeals to his sisters.

"Wanna bet?"

"Too complicated. They're married. Married people have to make their own lives."

"They may not stay married."

"Why do you say that Cass?"

By now they are all sitting at the table. "For one thing, I don't think Alex wants the baby. In films, you always see the husband taking care of the wife when she's pregnant, you know, making her put her feet up, not letting her carry the coal in."

Greg, with his mouth full, "Coal?"

"You know what I mean. Look at the way dad always makes Faith sit in the big chair and puts her feet on the stool, fusses round her—in a nice way Dad. You never see Alex doing any of that. He practically ignores her. Besides, I can't see what they've got in common. Dad agrees with me, don't you?"

"There are plenty of successful marriages between people with apparently little in common. Lots of men aren't interested in babies until they have a child of their own. Besides, Faith and Alex haven't been married all that long, they haven't had enough time to grow together perhaps."

"What, you mean like mistletoe and oak trees?"

45

Chris laughs, "Something like that." He's thinking how nice it is just being by themselves again.

—

When he hears the phone, he realises he's been dozing by the fire. He gets up to answer it but somebody already has. He looks in the kitchen—no-one there—so he fills the kettle and put cups on a tray, meaning to take tea up to Verina. She surprises him by coming out of the studio.

"I thought you were resting."

"I was. Then I thought I'd left the gas on."

"Who was that on the phone?"

"Only Faith, to thank us."

She looks flushed and her eyes are red. Has she been crying?

"You all right?"

"Yes. Why?"

"You seem . . . I don't know . . . Not quite yourself."

"Well I was asleep for a little while. I expect I need to wash my face."

She splashes cold water on her cheeks at the sink and lifts the tea-pot down from the shelf. It slips out of her hands on to the floor and smashes.

"Oh damn. I haven't dried my hands properly."

"And you're tired. You've been on the go non-stop for nearly a week. Go and sit by the fire. I'll clear this up, we never liked it anyway. I'll make tea with tea-bags. Let's take the kids out for rubbish food this evening—save you cooking.

—

There is a documentary on television about South East Asia that Chris wants to see. The children have gone to bed and Verina said she was going too but he can hear her rattling about in the kitchen and walking in and out of the studio. Eventually she comes in to pour herself a drink "I need something to help me wind down."

"The point of taking you all out was so that you could relax this evening but you still seem to have been busy. I thought you were going to bed before my programme started." He switches off the television.

"Don't turn it off because of me."

"It's finished. I feel guilty, watching the box while you whizz round."

"I wasn't doing anything in particular. I'm just restless."

"Anti-climax after Christmas I expect."

"Probably" she settles herself into her chair.

This might be the moment to talk to her. He needs some Dutch courage and pours himself a brandy.

"You ready for a top-up?"

"No, I'm fine thanks."

'He doesn't know how to begin and sifts through several ideas. "So, are you coming to terms with the fact that we're soon going to be grandparents?"

"The children are looking forward to it."

"Are you? Is Alex?"

"Of course. It was Faith's pregnancy that made him want to find me."

"Hasn't worked out all that well for little Faith though."

"In what way?" her voice has taken on a hard edge.

"Her pregnancy made him want to find you and finding you has moved her almost out of the picture."

"Chris, that's nonsense. You're being over dramatic. Faith is a very self-contained girl."

"Do you like her? You don't talk to her much."

"I'm not sure I talk to anyone much when I'm busy. Of course I like her. I suppose I treat her a bit casually as if she was one of the children but I think she likes that."

"But I don't imagine she likes the way you take up Alex's time and attention."

"I don't purposely set out to take him over. He wants to be at my elbow all the time. He's only just found me; he's pleased with me and wants to get to know me. I'm sure Faith understands that."

"I'm sure she does but you and Alex shouldn't forget about her."

"Look, we know we mustn't let the rest of you feel left out . . . no, that's not what I mean to say . . . that sounds as if we've been discussing it—we haven't. Alex is young, he's finding his way. So am I. It's an unusual situation."

"Yes it is. No-one wants to spoil things for you and Alex, it's obvious how happy you both are and that's all the more reason why you should make sure Faith is happy too."

"Are you saying she isn't?"

"I sometimes suspect it . . . It's often the little things that chip away at a relationship."

"Little things like what?"

"Perhaps waiting for Alex to join her at bed-time, when they've spent no time together all day, might cause her some disappointment."

"Oh I see. All this concern for Faith is really about you."

"That too. But you don't want Faith to experience any stress at this time, do you?" This is difficult but he pushes himself to go on. "You and Alex are so taken up with the excitement of being reunited and getting to know each other and that's fine but you need reminding that Faith still comes first with Alex and I and our children come first with you."

"That goes without saying."

"Does it?"

She won't meet his eyes. "You said just now, that no-one wants to spoil things for me and Alex but that's just what you are doing. I think you're jealous Chris. I never would have thought you could be a jealous man."

"Anyone can be jealous. I've never had reason to be before."

"You haven't reason now. Alex is my son—not another man in my life."

"So darling, try not to behave as though he is. Don't take half an hour saying goodnight to him in the dark. You must realise that seems odd. And it makes me mad. 'It doesn't matter about old Chris, he'll put up with anything.' Faith and I have given you both a lot of leeway all these weeks, now I think you should give us some thought. Try and behave a little less like a love-sick girl around him."

She takes a few minutes to reply. When she does, her voice tells him she is keeping back tears "Thanks. I shan't be able to look Alex in the face next time he comes. You've just ruined for me all the effort I put into trying to make an extra special Christmas for us all. Why are you being so cruel Chris?"

"I've seen the way people stare at the two of you sometimes and I want to avoid a disaster. It's not easy to say these painful

48

things to you Vee but you clearly can't help yourself at present, you're still in a state of shock and it's up to me to take control. We've had them here for Christmas, now let's have a little rest from them. By all means ring and see how they are but they'll be parents any minute now, they need to settle back into their life and get prepared."

"I said they could come for New Year."

"Well cancel."

Her face is sorrowful.

He sighs heavily, "All right. Let them come but Vee please do try to get things on to a more normal footing. I'll help you. I'll take Alex off for a pint sometimes with Joe and you get to know Faith a bit more. I'm worried that Alex is developing an obsession about you, we ought to help him."

She sits with her head lowered. He goes over to her chair, crouches, puts his arms around her and draws her head against his shoulder. She's unyielding.

"I'm sorry if I hurt you or make you angry but we are always honest with each other. I hope you can see I'm trying to take care of you—of all of us. Let's go to bed."

They lie side by side in silence. Chris re-runs their conversation for himself *did I say what I wanted to?* Some of his words flame out in the dark *did I go too far?—thank God I bit back the words 'and you're developing an obsession with your son'—saying that would have cracked all the china in the house—but I believe it's true and it's torture—trying to prevent a catastrophe here—but have I conjured up something unspeakable myself?—am I damaging our marriage with my jealousy and black imaginings?— what we have built up between us is surely enough to . . .?—but Verina's withdrawn from me. Oh God, if only I could sleep.*

—

Cassie and Gemma are up in the girls's room, sitting on the beds.

"So what do you think?"

"About your brother? You know I think he's drop dead gorgeous. If I was married to him, I'd be nervous all the time that someone else would steal him."

49

"It's funny, isn't it, how really good-looking men often marry fairly . . . erm . . . ordinary girls?"

"Yeah. I suppose it's to show themselves off. I don't think Faith's ordinary though, I think she's pretty but she doesn't make the best of herself."

"I know. I think if she put some blonde highlights in her hair and wore a touch of mascara, she'd look great."

"When do you think we could start wearing mascara?"

"You don't need any, your eyelashes are five miles long and very dark."

"Thank you."

"I do though." Cassie sighed at her reflection in the mirror.

Verina calls them for lunch but they don't go down straight away.

"Gem."

"What?"

"It's not really like having a brother."

"How do you mean?"

"Well, this is a secret between you and me right?"

"Of course." Gemma sits up.

"I feel . . . funny . . . sometimes when Alex is around."

"Funny?"

"Yes. Especially if we're ever alone for a few minutes. I feel as if he looks at me—as a girl I mean."

"More like you're looking at him!"

"Shut up Gem. Listen, there's a sort of atmosphere. I can't explain it."

"Cass. You don't think you're . . . attracted to each other?"

"Sometimes it does feel a bit like that. It's very embarrassing. Oh Gem, you'd never tell anyone would you? I'd die."

"Need you ask?"

"Sorry . . . but you can imagine . . ."

Verina's voice comes again "Do you girls want lunch or not?"

"Coming mum."

Gemma squeezes Cassie's wrist, "Don't get yourself in a state, Alex isn't like a brother yet because you've got to get used to him. Then it'll be all right."

"Do you think so?"

"Of course"

—

Chris is glad to be back at work. At home, Verina moves around the house sad and silent. He can't get near her—*my own fault—if I'd been a bit patient, she and Alex would have grown used to each other and everything would have settled down by now—went about it all the wrong way and when I want to try and put things right, I take one look at her frozen face and can't do anything—I'm sure over and over in her mind, she's constantly playing back the things I said the other night, and she doesn't like them and she doesn't like me—if I try to start a conversation, she says as little as possible—if we have an argument, we've always been able to find our way back to each other at night—not now; she walks about in a trance and gets into bed with her back turned and goes to sleep or pretends to—daren't talk to her or to try to touch her—can't believe this is happening to us.*

—

The evening the children are out at a pantomime with Chloé and Joe, he seizes the opportunity to force communication.
"Are you not speaking to me Vee?"
"Why do you ask?"
"You seem a bit distant."
"You're surprised?"
"This is because of our discussion the other evening?"
"Oh, was that a discussion? All I remember is you accusing me of unseemly behaviour with my son."
"I was not accusing you, I was trying to tell you how things look. I was honestly trying to help you . . . us . . . to adjust to the changes in the family."
"I think the only one having problems with adjusting is you!"
"You don't know that. I did suggest to you that Faith might be feeling a bit insecure too. She's only young. She's expecting her first baby and she needs support. I've seen her face once or twice when you and Alex behave as if you're are in a private world and I'm sure she feels forgotten."
"Chris, you said all this the other night. I have been thinking about it. I don't want to go over it all again."

51

"They're still coming for New Year though?"

"That's the general idea."

"Then I think you and I need to sort a few things out, otherwise it's not going to be a happy week-end. Do you realise this is the first time we have ever been . . . not together? I'm miserable. Aren't you?"

"Of course I am. A few days ago I was gloriously happy. My son was restored to me, we were all together for Christmas and now you seem to want to rob me of him all over again."

"No-one wants to rob you of anything."

"Alex is not going to like being spied on and criticised. You know Chris, if you keep this up you'll destroy our marriage as well as my relationship with my son."

"Vee, this is me you're talking to. Try not to be so angry. I don't want to destroy anything. I'm trying to build. We have a lovely family and now we're trying to graft on new members. It should be possible but we have to work together."

She says nothing.

He goes over to her "Please come back to me. Let me help." She stands up abruptly and is going to leave the room but he gets her in his arms. "Darling, please listen. Not to my words. I don't know what to say any more. I'm sorry you're so hurt. It's just what I wanted to prevent."

She lets him hold her for a minute then gives him a half-hearted hug and sits down again. "It's all so complicated. I get angry because I know some of the things you say are true. I have been neglectful. Alex is such a wonderful surprise for me but it doesn't mean I don't still love you and the children. It's just . . . I suppose I don't really know how to behave. I'm Alex's mother but because I didn't bring him up, it doesn't feel as if I am."

"It won't ever feel the same as with the other children but it will gradually become easier, ordinary."

"The children have accepted him."

"Yes, I think they have."

"So it's only you now."

"Vee, I've accepted him, or at least tried to, but as you're discovering yourself, emotions are not always easy to control. I'm sure you don't mean it but I get hurt."

"I'm sorry, she is looking into the fire, "it's all a bit unreal."

At least they're talking almost normally again but Chris is not looking forward to the week end. He's learned of the violence in himself, he wants to kill Alex.

—

Passing a florist on the way home, he notices a stem of Madeira orchids, the pinkish—wood colour that Vee loves. He scoops some drawings out of his brief-case and the girl in the shop cunningly packs the flowers so that he can sneak them into the house without Verina seeing.

She is busy in the kitchen and doesn't see him carrying his damp package into the studio. He finds a tall, narrow vase and as he stands it on her table, he spills a little water and grabs a cloth to mop it up. Wiping carefully round the gold frame she is working on, he sees a tiny piece of paper wedged under a corner. Worried that he might have wet a receipt, he eases it out. It's a note: **You left your smile in the car so I've stolen it to keep under my pillow. A.** He tucks it back and goes to his workroom.

Greg comes to fetch him at dinner time. "Why are you in the dark daddy? You all right?"

"Yes thanks." His arms and legs feel heavy, he has to push himself up . . . "Just tired. Boring old dad."

"You're not boring. Mike Taylor wishes you were his dad."

"Why's that?"

"His dad's only little, smaller than his mum and he's always cross."

Verina, sees his expression and says "Keep the volume down you lot. Daddy's tired and so am I."

They have an early night. Verina falls asleep quickly but Chris lies awake thinking for what seems hours. He hears Greg thump to the bathroom. He listens to the metal knockings in the central heating. He goes over the day's work and wonders whether he'll be able to dream up something interesting for the new campaign being planned. Verina makes a snuffly sound and turns over on her side. She loved the orchids anyway.

—

53

Even if he hadn't seen their car outside, one look at Verina would have told him that Alex and Faith had arrived. Verina shines with happiness. He recognises gratitude in her welcoming hug and allows himself to hope the week-end will go well.

During the evening, he observes Alex being attentive towards Faith. It's clearly making her happy.

"Do you like Faith's new hair-cut dad?" Nan is looking proudly at her.

"Yes I do. She looks like Shakespeare's Ariel."

Cassie bursts out laughing "Trust <u>you</u> dad. She wants to look trendy, don't you Faith?"

"I suppose so. Short hair should be easier to cope with in hospital anyway."

Verina gives Greg and Nan crackers for the table.

"How many are we then mum?"

"Chloé, Joe, Faith, Alex . . ."

"Nine" interrupts Nan, "I've already counted."

Faith's baby gives a kick and the drink she was resting against her side goes everywhere.

Greg's delighted, "He's saying, don't forget <u>me.</u> That makes ten!"

Joe and Chloé arrive.

The evening passes in a happy haze, like so many over the years. While they are waiting for midnight, Chris looks around at them all. Chloé is telling Alex about the countryside round Tours where she grew up, Joe and Verina are discussing a job, Nan and Cassie are whispering with Faith and Greg lolls sleepily across Verina's lap. Chris leans over to her "This year's been eventful."

She smiles and looks at Alex "This next one will be too."

"You mean because I'm going to be an uncle?" Greg is not quite asleep.

And now it's midnight and everyone is kissing everyone else. Alex says "Happy New Year Mummy-Verina," Chloé hugs Faith, "Happy New Year Faith and bump-whoever-you-are."

The younger children go off to bed. Cassie announces that she's not getting up until mid-day. She looks shyly at Faith "May I tell them?"

"Yes of course."

"And it is Alex's idea too?"

"Yes."

"Faith's asked me to be godmother."

"That's special" Chloé says "what a privilege Cass."

"I know. I'm delighted. Goodnight everybody. Happy New Year."

"I must go to bed myself" said Faith. "When it's been such a lovely evening, you don't feel like ending it." She smiles at Verina "Verina and Chris and" turning to Chloé, "you two, thank you for making us so welcome. We feel part of the family now, don't we Al?"

"We do. Come on you, I'd better heave you up the stairs." He gently helps her up out of the chair. Her slight frame staggers a little with the weight of her stomach.

"Goodnight."

"Goodnight. Sleep well." The door closes behind them.

"How much longer has she got to go? Joe asks Verina, "the poor kid looks as if she's got twins."

"Only a few more weeks I think."

Chloé rubs her hands together smiling at them all, "It's exciting isn't it? The life cycle. And fascinating."

Joe stands up, "Come on Angel before you start philosophising, we must go home and let these people get some sleep."

When he and Chloé turn back to wave, Chris and Verina are at the top of the steps, an arm round each other's waist.

"They're all right."

"You think so?" Chloé sounds less sure.

—

Verina pushes open the heavy pub door and eases her way into the warmth. The bar is packed, and noisy. Alex is waving to her from a booth near the window.

"You look like a beautiful Russian spy in that hat" he gives her a fierce hug, "you smell of fresh air and posh scent." He pulls her down beside him "I've been dying to see you."

"I can't stay long."

"Don't say that, you've only just arrived. What are you going to drink?"

"Could I have a brandy and ginger to warm me up please?"

He brings it for her and squeezes back in beside her, beaming delightedly" This is a real treat on a boring work-day."

"Oh come on," Verina smiles at him "don't be such a fraud, you love what you do."

He lifts her chin with a finger and tilts her face towards him, examining every detail of her face, "Hallo my lovely. It's been a long wait. I don't see nearly enough of you."

She gives an embarrassed little laugh, "Alex! You and Faith are over practically every week-end."

"Exactly! Me and Faith. I never get you to myself—like this—I always have to share you with loads of other people."

"You would have had to do that if I had brought you up." She picks up her glass.

"It would have been different. I'd be used to it. Now I want you all to myself. I can't help it. I've found you at last and I don't want to have to share you all the time. I want to find out everything about you. You don't have to hide anything from me you know, don't have to show me your best side all the time." He pulls her closer so that their faces are almost touching "The more I see you, the worse I feel about all the time I've missed having with you."

"Don't you think I feel the same?" She slips her arm through his "We're together now."

"You like it too when there's just you and me."

"Yes . . . but we've got to be a bit patient, we've got the rest of our lives to discover each other."

"If we're allowed."

"No-one's stopping us but we do have to be sensitive about Chris and Faith. I want to talk to you about that."

"No. I don't want to waste our precious time together talking about those two again. They're adults, they can learn to give a little."

"You're expecting a lot from Faith in her present state. How is she?"

"Belly-aching a lot. I don't understand her. She was all for me tracing you, now she seems to want to drag me back into a cosy little prison with just her, me and this bloody baby when it comes. She's so possessive. I didn't realise it 'til she was pregnant. She rings me up at work all the time now, never for anything important, do I think we should buy a new carri-cot or make do with a second-hand one from a friend? You know, really big decisions."

"She's nesting, it's natural."

"Nesting?! Disgusting word! When I hear her voice on the phone, I see these pale, clutchy fingers of hers clawing at me through the air. It's like being pursued by a sickly sea-monster."

"Alex!"

The music blares loudly and it isn't possible to hear each other speak until someone complains and the volume is turned down.

He takes her hand and links his fingers with hers. "Don't be cross with me Mummy-Vee, I do look after Faith."

"I hope so. You love her, don't you?"

He blows out a long breath.

"It's not easy when a wife's pregnant. It's even worse when the baby arrives and you lose your sleep for weeks but none of it lasts and it's all worth it. Once you hold your little one in your arms, you'll love him and although things are never the same again, you and Faith will settle into a new phase and be very happy. Aren't you looking forward to the baby?"

"I can't get my head round the idea of it yet. There's so much else to think about."

"I know what you mean," she strokes his cheek, "we haven't got used to this yet and now you're about to become a daddy and me a granny. We're not ready, are we?"

Sliding his glass round and round on its mat, he doesn't respond.

"What's the matter? What are you thinking?"

"I was thinking that once upon a time, you were the shape Faith is now and the baby inside you was me. Strange thought."

"Yes . . . could we open this window a bit?"

He pushes the window up a few inches. Icy air strikes their faces. He closes it again. Verina looks down into her glass.

"Can I ask you something?"

"Of course" she's tense, "what?"

"Did you really not know who raped you at that party?"

"Why are you asking me that? Don't you believe me?"

He's twirling a beer mat like a top. "I just wondered if you'd been flirting a bit maybe . . ."

"Asking for it you mean?"

57

"Oh God no. I'm sorry. I didn't mean that. I'm really sorry, I know you were only a kid."

Her eyes are brimming with tears. She gulps her drink. "Why must you constantly put me through all this? I'd better write it all down for you then you can read it over and over. You could even take it to a graphologist and find out if my writing shows a tendency to lie."

"I know you don't lie."

"So what do you want to know that I haven't already told you?"

"I thought you might be shielding somebody."

"No, I'm not shielding anybody. How long have you been waiting here for me?"

"Why? What's that got to do with anything?"

"I think you've already had too much to drink. You're being irrational again and aggressive. I think I'll go."

He grabs her arm "Please don't go. I'm sorry I've upset you again. What's the matter with me? I don't know why I do this. Don't take any notice of me. I'm an idiot."

She rushes away to wash her face.

There's another brandy waiting for her when she gets back. Alex makes her take a sip. "It's because we tell each other everything that I'm such a motor-mouth with you. There's a lot going on in my head. It's frustrating not knowing who my father is." He looks at the men standing at the bar as if trying to find one he might resemble.

"Whoever he was, at least he gave you life. That's one way to look at it."

"Christ! You're defending him now. I want him to know how much he's made you suffer—and me—and then I want to kill the bastard."

"Alex calm down. It's pointless digging up the past, you won't find any answers. You have to accept what happened just as I did."

He hugs her to him. "Poor Mummy-Vee, what you had to go through I don't deserve you. I always long to see you and then when we meet, I bugger it up. I'm like a tiresome teenager but you are still glad to have me, aren't you?"

"Yes."

"Let me see you smile then."

She gives him a shaky grimace. "Alex, try not to spoil things. All the badness and sadness has gone now. Try and stop tormenting yourself and me."

"When you met Chris, did you tell him you had a baby?

"No. I wish I had."

"I was your horrible secret."

"No. You were my beautiful child. Giving you up was an agony. When I met Chris, I was like a robot. He's a special man Alex, he didn't know it but he gave me back my life. I'd never want to hurt him . . ." she sighs "though it seems I have lately, without meaning to."

"Something to do with me?"

"Mostly thoughtlessness on my part. Chris says that when you and I get together, we're inclined to forget about everyone else."

He takes both her hands and holds them tight. "We need another drink. The same?"

"No. We're drinking too fast. I've had enough, I'd better not have any more."

"You're all right. You won't fall off the bus. I'll get some crisps."

He puts the glass down in front of her. "I don't like the idea of Chris making comments about us, I think he wants all your attention."

"He's never had all my attention poor man but he would like some, I am his wife."

"You're also my mother, the mother I didn't have all the years I was growing up."

"Phil and Lilian were good to you, weren't they?"

"What did you do after I was adopted?"

"I went on holiday with my mother, then back to school—a different school."

"So life just went on."

"Not exactly. I lost my friends and my girlhood."

"You should have refused to go through with all that. If you'd had an abortion, you could have gone on with your conventional little life pretending I'd never existed."

Verina leans back wearily and closes her eyes. "I wish you wouldn't do this. Why do you have to?"

"I don't know. I honestly don't know."

59

She hears the break in his voice and opens her eyes. He is fighting back tears now. She draws his head towards her and cradles his face against hers.

"I know I torture you Vee but I hate it if I think anyone is trying to stop us seeing each other. Still, if we can sometimes meet like this on our own . . ."

"It's not such a good idea."

"Why?"

"You can see for yourself, we get too . . . wound up."

"We won't in future. It's my fault today. I'm in a funny mood. I don't see why we can't meet for a drink now and then. Nobody has to know. We need time to ourselves. I must see you. I think about you all the time. You want to see me too."

"Yes but we should go gently. I have to safeguard the rest of the family while I try to help you gradually become a natural part of it."

"There may not be time."

"What do you mean?"

"I may be going abroad. The company's asked me to think about setting up a branch in the Far East."

Her face has lost all colour. "You haven't mentioned this before."

"I wasn't seriously considering it before but it seems to me if I can't see you whenever I want to without someone causing dramas, we may as well not be living on the same planet."

"I must have expressed myself badly, you don't seem to understand what I say to you. Do you listen?"

"I listen and I understand very well what you say and what you don't say. You put on a great performance at week-ends, having us over making us welcome, real little earth-mother. But then you go and hide in your work and the family. You can't fit me properly into your life. Let's face it, that's really what you've been trying to tell me for ages."

Verina hangs over the table, covering her face with her hands. Anyone pushing past could think she's shaking with laughter. The heavy drum-beat in the music drowns her sobs.

Alex ignores her for a moment then pulls her up and smoothes her hair back. He kisses her forehead and her closed wet eye-lids. Tears stream down her face. She shakes her head, "I can't bear this. I can't bear it."

60

"It's all right, it's all right. I won't go. I can't go. I won't ever leave you. How could I? Hush now. Come on."

"I can't drink in the middle of the day. I feel a wreck."

"You don't look it" he kisses the tip of her nose.

"I'll have to go in a minute."

"I know. So will I. When can we do this again?"

"What? Fight and cry?"

"I won't make you cry any more. I'm sorry."

"You wear me out."

"I know, I wear myself out. Vee, the one thing that keeps me going is looking forward to being with you whenever possible. I'll try and behave better if you promise me we can be by ourselves again soon . . . I won't let you go 'til you do." He's holding her arm and squeezing it hard, "Please."

"All right but I can't say when. I'll ring you."

Anxieties

Getting off the train, Faith hopes that his meeting might have finished early and that Alex would come and pick her up with the car but there's no sign of him at the station so she pulls her coat tightly round her and sets off walking *exercise'll do me good after sitting with Lilian all the afternoon—huge hug Phil gave me but I know they were disappointed Alex wasn't with me—that was a surprise—his ringing them every week to keep them up to date—funny person, so edgy sometimes then he'll do something nice like that—Phil and Lilian deserve it—they must feel bit out of it now Alex has found Verina but they don't show any sign—Lilian's so sweet, genuinely happy for him—odd situation for Al, suddenly so many parents in his life—when you look at Verina, you think she can't possibly be his mother, she looks so young—some people have everything—and now she's got Alex and he delights her—well, he would, he's good-looking too and clever—makes me smile, his sort of innocent vanity—why on earth did he marry a plain Jane like me?— must've subconsciously picked me as a foil—wish I hadn't encouraged him to contact Verina—never could have imagined it could take away interest in his own baby—he was so proud at first, telling everybody he was going to be a dad—not just Verina though, those nightmare weeks when I was being sick all the time put him off, made him queasy too he said—no patience with illness—can't stand the size of my belly now—but there's someone in there—someone who's going to arrive soon and will need taking care of—who will he be?—what will he be like?—thinking about the birth scares me but when I daydream about cradling my child—the welcome we'll get from the children the first time we take the baby over to Chris and Verina!*
    The hall light is on but Alex is not home yet. As she hangs up her coat, the phone rings, the caller puts the receiver down

when she answers. This happens a lot and is irritating. Could it sometimes be Verina?

It's eight o'clock, Alex will have eaten. She makes a sandwich and a cup of tea and curls up to watch television.

He comes bounding in "Hullo, Humpty-Dumpty. Oh good, you've made food. I'm starving, I've been to the gym."

"I haven't made food exactly, only a sandwich."

"Didn't you make any for me?"

"I didn't know where you were or what time you'd be in. I thought you'd have eaten by now."

"I did have something earlier but now I'd like a sandwich with you but if you don't want to look after me . . ." He pulls a pathetic face at her.

Faith pushes herself up and goes to the kitchen.

He flings himself down and starts playing with the remote control to search the channels.

"Here you are, your favourite, tuna and mayo."

"Thanks. What time did you get back?"

"About twenty minutes ago. Lilian and Phil send their love. I had to tell Lilian all about Verina. She was very shy about asking, she didn't want to seem nosy-poking. I could tell she was anxious."

"What about?"

"I suppose about the fact that she's always been your mother and now you've got your real one back. She may be worried in case you grow to prefer Verina and forget about her. She adores you."

"You mean she's another one who's jealous?"

Faith decides not to pick up on 'another one, "No. Lilian hasn't got an ungenerous bone in her body as you should know. She's happy for you and Verina. I think she may need some assurance that she is still has her place in your life and always will."

"What did you say?"

"I did my best to make her feel that your relationship wouldn't change. Verina can't ever be your mother in the sense that Lilian has been. That's her tragedy."

"Did you remember the photos?"

"I did. I promised Lilian that we'd have copies made and send them back. They're very precious to her."

"Let's see them then."

"What now?" She has kicked her shoes off and put her feet up.

"Yes. Now." He flicks his fingers at her.

Faith gets herself up again and goes to get her bag. "Lilian has written a note to Verina."

"Has she? I bet it's full of mawk. Let's see."

"Why should it be? You're talking about Lilian, an intelligent, sensitive woman who's been a good mother to you." He's tearing open the envelope. "And you shouldn't read other people's letters." Unfolding the single sheet of paper, he blows a raspberry at her.

Dear Verina

These photographs may cause you sadness for all you missed of Alex as a child but Faith tells me he insists on showing them to you. Perhaps I should have brought them to you myself and talked about them with you but that might have been too much of an intrusion. At least you will see that we took care of your boy. He was (still is) the centre of our lives. We both hope that you feel, however awful it was for you at the time, the right decisions were made. Philip and I have always been thankful for the chance to have a child to love and bring up. It made us into a family. We are so glad for you that your marriage is a happy one and you have those lovely children. Faith showed us some snaps of them in your garden.

You must be over the moon to have your son back. Faith is such a dear girl too and now we have our first grand-child to look forward to. We're all very lucky.

With warmest wishes from us both,

Lilian.

"I was right." Alex screws up the letter.

"That's an apalling thing to do."

"Vee won't want to read that drivel."

"I don't think you should make that decision for her." She retrieves the letter from the waste-paper basket and tries to smooth it out.

"Too late. She can't have it now."

"But Lilian will expect an answer."

"I'll handle it. I'll tell her Vee's not the letter-writing type but thanks her blah, blah, blah."

"Lilian cried, sorting those photographs, thinking about Verina and how she might feel."

"Yeah well, she's always been a bit soppy'

—

Chris and Alex have been out for a pint. As they come into the house, shrieks of laughter are coming from the kitchen. Greg is walking to and fro, his arms raised to hold up a fluorescent-lemon garment he's wearing over his clothes. It's knitted in enormous loose stitches and trails behind him on the floor.

"What's that?"

Faith is pink in the face and gasping, "An old lady who's known Alex since he was little made it for the baby. We shouldn't be laughing, it was very kind of her but I think she's forgotten how small babies are and I don't think her eye-sight's too good."

"Nor's her knitting."

"Let's eat" says Verina, "You're just in time to carve Chris."

Cassie reminds the table that a dinner lady at school had taught her to knit with meat skewers.

Verina remembers "You were going to knit a scarf for daddy, it was about an inch wide."

Nan starts telling Alex about wanting to make a bath mat with her French knitting when she was six.

Faith sees he's bored and so that Nan won't feel snubbed, she changes the subject. "Did you get the work from Knole, Verina?"

"Yes I did, five massive frames to restore and re-gild."

"Does that mean I can have the skate-board?" asked Greg.

Verina smiles at Faith, "You'd better prepare yourself, that's what children are like."

"Thanks."

"Not you Cass."

She beams at her mother. Alex winks at her. She blushes and starts talking earnestly to Faith.

Greg is enjoying himself, describing to Alex how he had scored the decisive goal in a match against a rival school. Alex isn't listening, he's watching Verina.

65

Chris looks around the table at the chattering family gathering; he sees Alex and Verina exchanging glances and knows they are not part of it. He carves more meat for everybody but can't finish what's on his own plate, there's a dead weight at the pit of his stomach. The noise level is rising and he hears himself shout above it "Pipe down a bit you kids! You're making an awful racket."

The children stare at him.

He forces a smile, "Eat your food,"

Verina has made an apple pie. Cassie tries to lighten the atmosphere, "Now you're going to see, Faith, why I'm never going to leave home, my mum makes the best pies in the world."

Greg and Nan rush off about their own affairs as soon as lunch is over. Cassie stays for coffee with the grown-ups.

Alex turns to Faith "Before you go up for your rest, could you get those photographs?" He holds his hand out, fingers clicking.

"They're in my bag." She hands him the bulging envelope.

As if tossing a pack of cards on the table, he spills the contents in front of Verina:

Alex as a tiny baby,
Alex learning to walk,
Alex the cub scout,
Alex up a tree,
Alex on a bicycle,
Alex sitting on a step, embracing a basset.
A beautiful child.

Faith waits in the doorway. Verina sifts through the photos. Alex looks on. Chris watches them both. Verina puts her hand over her mouth. Alex hurries round to put an arm across her shoulders "They're not making you miserable, are they? I thought you'd like to see them."

Faith begins to collect them up but Verina puts a hand over them, "Leave them Faith. It's all right."

Chris sits down beside Verina and picks up some of the snaps. They look at a few together. Here is Alex, about three, twisting round in the seat of a miniature train, smiling disarmingly at the camera. Verina makes an odd little sound.

Chris puts his hand over hers but she jumps up and runs to lock herself in the downstairs cloakroom. They can hear her crying as if her heart will break.

Chris looks at Alex "Thank you very much."

"What do you mean?"

"You know perfectly well what I mean. Come on Faith, you go and rest. Don't worry about Vee, I'll look after her." He leads her to the stairs then returns in a cold rage to Alex. "Could you get out of my sight for a while?"

"Why? What have I done?"

"You know what you've done—exactly what you intended when you threw those photographs at her without any warning. You wanted to punish her."

Cassie is white-faced, "Daddy, I can't bear to hear mummy crying like this." She's in tears herself, "Please make her stop and come out."

Alex packs the photographs back in the envelope and walks out of the kitchen. They hear the front door close.

Chris comforts Cassie "Don't worry sweetheart, this is an emotional time for mummy but we'll help her through it."

At the sound of the cloakroom door opening, Chris goes to meet Verina and takes her in his arms.

"I'm sorry Chris, it was suddenly all too much. Where's Alex?"

"Gone out. Come and sit down. I'll pour you some more coffee."

"Thank you. I hope Nan and Greg didn't hear me yowling. I'm sorry you did Cass."

"Nan's upstairs playing her music and Greg's down the other end of the garden."

"Good. I can explain to you two. I've got three scrumptious children and I love them to bits as you know but I saw nothing of Alex's childhood and it makes me distraught that I wasn't there at such a precious time." Near tears again, she drinks some coffee. "You know Chris, I felt as if Alex was reproaching me just then. It was as if he deliberately wanted to hurt me."

"He did."

"Yeah, I thought he was a bit rough mum, the way he banged the photographs down on the table. Perhaps he was fed up because we'd been talking about when we were little."

67

Chris makes Verina settle herself by the fire with the papers while he and Cassie clear the kitchen. Father and daughter are quiet.

Cassie starts arranging tea things on a tray when a ring on the door-bell sends her out to answer the door. Alex is there with chrysanthemums. He pushes past her and goes to confront Chris.

"Will you let me give these to Verina?"

"You can give them to her. They won't make her feel any better. I don't know what you're playing at but I won't have you upsetting her."

"I'm sorry. I didn't mean to. Do you want us to push off home when Faith comes down?"

"There's no need," Verina has appeared.

Alex hands her the flowers. She puts them in water and goes back to the sitting room followed by Chris.

Cassie fills the kettle, knowing that Alex is uncomfortable but unable herself, to find any helpful words.

Greg rushes in from the garden "Alex, you'll never guess what I've found for you in the garden—a white horse." He runs to the sink "Have to wash the earth off. Look at its curly mane. I think it's an Arab steed, they're the best in the world you know."

When the phone rings Cassie answers. "It's for you dad, someone called Dean?"

Chris groans.

"Chris, 'sorry to ring you at home. I've managed to resist calling you all day but I've been brooding about the whole business since Friday night and I'm driving myself mad here."

"What 'whole business'?"

"I know you'll think I'm paranoid but I can't get Fletcher's remarks at that meeting out of my mind. I'm sure he was referring to me. He doesn't think much of my capabilities. I think he's going to put the mockers on any ideas I put forward so I need a strategy to deal with him. You know him much better than I do, could I possibly come round for a chat? I won't stay long."

"We've got rather a houseful here." Chris hesitates," It would probably be better if I came to you—after supper perhaps, about nine say, something like that?"

"Thanks Chris. I'd really appreciate it. I hope your wife won't mind."

Before going out to see Dean, Chris seizes a moment to ask Verina privately if she's really feeling all right again."

"Yes of course. It was just seeing those baby photographs out of the blue, that knocked me sideways. He's apologised for being insensitive."

"You won't feel I'm deserting you if I go out for about an hour?"

"No. If Dean needs your advice, you go and see what you can do for him. But don't let him keep you too long while he maunders on about himself. You're too kind for your own good most of the time."

A little after midnight, Chris lets himself in, feeling dissatisfied with his handling of the talk with Dean—*waste of time, he doesn't listen—in any case couldn't dredge up anything useful to say, too worried about Vee—and need to think about Alex's behaviour—throwing the past at her like that when she's still trying to adjust to the present—she could lose her balance—leaving them to it this evening, partly an act of faith, wanted to give them space to sort out the kerfuffle.* He checks the garden door and puts out the kitchen lights. Better see if the fire's died down. He opens the sitting-room door.

Empty bottles and glasses in the hearth. Verina and Alex lying on the floor, tangled up in each other. They roll apart and look up at him sleepily, unfocused.

"Come on, bed-time." He helps Verina up.

Alex pushes himself into a sitting position.

With his arm round Verina, Chris puts out a hand to him.

"I'm okay. I'm okay." He manages to get up, stagger to the door and throw himself up the stairs.

With Verina's head heavy against his shoulder, Chris gets her up to the bedroom and on to the bed. He pulls off her dress and removes her shoes. She's already asleep so he pulls the covers up over her and puts out the light.

Down in the kitchen, he mechanically makes himself a cup of tea—*my Verina, weeping bitterly and pissed paralytic all in one day, she's going to feel terrible tomorrow—I feel terrible tonight.* He allows himself to see Alex and Verina again as he has just found them—*okay, like lovers.* He repeats the phrase, running it like a sub-title under his mental images—*it doesn't necessarily mean anything—things always look worse in the middle of the*

69

night and I'm exhausted. The tea grows cold at his elbow. In the lonely kitchen a tear rolls down his face. The heating's off and he shivers—*can't face my warm bed—strange woman in it—not my Verina, she's gone—don't know where—bugger everything—should've stayed home tonight and looked after her, then she and Alex wouldn't have got pissed and ended up rolling about on the floor—that business with the photographs was a ploy—he likes distressing her so they can have reconciliations—they're so out of it, they won't remember a thing in the morning while I'm left with this picture nailed to my mind and I can't escape from it—how do you switch off thought?—what should I do?—what can I do?—it's like watching two people in a car with failed brakes, careering down a hill while you stand helpless at the side of the road, waiting for the crash—oh God, listen, if you exist, help me please—help all of us—show me what to do.*

—

Verina is coming down the stairs as Chris walks in with Greg.

"Hey mum, you didn't see me this afternoon when I waved to you."

"What? When did you wave to me?"

"When our class was coming back from the Science Museum. I saw you on the platform with Alex but you didn't see me."

"Oh, sorry darling."

Chris helps Greg hang up his school bag and follows Verina into the kitchen. Nan is slumped over the table, her head buried in her arms.

Verina goes to her "What's wrong Nan? Don't you feel well?"

No answer.

Verina tries again, "Please tell us what's the matter darling. We can't help you til we know what's wrong."

Nan keeps her head down. "I hate Alex."

"Why? What's he done?"

"I really hate him" she lifts a red, tear-stained face, "you said you couldn't come to hear me read my poem in the competition because you had to see an important client but you had time to see Alex." She hides her face and starts crying again.

70

Verina pulls a chair near to her and sits stroking her head, "Sweetie, I did have to see a client—a very important person who's going to give me a lot of work. I met Alex by accident."

Cassie comes in. "What's up with Nan?"

"I didn't get to hear her read her poem in school today. She thought it was because I'd been with Alex, I met him accidentally at the station."

"I'm beginning to think our new brother is not such good news, he keeps making people cry."

"Don't exaggerate Cass."

"Well poor Faith was in floods of tears too on Saturday afternoon. I heard her when I went upstairs for your cologne."

"That was probably my fault" Chris says. "I was a bit cool to Alex in front of her because of the business with the photographs."

Verina sighs, "Oh Chris, I over-reacted"

"Well I hate him" Nan repeats from under her hair.

The telephone is ringing. Chris goes to answer it *what was Alex doing over here on a weekday afternoon when he works in central London?*

Joe's voice, "Fancy a pint Chris?"

"Perfect timing."

"See you in about ten minutes?"

"You're on."

"Blimey Chris, you've lost some weight!"

"Have I?"

"Yeah. You all right?"

"A lot of pressure at work just at the moment."

"You wanna take things a bit easy mate. Life's too short. You find us a table, I'll get these."

"How's Verina and the kids? That cuckoo still trying to get into your nest?"

"You don't miss much Joe."

"Well I can see it can't be easy."

"It isn't. I'm out of my depth to be honest."

"I can imagine. I would be too. Are the kids jealous?"

"Not only the kids."

"Still it's bound to settle down, it's not as if Alex is 'the other man'."

"I don't know. A lot of the time it seems as if he is. I think he's always on the phone to Vee. Often I'll come into the room and she'll put the receiver down."

"Could be a customer."

"No, it's sort of secretive. I'm not imagining it. I sometimes wander in and she's mumbling into the phone or arguing quietly and my sixth sense tells me she's talking to Alex and he's giving her some kind of grief. If I ask her who it is, she'll say a supplier has let her down or something."

"You mean she's lying to you?"

"She wouldn't see it as lying. She knows how jealous and fed up I am at present and probably wants to avoid giving me any more aggro."

"Of course, when you are jealous, it can make you imagine things."

"I know. I'm suspicious all the time these days. Vee is often out on mysterious little errands these days. I'm sure she sees Alex on the quiet."

"Joe thought about this. "If she does, it could be so as not to wind you up—you and Faith. You know, get things out of their system without having to worry about you two. It's all still a novelty for them."

"Yes but if they're meeting in secret, then it all gets heavy-heavy, know what I mean? Vee and I have always been open and honest with each other but now when I ask probing questions—and I can't stop myself—she shuts herself off. I suppose I deserve it, I do sort of spy on her. I don't want to think of them having meetings on their own when I'm trying to help Vee keep a sense of proportion about the boy. You've seen for yourself how they behave."

"Yeah, bit too touchy-feely."

"It's hard on young Faith. Pity he had to find Vee now while she's pregnant, she isn't getting his full support."

He tells Joe about the incident with the photographs. "Vee goes up and down all the time these days. She told me something the other day, she saidshe's spent her life looking for her son. Not actually doing anything about it but she'd see a boy at a bus-stop or cruising past her on roller-skates and she'd wonder if he was hers. Only natural I suppose but I never knew anything about it. You think you know the person you're married to. I always thought she was happy, while all the time, she was keeping this to herself."

"She has always been happy and so she should be."

Chris got up to get them another pint.

"Thanks mate. Listen, who knows what goes on in women's minds? I daresay Vee did think about the kid now and then but the memory didn't impinge that much. If you don't mind my saying so, I think she's making a bit of a drama of it now to cover up some of the carry-on between her and the lad. You're a good husband to her, she's got three lovely kids and a comfortable home. What more could she want? Marriage is a see-saw, sometimes when one's up, the other's down so you shift around a bit until there's a balance. You and Vee can get through this."

"I hope you're right Joe. I never would have believed anything could shake us. I've watched her suffering all sorts of reverberations from the shock of Alex turning up. It's complicated. She's delighted with him but I think he's made her relive the whole bloody business. He certainly seems to like making her feel guilty. And she's no reason to but if I ever venture the slightest criticism of him she's like a tigress with her cub."

"Don't you like him?"

"Well I could like him, I suppose, if he didn't cause trouble in the family all the time. He's probably unaware because he's totally self-centred."

"Aren't we all?"

"Yes. We all fight for our share."

"Why don't you take Vee away for a few days? It sounds as if you could do with some time to yourselves. You might get a better perspective on things. Chloé and I would have the kids."

"She'd be bound to think I was trying to get her away from Alex."

"So?"

"I dunno. It's good of you but . . ."

"It's enlightened self-interest mate, anything that affects your family affects us. It sounds as if Alex is trying to cut your balls off."

—

73

They are in The Crown at Framlingham which Chris chose for its happy memories. To persuade a tired and overwrought Verina to leave the children and go into the country has proved surprisingly easy. She is taking the opportunity to rest as much as possible. Leaving her half-dozing over a book, Chris goes off for a walk on his own.

She watches from the window to make sure he's well on his way, then sits down and writes a note:

My Darling Boy,

I'm snatching a few moments while I'm on my own. I didn't call you again before we came away because the words you left me with on Thursday were too precious to be followed by one of our difficult conversations on the phone. The things you said lit up the lamps down our street.

Do you know what I do at night now? I let you slide sideways into my sleep so that I can have you with me.

This is not being a successful break, I don't want to be here. I'm using up the days by sleeping. I can see your face as I write and feel the clasp of your fingers.

I'll slip out and post this now.

V. xxx

Looking at her across the table over dinner, Chris is remembering the first time they stayed in this hotel. They were so mad about each other they woke in the morning, smiling with happiness and snuggled together unwilling to get out of bed until the maid came to do the room. From their window, they laughed at a duck and a drake waddling across the cobbled square together like an old married couple. They bought their first water-colour here in the gallery across the square. Is Vee reliving any of this? Where is she in her thoughts? Far from him. She doesn't look at him when he speaks to her, it's as if she's being dragged back unwillingly into an unpleasant world. "Shall we have our coffee out there by the fire?"

"If you like."

He is moving through a dream himself—a nightmare—in which he has to confront an invisible demon. There must be

74

a formula for defeating it but he can't work it out with this fear clouding his mind.

One ill-chosen word and Verina will pack her bag. Yet he's been so careful.

"This little break isn't really working Vee, is it?"

"What do you mean? What did you expect?"

He tries to will her to look at him, encourage him. "I hardly know. It's as if I've gone blind and I'm groping around trying to find my bearings."

Irritated, she shrugs.

He presses on. "I suppose I was hoping for habit to do the trick somehow—for us to get back to normal. For you to come back to me."

"This is hardly the place for this conversation."

"There's no-one else here. Seems as good a place as any."

She is slumped in her chair, looking into the fire.

Chris pours the coffee and hands her a cup. "It would probably all have been much easier if Alex had been a daughter."

"What are you talking about?"

"Mothers and daughters spend endless time together in the ordinary run of things, like you and Cass. You wouldn't have needed to arrange private rendezvous.

"Who said anything about private rendezvous?"

"No-one. I guessed. It's true though, isn't it?"

"You've brought me down here for another inquisition."

"I'm trying to hold our family together."

She looks directly at him for the first time all evening. "All right, it is true. I do see Alex occasionally. There's nothing wrong in that. We need to get to know one another in peace."

"You can do that within the family . . . and it's safer."

"Oh for God's sake Chris, you and your psychobabble. You think you know everything."

"It's because I don't know everything that I've been thinking perhaps you and Alex should go and get some counselling."

"Counselling? Are you mad?"

"Not far off, I could do with some counselling myself. But please do think about it Vee. It might help you both."

"With what?"

"With keeping the strong feelings you have for each other within appropriate bounds."

She's red in the face and turns away from him angrily.

"I don't like putting you through this and it's hard for me to say these things. I'm sure neither of you can help the way you behave. But please let's talk. I am your best friend."

After a long silence, she replies in a husky voice, "No wonder I'm so tired. There's Alex all intense and demanding on one side of me and you tormenting me on the other."

"I don't mean to do that. You've had stars in your eyes for weeks and I don't want anything to change them to tears."

"Can I have a brandy?"

"Of course." He orders brandy for them both. "Look, I expect I'm saying the wrong things but if I am, it's out of panic. I am afraid for you, for all of us. I feel helpless watching the pair of you. Please go and get some advice before everything goes pear-shaped. I've been on to the Post-Adoption Society on my own behalf. I've got the name of someone you could go to. Will you do that?"

"If that's what you want."

"It is but don't just do it for me—or even the children—do it for yourself. You're like a woman bewitched. I'm worried about what might happen if the spell should break."

"Could we stop talking about it now? It's doing my head in."

"All right but please try and persuade Alex to see this man too."

—

The three of them are chatting in Gemma's room. Cassie is lying on her stomach on the bed and Sheldon is stretched out near her on the floor.

"So you don't need me as an honorary brother anymore?"

"Frankly, I never did."

"Perhaps I'll give you a couple of years to blossom into something fancyable and then I might ask you to go out with me instead, you lucky girl."

Gemma, who is looking through some sheet music, snorts "Puh-lease, this is my friend here. She's got more taste than to ever go out with you!"

"What's wrong with me? I haven't got spots and I've got a brilliant future ahead of me."

"'Brilliant future'? You haven't even got your 'A' levels yet."

"They're in the bag."

"Modest, isn't he, my brother?"

"I wish I was that confident."

Sheldon pats Cassie's head, "Comes with age and experience my dear. So what's he like, this big brother of yours?"

"He's all right."

"All right?" Gemma's amused, "He's gorgeous—to look at anyway."

"I don't like the way he enjoys teasing Nan."

"Does he tease her?"

"Yes and you know how friendly and affectionate she is. When she was little, mum used to have to stop her kissing the gas-man."

"Kissing the gas-man?"

"She thought you had to love everybody. She still does, only she really means it. She thinks Alex is wonderful. He helps her with her homework sometimes—to impress mum I'm sure—but then he'll ask her a question and when she's trying to explain things, she goes red and waves her arms around in the air so Alex calls her 'Lobby-loo', short for little lobster. He embarrasses her and then she loses her words."

"Does he tease you?"

"Oh yeah, calls me 'Catastrophe'. Cassie, catastrophe, geddit? He tries to put me down in front of mum. He's jealous because we're so close. I can tell he doesn't like it if I hang around when he wants to talk to mum."

"How about when you want to talk to your mum?"

"I admit I'm just the same. I don't want him taking up all her time. Like . . . I'm used to getting home earlier than Nan and Greg a couple of times a week. That's always been a time for mum and me to have a quiet cup of tea and talk about things. Now, I often find Alex has popped in, or worse still, mum has popped out and I often suspect she's off somewhere bonding with him."

"What's he like with your father and Greg?"

"He's respectful to dad and I can see that makes dad feel old and he calls Greg 'sir' which makes him crack up. Greg thinks he's the best thing since sliced bread."

Gemma fished under her bed and found a half-empty box of twiglets which she offered the other two. "You like Faith though?"

"Faith's lovely, she just fits in. Alex is horrible to her. He seems to be annoyed that she's pregnant as if it's got nothing to do with him. He still expects her to do everything, as soon as she sits down he starts ordering her about, 'Make me some coffee, ring and cancel this or that' he never says please or thank you. He talks to her as if she's a dumbo. She's only got an MA from Oxford! Dad reckons she's quietly on the ball and knows a lot more about everything than Alex and is more intelligent."

"Why does she let him push her around?"

"To keep the peace I think. Then when he wants to go off for hours to sit brooding over mum while she works, he comes over all solicitous and packs Faith off to rest upstairs. Poor mum, I bet he bores her to death talking about winning the painting competition when he was six and how he got into the cricket team. He loves talking about himself."

"Sounds like Sheldon."

"Watch it!"

"But Cass, be fair, it's natural he wants to tell your mother everything."

"I know. I'm just not a very nice person."

Angela calls up the stairs "Gemma, Mrs Welland is here."

"Thanks mum." Gemma jumps up. "Got to go for my piano lesson. Back soon."

She has left the door open and they can hear her clattering down the stairs and then the strains of Liszt. Cassie drops her head on her arms, settling to listen.

Sheldon puts his hand on her shoulder, "You are a nice person."

"What?"

"You said you're not a nice person, I'm saying you are."

"Thanks but don't start being embarrassing."

As Gemma plays, Cassie relaxes to let the music pour through her, she begins to feel drowsy. Sheldon is smoothing her hair and his gentleness seems all of a part with the music, as though he senses that deep down she's miserable and this is his wordless way of showing sympathy. She's grateful for his silence until he slides his fingers under her hair and begins to stroke her neck, "Sheldon! Leave off!" She raises her head, the old sweater belonging to her father is hanging off her shoulder

78

and before she knows what's happening, he's pushed his hand down the front and managed to get his fingers inside her bra.

Shock paralyses her for a second, then outraged, she pulls away from him and flies down to sit on the stairs outside the music room.

With thundering chords, Gemma seems to be calling up out of the piano, the frenzy inside Cassie *why is everything so vile these days?—feel like banging my head against the wall—sodding Sheldon, pretending to be sweet only so he could take liberties—want to dive out the door but got to behave as though nothing has happened.*

Shrinking herself into the smallest shape she can against the bannisters, she concentrates on her loathing of Sheldon.

Angela crosses the hall with a pot plant, "I hope you're staying for tea Cass?"

"Thank you Angela but I can't, I've got to get back to give Chloé a hand. I'm only waiting to say goodbye to Gemma."

—

Verina has given Cassie a pile of underwear to put in Nan's drawer. Cassie comes back down looking troubled.

"What's the matter?"

"Well, it's probably all right mum but Nan's got Chloé's amber earrings and bracelet in her drawer. Do you think Chloé might have lent them to her?"

"Doesn't seem very likely." Verina goes up to see for herself, then rings Chloé.

"I didn't realise they were gone. Don't be cross with her please Vee. She wouldn't steal from me. Shall I pop round and talk to her about it?"

"We should come to you really."

"She'll feel better in her own home, don't you think?"

"Perhaps you're right. Bless you Chloé. You're so good to take it like this after all you do for these children."

Nan, hearing Chloé's voice when she arrives, dashes down the stairs to give her a hug.

Verina asks her to come through to the studio with her and Chloé. "What can you tell us about these?" she asks quietly, pointing to the jewellery on the table.

"I didn't steal them."

Chloé says quickly "Of course you didn't darling. You just wanted to borrow them I expect."

"Yes. I wanted something of yours to keep with me when we had to come home again. I should have asked you. I don't know why I didn't. I shouldn't have touched your things. I'm sorry." She starts to cry. Through her sobs, she manages to say "You won't want to be my god-mother any more now."

"Yes I will and I've always told you that my things are your things because you are special to me, so you haven't done anything terrible at all."

"I hate myself. I've spoiled everything. I was going to put them back. You do believe me, don't you?" Fresh tears threaten.

"I believe you. It's just a muddle. We all do strange things at times and we don't understand why we do them. Isn't that true Verina?"

"For some people, perhaps it is."

"Oh mummy, do you mean loopy people?"

"Mummy's not talking about loopy people Nan. You're not loopy but sometimes if we're feeling confused or unhappy, we don't think straight. Then we do something all of a sudden that we wouldn't normally do. Are you worried about anything Nan?"

"I don't think so. I don't know. I'm so sorry Chloé. Please forgive me."

"Darling, you are forgiven. Let me tell you a story. When I was eight, my best friend was in hospital with leukemia. One afternoon I was with her and she asked me to pass her a pear. It was the last one in the bowl. I picked it up and I remember staring at her white face and big, sad eyes and trying to imagine what it must be like to die when you're only a little girl. Then I started to eat the pear and the juice ran down my chin. When I had eaten nearly all of it, she asked me for a bite and I burst into floods of tears. I couldn't understand how I could have eaten the pear my friend asked for when she was dying. It was an appallling thing to do but worrying about her made me forget what I was doing, I didn't particularly want a pear, didn't even realise I was eating it. Do you see what I mean about not thinking straight, not thinking about what you're doing?"

"Yes. Did she die?"

"No and we had many a laugh about it all when she was back in school. I told you the story so you wouldn't feel so bad about yourself. Have a good think, and if you are worried about anything—perhaps there's a problem at school—talk it over with mummy. And you're still my special girl, all right?"

They are setting the table for supper. Cassie says "Mum, can I ask you something?"

"Yes?"

"Why didn't you speak to Nan before you rang Chloé? I was quite surprised. I hope you don't mind me asking only Nan got an awful shock you know."

"I suppose I should have done really but I was horrified. If Nan got a shock, it's no bad thing, she won't help herself to other people's things again in a hurry."

"No but . . ."

"I don't want to talk about it anymore Cass. Nan will get over it. You make the salad—dressing please."

There is someone at the door. Cassie runs to open it and is delighted to find Gemma standing there—until she notices Sheldon behind her.

Nan grabs Gemma's hand, "Come and see our baby guinea-pigs."

"I will in a tick."

The girls leave Sheldon to close the door and they hurry into the crowded kitchen.

"We've come to invite you to our party on Saturday Cass. And Vee, here's a note about it from mum."

Cassie is already on her way out of the kitchen.

"Hey Cass, where you going? You haven't said you'll come on Saturday."

"That's because I won't. But thank you."

"What?" Gemma is puzzled, "You are joking?"

"I don't like parties much actually."

"Since when?"

Sheldon says "Perhaps she doesn't like me."

Cassie looks past him, "You said it."

There's an awkward moment while everyone takes this in.

Verina breaks the silence, "Come on you two, have you been having some sort of row?"

"Cass, you're not seriously saying you won't come. Please come for my sake. You can ignore Sheldon if you want to."

"Sorry Gem. I don't even want to be in the same room with him."

"Aren't you being a bit rude Cass?" Verina's annoyed

"Oh, sorry. I'll try and be more polite. My dear friend Gemma, my very best friend, I thank you for your kind invitation and I don't want to hurt your feelings but I have to tell you something painful to your ears. I'm afraid I do not care for your brother and so I am unwilling to come to your party. Excuse me." She goes out closing the door.

Gemma rounds on Sheldon "What the hell have you done to Cass? How can we have a party without her?"

He opens his eyes wide, "I dunno what's the matter with her."

"Stay here, I'm going to ask her."

"Cass? Can I come in?"

"You can."

However, she can't get Cassie to say more than "Look Gem, this is an absolute secret between you and me, Sheldon embarrassed me the other day when you went off for your lesson. I don't want to say what he did. I don't want to talk about it and cause a major drama, I don't want to give him the satisfaction. And please don't you ask him anything or I'll feel even worse. I'm sorry because he's your brother."

"Don't worry about that. I know he can be maddening. I'm angry with him too if he's done something to upset you. But if you don't want to talk about it . . . I don't want to have the bloody party now if you're not coming but mum's already asked the cousins. She'll be mad at Shel. What do you want me to tell her?"

"Please don't mention him. Tell her I've fixed to stay with Faith and Alex Saturday night. I offered to go with Faith to get things for the baby. Alex hates shopping. I'll go this week-end then it won't be a lie. Sorry to disappoint you Gem. Normally I'd love to come."

"You're sure you didn't misunderstand something Shel said or did?"

Cassie raises her eye-brows.

"Well it's strange because I think he really fancies you. He's always saying you've got brains."

Cassie shrugs.

Over lunch, Verina mentions the party again, "I can't understand why you don't want to go Cass. Whatever Sheldon is supposed to have done, it can't be that bad. Besides, it's a bit awkward when we're such close friends."

"Oh mum. Please stop going on about it."

"I'm not going on about it, I just."

Cassie cuts in "For goodness sake! I should have thought you'd prefer me not to go. Look what happened to you when you went to a teenage party."

"Cass!" Chris thunders.

Cassie escapes up to her room to fling herself on her bed. There was a time when she could have had a quiet word with her mother and explained. Now she can't *Mum's always preoccupied these days, she doesn't seem to listen—surely she does still care about all of us?—don't want to talk to dad about Sheldon, we love each other to bits dad and I but we're both a bit shy—feel so humiliated—could absolutely kill Sheldon—shouldn't have shouted at mum like that—hope it didn't make her cry again—made dad angry too—I wish I was dead.*

Nan brings her up a cup of tea and some chocolate biscuits. "It's all right. Mummy knows you're miserable about something or you wouldn't have said what you did. Why don't you go and say sorry."

"Oh Nan, I feel all shaky."

Nan hugs her. "We're all going down to the river. You coming?"

"I need to be by myself for a while. Okay?"

"Course. See you later."

Verina goes to her room to brush her hair after the walk and opens her door to the scent of freesias. They're arranged in a small vase on her dressing table with a note:

Sorry Mummy. I didn't mean to hurt you. Anyway, good came out of it all in the end, Alex I mean.

Love Cass. xxx

They've finished supper and Verina tells the children to go and get on with their homework.

"You said you were at the school today?"

"Yes."

"So what was that all about?"

"Nan's been caught stealing. She's owned up now but she lied at first so they're not letting her go on the school trip.

"I thought she was very subdued this evening. She'll be bitterly disappointed."

"She is."

"I wonder what's made her start stealing. What sort of things has she been taking?"

"Oh she took someone's birthday present—a Parker pen—and some crisps or something from the confiscation cupboard. They want her to see the ed. psych."

"I'm sure that's not necessary. You don't want that, do you? Poor little Nan. I can't understand it. Still, if she's disturbed, it's up to us to sort her out." Verina's face is set hard. "It's not your fault you know. It's more likely mine, I don't give the kids much time in the week. I tend to leave everything to you."

He waits for her to say something. "Look, why don't we have a quiet couple of days with just us this week-end? Perhaps we need to concentrate on these three a bit more. After all, they're used to life more or less revolving round them. They might be feeling a bit neglected. Let's take them out somewhere for a treat."

"I knew this was coming."

"What?"

"I knew you would try and make some connection between Nan's attention-seeking and Alex."

"Attention-seeking?"

"The Head said stealing is often just that."

"I wasn't trying to make any connection but there may be one. Nan adores you, she may well be feeling she's lost you to Alex."

"You really want me to feel guilty, don't you?"

"No, I don't. But aren't you concerned for Nan? I just want us to do what's best for her at the moment. If this is a bid for attention, we must give her some attention. There's obviously something going on in her head which is making her unhappy. It may be nothing to do with Alex."

"Cassie and Greg are fine."

"You can't always tell. I think Cass sometimes feels displaced and hurt. As for Greg, a lot goes over his head but we shouldn't we complacent. Children always know when things are not as they should be. How about my idea for the week-end?"

"I'll think about it."

"You mean 'no'."

"It would look odd."

"Who to?"

"The last thing we should do is make dramas I think."

Chris sighs, "We already have one. Taking the children out is a natural way of trying to deal with it. Faith is the first person to understand that. In any case, I'm sure she doesn't want to come waddling over here all the time, especially now. And she must sometimes want to have Alex to herself at week-ends. Anyway we owe it to little Nan to give her some special time for a while, show her we still love her and have faith in her. We need our space. I'd like a break from having other people around all the time."

"I suppose you're right. Faith did murmur something about perhaps not coming every time, she does get tired now."

"Does that mean Alex will stay home with her?"

"I've got an idea, maybe he should talk to Nan. She looks up to him."

"No." Chris is furious, "No-one's going to talk to Nan but you and me. I won't have her humiliated. And please Vee, just for a week or two, I don't want Alex here."

"Too bad." She raises her voice now too. "You can't start laying down the law like this. It's unreasonable. I want him here. He's my son and he's coming."

Chris picks up a heavy glass bowl and hurls it at the door. The crash shakes the room. Splinters of glass fly everywhere.

Verina picks her way through the fragments and leaves him standing there.

Nan's terrified face appears round the door.

"What was that noise daddy?"

"I was angry about something and I threw a bowl across the room. I shouldn't have done. Dangerous and stupid."

Cassie has run down the stairs and is staring in too.

"Your old dad lost his cool for a minute Cass."

"Was it because of me daddy?"

"No Nan, it wasn't because of you. Don't come in here either of you until I've cleared up the glass."

The feeling of being out of control invades him. As he empties the newspaper and glass into the kitchen bin, he speaks to Verina. "Do you remember when life was simple?"

"It still is. You're the one who creates complications."

Chris looks at her in silence *I do still love you but I'm also beginning to dislike you.*

—

Cassie receives a hand-delivered note. She recognises Sheldon's writing, and nearly doesn't open it.

Cass,

I was out of order the other day. I'm sorry. You seemed a bit miz and I honestly started out just wanting to comfort you, that's all. Then some devil got into me and I know I was starting to go too far. I wanted to explain when Gem and I came round but you didn't give me a chance. I don't blame you. You're not a girl who gives anybody the 'come on'.

Our party was a washout and though you hate me being embarrassing, I've got to admit, it was because you were not there.

I know you think I'm a rat but if you can't forgive me for the other day, could you at least try to forget all about it please? I promise it won't ever happen again. Can we go back to being mates?

Sheldon.

Reading it, she thinks *at least he can say sorry—seems genuine— still feel so mortified—'spose I'll have to try and forgive him—always liked him up til now—enjoyed his cheek.*

She rings Gemma who asks her round. While she's describing her week-end with Faith and Alex, Sheldon pops his head round the door to ask his sister to lend him some scissors. As if surprised to see Cassie, he says "Oh, hi Cass."

Looking past him, she replies cooly "Hi Sheldon."

86

Gemma says, "Shel and I were thinking of going to the new James Bond film Sunday night, d'you fancy coming?"

She can feel Sheldon waiting for her answer so Cassie lets him wait a few seconds "Yeah, if I can."

He comes right into the room at that, extending crossed fingers to Cassie "Pax? Is it Pax then?"

She makes the same gesture back to him and still without quite looking at him says "Yes, it's pax."

"Great. See you Sunday."

Secrets

Chris hears the bell and goes to open the door. Faith is standing there. "Alex and I had a row. He's not here, is he?"

"No. There's nobody in but me. Come in. Did you drive over?"

"No. Alex has got the car."

"Sit down Can I make you some tea or would you like a drink?"

"I shouldn't but a drink might stop me shaking." She crumples into a chair and looks miserably at him

"I'm sorry to disturb your afternoon peace Chris."

"You're not disturbing me, I'm pleased to see you though I'm sorry you're so upset. G and T?"

She nods, "Please".

"I'll join you." He pours the drinks and sits full of foreboding while she takes a few gulps.

"I had to get out of the flat. I didn't plan to come here but I didn't know where else to go. I thought I'd find Alex . . . and Verina and I hoped you'd be in and we could have some kind of showdown because I don't know what I'm expected to do." Her hair is unbrushed and desolation stares out at him from her eyes.

He waits for her to continue.

"Chris, do you know for God's sake what's going on? Because I don't. Alex tells me he's going to be living with Verina soon. Do you know anything about this?

Chris shakes his head, "He said that?"

"I can't make out whether he means he's coming to live here with all of you or what. I'm sure you don't want him here, do you? And what about me? And the baby?" She touches her stomach. "And the children? I'm so confused, I feel as if I've been drugged. He's trying to make me go along with something extraordinary and horrible." She finishes her drink quickly to stop herself from crying. "He says now he's met Verina, she has to come first. He can't help it, he says. In any case, he thinks it's perfectly natural. He's full of theories and explanations. He says, when a man marries, the wife becomes paramount and the mother stands back but in our case, the situation is reversed. He says if I really care about him, I should understand this. He seems to be telling me to get out of the way." She sips her drink, very near tears again.

"Chris, you don't think they could possibly be planning to go off together and leave us all, do you? If you'd heard him going on last night, you'd have thought the same thing I'm sure. 'Sorry, this has gone to my head." She puts her glass down. "Am I mad or is he? I can't get angry with him although he gets angry with me. I can see he's not himself, it's as if a devil's got into him and changed all his thinking—all his feelings. He speaks very clearly as though what he is saying is simple and normal but every word he comes out with frightens me and muddles me more and more." She breaks down.

He lets her cry, hoping it will relieve her. Listening to her despairing sobs, he tries hard to think of a way to comfort her.

"Chris, I don't even know what I'm talking about. None of this seems real. Alex shouted at me today that I'm a bad wife who will make an awful mother because I'm inhuman. Then he left me and I've been worried because he drives erratically when he's in a temper."

She looks like a child, pink smudges under her eyes, and strands of her short hair sticking up.

"Oh Faith, none of us is equipped to deal with all this. To tell you the truth, I'm floundering myself."

"Oh God. Sometimes I feel I hate Verina. I don't, of course. Any more than I hate Alex. But I do hate the equation of Alex plus Verina. I'm frightened to say too much or even think too much but it's not right, is it? What do you think of it all?"

He doesn't answer. He looks at her as though he's not seeing her. To hide his own turmoil, he turns his head and stares out of the window. "You used the word 'drugged' just now, I've been feeling like that too for a long time. It's the strangest situation I've ever been in. Certainly the saddest."

"Here am I, bleating on and you're wretched too. I'm sorry, when we all first met, you and Verina and the children looked like the ideal happy family to me. Now Alex and I have come along to ruin it. I have tried to prevent things going wrong."

"So have I."

"Whenever I try to talk to Alex, I manage to say the wrong thing and end up making matters worse. Perhaps I could have coped better if I hadn't been pregnant. As it is, I can't sleep. It takes me all day to wash up the breakfast things. I worry that all this emotional upheaval might affect the baby."

She gets up from her chair and wanders over to the window, then comes back again and sits down. "I . . . am . . . going . . . mad. Part of me wants to smash the glass and walk out the window . . ."

"Oh Faith, don't frighten me like that. You must take care of yourself, whatever's happening."

"I couldn't really do anything to harm the baby. It's just wild talk. I'm so frantic."

"Things will change, you know."

"You mean, you think it will pass Chris, that this is only a temporary . . ." she's searching for the least painful word, ". . . fascination? I'm sorry I'm being so selfish. I'm trying to get you to reassure me and you need help too. I even rang the Samaritans last night, or rather at three am."

"Did they help?"

"Well, I couldn't stop crying and was afraid Alex would wake up and start shouting. The woman said I should ring back when I felt able to talk. I actually managed to fall asleep after that but then I woke up late this morning feeling drained and Alex wanted me to cook him an omelette; just the thought of it made me heave and he accused me of being lazy. We both shouted rubbish at each other and he banged out of the flat to go and get breakfast in the cafe round the corner. I waited a couple of hours to see if he'd gone to the gym and would come back or ring me but then I saw the car was gone. I thought he might have come here."

They sit in silence for a while.

"Everything's completely changed, he doesn't give a damn about me or the baby any more. He knew I was devastated last night." The tears begin to roll down her face again.

"We need some sort of plan—a plan of action. If it's okay with you, I'll talk to Don. He's a good friend besides being our doctor. He'll advise us. Perhaps I should have spoken to him sooner. I kept thinking—hoping—things would settle down. I'm very worried about you. You don't need all this stress so near the baby's birth. Is there no-one you could go and stay with for a while to get a bit of rest? What about your parents?"

"I couldn't go away. I've got to know what's happening. I shouldn't have come here and bothered you. I think now it's better if Alex doesn't know so please don't tell him."

"Don't worry. Why don't you close your eyes for a while and try to doze off? You look exhausted."

"What if Alex shows up? I don't want him to find me here. I ought to go home."

"If he does, I'll think of something to say to him. Just have a little peace and quiet, then I'll put you in a taxi." He's already lifting her feet on to a stool and placing a cushion behind her head. Again he's struck by how young she looks—a tearful child.

"Thank you Chris. Actually, that drink has made me sleepy." He banks up the fire and goes to get a car-rug. She's asleep before he folds it round her. He feels he must guard her and sits gazing into the fire, worn out himself and repeating in his mind the words 'God help us, God help us' like a mantra. How would he broach the subject of all this with Don?

He doesn't hear Cassie come in. "Hi dad. Oh, Faith's here. Sorry, did I wake you?"

"No, I was just cat-napping."

"How are you? You look tired."

"I'm all right."

"Where's mum?"

"At the hairdresser's—she won't be long."

"I'll put the kettle on, shall I?"

"Good idea."

"Do you mind if I just go Chris? I won't have any tea. Explain to the children."

"You want to go just like that?"

"Please."

"Okay. I'll ring for a cab."

Greg and Nan come in from school arguing. "Oh hallo Faith, Nan says the Ancient Egyptians had dreadlocks. Is that true?"

91

"I don't know Greg. I think they did their hair in thick plaits that might have looked a bit like dreadlocks." She's on her feet, picking up her bag.

"Aren't you staying?"

"Not today Nan. I only popped in to . . . get some advice from your dad." She looks urgently at Chris.

"Your taxi's outside." He goes to the door with her.

"It's like a bad dream Chris."

"It is. We may be lucky and wake up." He hugs her. "Let me give you some money."

"No thanks, I've got some."

"Are you going to be all right on your own? Would you like Cassie to go home with you?"

"No, really I need to be by myself at the moment."

"I'll ring you."

Verina's hair is different. Smoothed back from her face, it makes her look like a ballerina. Nan sits on the floor with her back against Chris's legs. Cassie is near her on the rug, arms clasped round her knees, warming her face at the fire. Greg squats on his heels so that he can easily bounce up and down for more food. While still finishing a mouthful, he suddenly asks "What's for supper tonight mum?" which makes everyone laugh.

It seems to Chris the laughter comes from dense woods miles away across fields. He's thinking about Faith, imagining her getting back to an empty flat, wanting for Alex to come home but perhaps afraid of whatever he's going to say.

"You look very thoughtful Cass."

"Mm. I'm worried about Faith. She didn't look well this afternoon, did she dad?"

"What d'you mean? Was she here today?"

"Yes but she went home as soon as we came in."

"Why was she here Chris?"

"I'll tell you later."

After the children have gone to bed, Chris tells her about Faith's visit. "She was in a hell of a state today. She and Alex had a row, he banged off out of the house and she didn't know where he'd gone. She hoped he might have come here. She wanted some kind of showdown."

"A showdown about what? Doesn't sound like Faith—bit hysterical. Why was she in a state?"

"Alex told her last night that he's soon going to be living with you."

"And she believed him? He was winding her up. When he's being childish, he often says he wants to come and live with me but it's only fooling about."

"Faith seemed to think it serious. She asked me if I knew anything about it. Does he want to move in here with us or what?"

"I've told you, it's all nonsense. They were having a row and he was baiting her."

"He's managed to upset her so much that she actually asked me if I thought you and Alex were planning to leave us all and go off together."

"What did you say?"

"I said I didn't know. Perhaps you are?"

"Don't be ridiculous. It was silly of Faith to make such a fuss. She'll only annoy Alex all the more."

"She knows that. She acted on impulse and she doesn't want him to know she came here. So please don't tell him." *Though I'm sure you will.*

—

Angela opens the door. "Hallo Chris. Come in. Don will be free in a minute. Come through." She leads him into the untidy little room she calls 'the snug'. It looks on to the garden which, on this January day, is utterly bleak. "I'll make us both some coffee with hot milk, you look cold."

He throws his coat over a chair. Just beyond the window, on a bare branch, sparrows huddle together as if trying to get warmth from each other.

Angela comes back with the coffee and winks at him as she slops whisky into his. Chris cups his hands round his mug and for a minute or two they sip the hot drinks in silence.

"How's the family?"

"They're all fine thanks."

"And you? How are you?"

He blows on his coffee. "Bit tired and a bit sort of punch-drunk to tell you the truth."

"I'm not surprised. You go out to celebrate your anniversary one night and you come home with a stepson, a daughter-in-law and an imminent grandchild. You and Verina haven't had much time to catch your breath. How is Vee adjusting to a finished-off, grown-up son would you say?"

"She is happy to have him back in her life but she's also unhappy about all the years between. She did what her parents told her was best for them both."

"I'm sure she did. Poor love."

"I don't know quite how to help her."

"I don't suppose you do. But really, it's not anything to do with you is it, her past? It's something she's got to deal with herself. Don could probably refer her to someone if it would help—and you too, if you like."

"She wouldn't go."

"You think not? Pity. We all need a bit of outside help at times" she smiles, "even if it's only from friends. I can imagine the boy has stirred up painful memories for her. I can't remember who said 'Life must be lived forwards but can only be understood backwards.' Given time, Verina will cope—all of you will."

"I hope so."

"You talk to Don. He's a wise old owl."

As if on cue, Don appears. "Sorry to have kept you waiting Chris."

"That's all right, Angela's been looking after me."

"And now I'm off to cook."

Don settles himself comfortably into his chair and looks encouragingly at Chris. "You wanted a chat?"

Chris lifts a serious face to him, "It's all getting a bit Aedipus in our house."

"Ah. I wondered if it might. You and Verina had no time to prepare yourselves, everything happened so quickly."

"Yes. Also the timing couldn't be worse for young Faith. She's been knocked sideways by it all. That's why I decided to come and see you. I can't help her. I don't know what to say to her. We're both as bewildered as each other. She doesn't understand what Alex is talking about much of the time. His latest idea is that she should move into the background— whatever that means—and leave him free to be with his mother. It even seems he's trying to find a way to come and live with us."

"God forbid! Of course, Alex and Verina will be partly operating on a symbolic level."

"How d'you mean?"

"Well, when Faith became pregnant, it was natural that Alex would want to trace his own mother. All sorts of unconscious and half-conscious feelings would have been stirred up. Whoever his mother had been, the reunion would have been traumatic; as it is, you've got two people bringing emotional baggage to each other and to make matters worse, they're both very attractive members of the opposite sex. An explosive mix I should have thought."

"You think they could be physically attracted to each other?"

"Do you think they are?"

"Yes."

"And you're almost certainly right. It's not uncommon in these circumstances and was probably inevitable. And that's their difficulty. In their particular situation emotions are extremely intense and very hard to control. They will be feeling as desperately confused as you and Faith."

"But you think they'd stop short of becoming incestuous?"

"I don't know. They may not. It does happen. They may feel—prefer to think—normal rules don't apply."

"They behave as though that's what they think. It's unreal around them sometimes. Faith, poor kid is absolutely distraught, that's why I promised to come and see you."

"Poor girl. If only we could tell her that next week Alex and Verina may well have decided they loathe each other."

"That's not likely, is it?"

"I'm not an expert in these matters but from the little I do know, people seem to go through extraordinary changes. It's the strain you see."

"I know all about strain. I feel as if I'm sitting on one of those roundabouts at the fair that spins faster and faster and I'm desperately trying not to fall off. I'm worried about Faith and sorry for myself."

"Quite honestly, Angie and I have been concerned for weeks but we didn't want to intrude. I'm glad you've come round."

"You know Don, you look around at some people and you see they've got enormous problems. We've never had any before. Vee and I have always been grateful for that and up to now, we've relished our family life with the kids. Which is why it's so difficult to understand how it's all turning so ugly . . . Of course you try and carry on as normal. I don't know whether the children actually realise we're living in a nightmare. The first rows that Verina and I have ever had, have been over Alex. I don't want him around the entire time. It's not fair on Faith or the children."

"Or you."

"Or me. And you're right, Vee is completely mixed up. She gets stressed out because she wants us to be as we always used to be, we try to come together and then she somehow slips away from me again. It's difficult to explain. Sometimes I find myself hating her. Can you believe that?"

Don gets up to let the cat out and touches Chris on the shoulder, "What you hate is the situation which you're finding so difficult to cope with. It's natural. Any man would feel the same. I know I would."

"I'm losing her Don . . . I can't believe I just said that. I watch her all the time now. Partly to catch her out."

"Catch her out?"

"Well, sometimes to find justification for my nasty thoughts . . . I've always loved the way her face gradually lights up like a slow fuse when you say something that makes her happy but nowadays I often want to say something to hurt her and dash her smile away because it's more likely to be for Alex than for me. She's on an emotional see-saw too though and it kills me to watch her and not know what to do. She can go from being hysterically cheerful to suddenly being quiet and anxious. It's all to do with him. I think she's constantly aware of what he might be thinking and how she might appear in his eyes. It's as if he's become her Svengali and she must dance to his tune. What's happened to my proud, confident wife? What's he done to her? What's going on in her mind? It's almost impossible for us to talk these days. Most week-ends I don't even want to be in the house I'm so angry and miserable. I even find myself envying the kids. They're always looking forward to something, whereas I'm anxious about what's going to happen next. I'm a pathetic bastard."

"Are you sleeping?"

"Not very well. And when I do sleep, I have wild, incomprehensible dreams and wake exhausted. I'm sorry to burden you with all this crap Don but it's rotting my life."

"You're not burdening me. You're treating me as a friend but while I'm a sympathetic and willing listener, I think you need more practical help from experts in this field."

"Well to be honest, I've already been to the Post Adoption Centre to try and get some general information. I didn't actually talk to anybody, I just picked up a few leaflets in case I was over-dramatising. Now, it's got to the stage where I can see myself suing my stepson in the divorce court. They do have a counselling service and I wanted to ask you whether you've ever referred anyone to them, if you know anyone there?"

"Well the answer to that is no but I think they'd be helpful. I could certainly make a few discreet enquiries to find out who on their team is particularly good. Though they probably all are. It does sound as if you need to talk to somebody familiar with these things."

"Faith too, she's in a hell of a state and that can't be good for her or the baby."

"Don't worry about the baby. Babies are tough. Who's Faith's doctor?"

"I don't know."

"Do you know which hospital she's booked for?"

"I don't know that either. I'll find out."

"Well do that and in the meantime, let me do some telephoning and get back to you. The Post Adoption Centre is a very good starting point. I take it you are here to see me on your own behalf as well Faith's?"

"Oh yes."

"So you will also go for counselling."

"With great reluctance, yes. I need to be prepared for all eventualities. Just for the moment, I'd rather Verina didn't know I've spoken to you."

"Understood. Understood."

"I never would have believed that anyone could come between Verina and me, would you? You've known us for years, give me your honest opinion Don, do you think we can recover from this? Verina and Alex are totally infatuated with each other."

97

"Well you know yourself what happens with infatuation."

"Yes. . . . I suppose then we'd have to pick up the pieces. I dread the outcome—whatever it is."

—

Chloé has brought Nan back from a shopping expedition to buy Nan a guitar so that she can join the school group.

"Isn't it great mummy?"

"Yes, it's lovely." Verina runs her thumb across the strings. "You can't make an ugly sound on the guitar, can you?"

Greg wants a try so Nan sits him down and rests the guitar across his legs. "You have to be very gentle. This is a delicate instrument."

He manages to make a twanging noise and beams with delight.

Nan hugs Chloé, "Thank you, thank you, thank you. I'm going upstairs now to learn to play something. I've got a bet on with Alex."

Greg follows her.

Verina smiles at Chloé "You spoil her you know."

"It's important to show her she's still special to me . . . you know . . . after that other business. She was so upset and I think confused, don't you?"

"Mm. I only hope she doesn't think you get rewards for stealing."

"It wasn't really stealing but you're her mother, I don't want to do anything you're not happy about."

"The thing is, she's been caught stealing in school now."

"Oh no!"

"Oh yes. Chris and I are trying to sort it out with her."

"So that's why he looks a bit down. I thought perhaps he wasn't well."

"Oh he's all right. He's got a lot on his mind that's all. There's a chance his firm's about to lose an important client. Could I give you a little frame for Joe please?"

"Of course."

The two women walk off into the studio.

"What happens if the firm does lose the client?"

Verina is packing the frame in bubble-wrap, "Chris will have to get out there and hustle for another account. These things

98

happen in business. Have you noticed, men run the world but we still have to mother them through every crisis?"

"We mother each other from time to time, don't we—in a marriage?"

"I know what you mean and I don't want to sound unsympathetic. Chris isn't lazy but he does hate change of any kind. Whereas I love it. I find it stimulating. He ought to enjoy the challenge of having to work on something new instead he's becoming a dead weight around the place."

"How do you mean?"

"He finds it hard to move on, develop. I can't shift him and I feel he's holding me back too."

"In what way? What's he stopping you from doing? That doesn't sound like Chris."

"Perhaps I'm being unfair, it's difficult to explain what I mean. Maybe it's nothing to do with Chris but I feel stifled. You do when you have a family always making demands on you."

She's fastening sellotape to the parcel so she misses the shiver across Chloé's face.

"I've always had the impression that he clears the way for you to do whatever you want." She picks up the package.

Verina is holding a small jar and absently looking into it. "Yes, well." Chloé turns to go, and hears her murmur "I think I've used up all the gold in that particular pot."

Something makes Joe glance over his paper at Chloé. Her eyes are full of tears. "What's the matter babe?"

"I'm sad. I'm sure things are going wrong with Verina and Chris and that it's affecting the children—especially Nan."

"Because of the lad, you mean?"

"Perhaps. I don't know. Verina's changed. She doesn't seem to care what's happening to Chris and he looks awful."

"She probably hasn't changed love, it's just that you're beginning to see her better. I'm as fond of her as you are but not so blind to her faults."

"What faults?"

He laughs, "There you go. Vee is out for Vee most of all. She can't be blamed, she's always been spoiled—by her parents, her friends and most of all, Chris."

"Everyone loves her, that's why."

"Yes but no-one more than herself. It doesn't stop her being a good mother and all that, it's part of her self-image."

Chloé is thoughtful, "When I said I thought Chris didn't look very well she just brushed it off explaining he's got some problems with work. She made out that he was being a wimp. She didn't use that word but that's what she meant. I think Chris is unhappy, he doesn't smile these days. It's making me feel insecure."

"Come over here." Joe tosses his paper on the floor and draws her down on to his lap. "You've got nothing to feel insecure about."

"I know. You love me, don't you? You're not going to change?"

"You want words? You need words?" He holds her close, his face in her hair. "You should know by now, it can't be put into words it just goes on all the time, like prayer."

—

They are round with Chloé and Joe, celebrating the completion of a big job Verina and Joe have been working on." The telephone rings, it's Cassie, "Dad, granny has just called and left a number. She wants you to ring her back immediately."

"Hang on Cass, I'll find a pen. Where is she?"

Chloé passes him a pad and pencil.

"I don't know, she didn't say. She just wants to talk to you."

"Not mum?"

"She said 'I need to speak to your father urgently'."

"Okay. Thanks Cass. I'll ring her now. You kids all right?"

"Well Nan and Greg are re-painting the sitting-room and I'm dyeing my hair blue, apart from that . . ." She giggles and rings off."

"There's nothing wrong with Faith, is there?"

"No Vee, it's your mother. She's been on the phone and wants me to call her." He dials the number.

"Oh Chris, thank you for ringing."

"Has something happened? Where are you?"

"At the hospital in Bury. David had an operation yesterday. He's on the mend but I thought I'd better let you and Verina know."

"He's had an operation? What for?" "I'll explain when you get here. You'll come and see him?"

"Of course. We'll come tomorrow." He looks at Verina who nods. "Which ward is he on?" He scribbles things down, "Right. Thanks for letting us know. See you tomorrow then."

"Dad's had an operation? What for? Verina is agitated, "Why didn't she ask for me?"

"I don't know. She didn't tell me anything. I think she was talking from his room and didn't want to say too much. We'll find out tomorrow."

"Don't feel you've got to come rushing back. I'll hold the fort after school and if you find you need to stay over, Joe and I will camp in the house til you get back."

"Chloé, you're an angel."

Joe is re-filling glasses. "You're not going til tomorrow, so we may as well finish the bubbly."

Verina is thinking aloud. "What's can be the matter with him? If he had an op. yesterday, that means he's probably been in hospital for some time. Why didn't she tell us sooner?"

"You've always said she's possessive about your father."

"Even allowing for that, you'd think she'd have told me he was ill. She knows I love my old dad. I hope it's nothing too serious. He's getting on a bit."

One look at him in the hospital bed next day answers her question. Her tall, broad father has shrunk, his face is tinged with yellow and his scalp shows through his hair. Opening his eyes, he tries to smile, "Verina my dear. Lovely of you to come. And Chris. But really, no need, no need." His eye-lids droop again.

"He's heavily sedated but he'll be up and about again soon," Verina's mother chirrups. She's holding his hand and patting it, with a bright, ghastly smile.

Chris meets Verina's eyes, they're full of fear. He says quietly, "I'll leave you for a while," and goes off to find someone who can spell out the state of affairs.

"I'm glad you've come" the doctor says when he tracks him down, "your mother-in-law doesn't seem able to grasp the full picture."

"Probably can't bear to."

"Exactly. She thinks because we're letting him home in a day or two, he's going to get better."

"And he's not."

"Fraid not. There's very little more we can do for him. He's left things too late. We have discussed chemotherapy but he feels, at this stage, it would only add to his miseries and I agree. We've done what we can to alleviate discomfort but whatever we do beyond that is not going to prolong his life, the cancer is too advanced. The best we can do is make sure he has sufficient pain relief. A Macmillan nurse will oversee that when he gets home. She will also help your mother-in-law to come to terms."

Chris blew out his breath, "Phew. We didn't know anything about all this. He must have been ill for quite a while?"

"I'm sure he has. Some people ignore symptoms, or don't take them seriously."

"And what? Just hope they'll go away? I bet my father-in-law has been praying about it instead of going to see his doctor."

"Maybe". His bleeper sounded. "You'll have to excuse me, I'm needed up on the ward."

Before they leave, it is arranged that he and Verina will drive down again at the week-end to take her father home and help her mother settle him in.

Chloé has saved supper for them and Cassie has waited up.

"How's grandpa?"

"Not well Cass, not well at all."

"He hasn't got cancer, has he?"

"How did you guess that?"

She shrugs "Don't know. He won't die before we have a chance to see him again?"

"I hope not. We'll try and arrange something very soon."

"So what's the next step?" asks Joe, "you gonna bring 'em up here?"

"No. My mother wouldn't hear of it. She feels dad's better off in his own home. She's probably right. He needs peace and quiet and wants to be near his garden. Chris suggested she makes up a day-bed for him in the conservatory so that he can go in there when the spring comes. That's of course, if he lasts that long."

"It's that bad?"

"Mm. And my mother's behaving as if he's had a nasty dose of flu."

"Her way of coping. You're going to have to be brave Vee, whatever age you are, you still feel orphaned when you lose a parent specially when you love them like you love your dad."

"Joe" Chloé protested, "She hasn't lost him yet."

"She knows she's going to soon. Then you'll have your mother needing all kinds of help."

"Well she'll look to her blue-eyed boy for that" she nods towards Chris. "I just can't win with her these days. She didn't want anything to do with Macmillan nurses—'They're for the dying, your father's on the mend'—but when Chris explained that they would take charge of his pain relief and see to it that he had reasonable nights and some quality in his days, she agreed to co-operate with them. She listens to him. You'd better go to bed Cass, school tomorrow."

"Don't remind me mum, we've got a maths test first thing."

"We'll push off too" Joe helps Chloé with her jacket, "Let us know how things go and don't forget, we're here if you need us."

When they've gone, Chris decides he wants a cup of tea. So does Verina. They sit at the kitchen table, each deep in thought.

The phone rings.

Verina leaps up to go and answer it. He hears her say "We haven't been back long." She laughs "Naughty boy. Go home . . . No, that's not a good idea, it's far too late. We're going to bed in a minute. Talk to you tomorrow. Goodnight."

"Alex?"

"Yes. He's been drinking with a friend from university and has no idea what time it is. He wanted to come over."

"By the way, did you ever get around to suggesting to him that he might have a chat with someone?"

"Yes I did. He won't have anything to do with it, says it's not necessary."

"Faith thinks it is. So do I. I was hoping he'd listen to you. He won't listen to her. She suggested they went to Relate together and he refused. Our situation is an odd one, it's difficult for us all, quite outside our experience. You can always talk to me and I wish you would but I have to admit, I can't look at things objectively. However repugnant the idea, I really think all four of us could do with some outside help."

She doesn't answer straight away and seems to be sorting her thoughts. "I honestly don't think it would help. I think I can see quite clearly what has happened and no counsellor on earth could magic any of it away. When you give up a child, you ache for it all its life. You go on carrying all that frustrated love inside you, hidden away but building up pressure without you realising, until something causes an explosion. Then you're shell-shocked."

"Extraordinary that you should use those words. I've had this recurring dream lately—you, stumbling about in the dark, in a bombed house."

"It is like that."

"I want to put out a hand to guide you back into safety."

"I don't deserve you."

"I think this is one of those 'for better or worse' bits we made promises about."

"I'm sorry I've been so selfish and preoccupied."

"Vee, you can be whatever you like, whatever you need to be as long as you don't cut yourself off."

"I'll try not to."

"And I'll try to be more reasonable."

"That's enough Chris. Don't turn into a complete saint, I feel guilty enough already."

"I'm not trying to make you feel guilty, I'm trying to show I support you. Which reminds me, would you rather I put off my Paris trip? I don't like leaving you with this news of your father."

"Oh no. I'll be all right. You'll only be gone a few days."

"And I can get back very quickly if you need me. I still think it would do you good to come with me. I've been imagining us having dinner at Maitre Albert."

"I couldn't go away at present. I'd be poor company. I can't get my head round the thought that my poor old dad is dying. But it'll do you good to go. You said the other day that the house was becoming claustrophobic. Set yourself free for a day or two. Try not to work all the time so you can enjoy it." She yawns.

"Come on. It's time we went to bed."

"I couldn't have managed without you today. Thanks for all you did."

It 's becoming a habit that as she sleeps, he lies beside her, solitary in the dark, going over words they have exchanged *we're like amateur actors—polite, wooden conversations, no real familiar closeness—that stuff about the baby may be true but you could be using it as a cover to hide the more worrying concern—the young man he's grown into—you're Phaedra, only he's not your step-son—my poor Vee.—Christ knows what's going to happen . . .*

—

Verina wakes and for a minute, thinks she's dreaming. Alex is sitting on the side of the bed.
"Alex? What are you doing here?"
"Visiting you. Are you feeling better?"
"How long have you been listening to me snuffling?"
"Not long. And you haven't been snuffling, you've been smiling in your sleep."
"I don't like being watched while I'm sleeping."
"Don't be cross. You looked so peaceful. Anyway, I've had my secret little gloat. You can't take it away from me."
"Why aren't you at work?"
"I've been to a meeting in Hammersmith so I thought I'd call in and see you."
"You look tired."
"I am. Faith can't get comfortable at night now, she moves about a lot so neither of us gets much rest."
"Poor you. And Faith. It won't be much longer."
"May I put my head down for a minute?"
"Of course. I don't suppose I'm still germy."
Lying beside her, his face against Chris's pillow, he regards her gravely then lifts her arm and settles it around him so that he can move nearer and rest his head against her. "Am I too heavy?" "No." He nuzzles into her "You smell lovely." "I can't do, I've been in bed all day." "You do, you do, mm, mm," he kisses her neck and her breast. She pushes herself up and tries to move away, "Alex, I don't think you should . . ." He's too strong for her and forces her back down "It's all right Mummy-Vee, it's all right. I'm your baby." He pulls her nightdress aside and

clamps his mouth onto her nipple. She closes her eyes, unable to detach herself.

Downstairs, the telephone rings several times then stops. She makes an effort to push him off but he locks on to her more fiercely, tugging at her with his lips. She gives a long, moaning sigh, and lies still.

No sound comes from the street below. Nothing stirs the total silence in the house. The drowning afternoon slows right down.

The muffled thud of the front door shakes the walls. Alex releases her, smoothes the covers up over her and goes to look out of the window.

A smiling Cassie hurries in "Hallo Mum. Oh!" Now she's frowning "Didn't know you were here Alex. I didn't see your car."

"I came by tube. I had an appointment nearby and called in to see how Verina was."

"It's very gloomy in here, don't you want your lamp on Mum?"

"In a minute."

Cassie touches her mother's forehead "You've still got a temperature, I think. I'll get some water to bathe your face."

"Can I do anything?"

"Yes please Alex, you can go down and put the kettle on."

She brings in a basin and washes Verina's face and hands. "Shall I switch the lamp on now?"

"Yes darling, thank you and pass me my hair-brush please."

"I'll do it. I love brushing your hair."

"I'm a lucky old mum to have a daughter like you."

"Yes, you are," she kisses her and picks up the basin, "and we're all lucky to have you for our mother."

In the kitchen she questions Alex "Did mum get out of bed to let you in?"

"No, I've got a key."

"Since when?"

"Cass," he gives her his 'guaranteed-to-charm' smile, "I am one of the family."

"I suppose you are. I keep forgetting."

"Can I take the tray up?"

"No thank you. Mum only really likes me around when she's not well—and dad of course."

Greg and Nan come clattering in as Cassie comes back downstairs.

Alex stands up, "I'd better go. I'll just nip up and say goodbye to Verina."

"She's gone back to sleep."

"You'll explain to her then, will you?"

"Yes. I'll tell her you had to go."

"See you at the week-end then."

"I don't know. We might be going to see grandpa if mum's flu is better."

"Oh, right."

Greg is disappointed "Can't you wait til daddy comes home?"

"No sir, sorry. Got to go and look after Faith."

"Give her lots of love from us."

"Will do."

—

Sorrows

Faith is lying under the duvet, watching Alex wander in and out of the bathroom. "That's a terrific hair-cut."

"Think so?"

"Mm. You look like a French film idol."

"I know". He poses for her, showing his profile. "Where are my jeans?"

"In the airing-cupboard."

"Shouldn't you be making a move?"

"I suppose I should." She slides off the bed, stands up and immediately sits back down again heavily. "Whoops!" "What's the matter?" "I feel dizzy," "Perhaps you got up too quickly. Take your time, try again." "I will in a minute."

She again tries to stand, holding on to the head-board but she has to sit down again. "Oh Al. I don't feel well. I don't feel well at all." "Do you think you've started labour?" "No . . . . No, I don't think so. I haven't had any of the signs." "So in what way do you feel unwell?" "When I stand up, I feel weak and awfully dizzy. Perhaps it's normal when the baby's nearly due . . . and it's been a busy day. I expect I'm just tired."

He's brushing his hair now and says into the mirror "Seems to me you're making a big production number out of this. Women have babies every day. It's not an illness you know."

"Of course it isn't but I don't think it would be very sensible of me to go charging off out tonight."

"You would pick this evening to feel ill! I suppose this is because you wanted me to take you out to dinner."

"Well I did, yes but that's only because we haven't been out together for ages and there may not be an opportunity for a long time once the baby's here. I thought Angela's birthday was next week-end. But it's not any of that, I'm not pretending, I honestly don't feel good."

"So you don't want to come with me?"

"I don't think I can. Al, I haven't cried off once during all these months though I sometimes wanted to, as you know but tonight I feel rotten . . . . would you mind very much if we cancelled?"

"Oh no! It's weeks since we've been able to get out of this dump at the week-end. I'm not cancelling. In any case we'll be in a doctor's house tonight so you'll be all right whatever happens."

"I can't go this evening Alex, I really can't. I feel odd, sort of nervous."

He sits down beside her and takes her hand "Of course you're nervous. You haven't had a baby before. But it's not going to be born tonight, is it? You said you've had none of the signs?" She shook her head. "Well then."

"I suppose I did too much in the flat today."

"Then that was silly."

She pulls the duvet up over herself.

He jumps up "All right. You rest this evening if you think you must and perhaps you'll feel well enough to come over tomorrow."

"You mean, you're still going?"

"Faith" he speaks slowly and patiently, "we are expected at Angela's. It's good of her to invite us on a special occasion. It means we're accepted as family."

"Angela will understand."

"I'll make your excuses. Where's her present?" He starts walking around flapping his hands, looking for it.

"I think you should stay with me."

"Oh? Bit selfish, don't you think? If all you need is to lie in bed why do you want to keep me hanging round? What am I supposed to do?"

"You could get us a DVD and a take-away. There's some wine. We could have one of our cosy evenings."

"Great! I'm to pass up a fun evening and Angela's marvellous cooking, to eat duff food and watch some crap film. I don't think so. Look, why don't I run you a bath? Slobbing in your pit and telling yourself you don't feel well is negative. Have a good soak, do yourself up a bit and you might feel more like going. Come on." He starts trying to lift her off the bed.

"Leave me alone Alex. My back aches. You're hurting me."

He lets her fall back. "I need a drink."

She calls after him "You go Al, I don't want to spoil your evening."

He's back in the bedroom, drink in hand. "One of us ought to go."

"All right but would you mind coming back tonight though? I'd rather not be by myself. Please?"

"Oh for Christ's sake! Talk about giving with one hand . . . You're saying I can go but I can't have a few drinks and relax because I've got to drive home again to my neurotic wife." He starts throwing things into an overnight bag.

"I'm sorry I don't mean to be dreary. Don't go off on a bad note." Her voice is purposely cheerful. "When you get to this stage, you've had enough. You just want the baby to get itself out."

"Then I suppose we'll have it screaming all the time. What a prospect!" He goes to the bathroom for his razor.

"He won't scream all the time, I shall look after him properly." She smiles, "I know you've had a bad pregnancy but once you see him, you'll think it's been worth it."

"Maybe. Seen my red sweater?"

"It was folded on top of your jeans."

He finds it and stuffs it into the bag. "Where did you say you put Angela's present?"

"On the coffee table."

He comes back and throws the package in on top of the other things and looks at his watch. "Do you want anything before I go—a cup of tea or something?"

"No thank you but if you're all set, I'd like to talk to you for a minute."

"Right headmistress. What about?" He sits on the bed.

"About what you said just now about the baby screaming all the time, babies do cry but I don't want you to be put off him before he's even arrived."

"I'm already off him."

"You don't mean that."

"Look at the inconvenience caused and it's not even born yet."

"Be serious for a moment please Alex. You do want our baby?"

"If you want the truth, at this particular moment in time, no I don't but there's nothing we can do about it."

"What? D'you really mean, you've changed your mind? You were thrilled when we first knew. I thought that deep down, you still were."

"I was pleased for you. You were happy. But you never asked me if I was or not, you just went ahead with it all."

There's a roaring in her ears. She stifles the need to scream and cry. Her voice quavers, "I'm sure that's not how it was. You were glad too and proud. You said the timing was right, we could afford it and the house would be nearly ready."

"What else could I say?"

"Are you telling me you would have preferred me to get rid of it?"

He pretends to yawn.

"I'd have thought someone who'd been adopted would make sure his own child was wanted."

"You spiteful little cow!"

"Don't talk to me like that Alex. I don't mean to be spiteful. I'm trying to understand you. When you came with me for the scan and we knew it was going to be a boy, you were delighted. I can't believe what you're saying now." She's near to tears and doesn't dare add *and you squeezed my fingers so much it hurt and when I looked at you, your eyes were wet—how could we have shared that moment looking at our unborn child on the screen and now you don't want him?* Boiling panic floods through her, she needs air *can't think about this til he's gone.*

"Come to think of it, perhaps it's better if you don't come tonight. You're not looking your best, you're very red in the face." He goes to get another drink.

There's a clink of glass from the other room and she calls out "Don't have any more to drink Alex, you're driving."

He leans in the doorway and looks at her "So you don't want me to kill myself?"

"No I don't, I'm not that much of a cow."

"Okay, I shouldn't have said that but you annoyed me. It's best if I do leave you alone tonight, you're obviously in one of your moods."

She says nothing.

"Ring me if you need me."

"I need you now."

"No you don't". He comes over to the bed and starts twisting a strand of her hair.

She pushes his hand away. "You don't give a damn about me any more."

"Here comes the drama."

"It's true though, isn't it? It doesn't matter to you whatever might be happening with me, you can't wait to get out of here and rush over to your precious mother."

"You've really got to try and do something about your insane jealousy."

"And you've got to try and do something about your unhealthy obsession with her! It's sickening. You're her son."

"You've got a nasty, commonplace mind Faith. Verina's a lovely person. She's fond of you. She always makes you welcome and."

Faith cuts in "Oh fuck Verina! Ha!" she gives a choking little laugh, "that's probably what you want to do anyway."

Alex smashes his fist into her face.

Blood spurts from her nose and tears overflow down her cheeks. She mops her face with the sheet and shrinks from him. He looks at her with hatred, picks up his bag and leaves.

She hears the car start and turns sobbing into the pillows—*so my little one, you're not going to bring him back to me—he doesn't want you now—but I do—can't wait to have you in my arms—he doesn't want me either—La Belle Dame has him in thrall.*

—

The client wants a Gallic feel to the art-work. Although he's tormented, worrying about what's going on at home, Chris seizes the opportunity of a few days in Paris 'to absorb the atmosphere'. Perhaps physical distance from events will clear his mind and Verina might miss him.

A smiling but untalkative young woman meets him at the airport and leads him out to a Renault Espace. He's her only passenger and he's grateful for the absence of chat and the smooth comfort of the car. As they pull away from the terminal, he studies the advertisements on the hoardings, admiring their wit. The road into Paris is dark, he settles back in his seat to doze.

When he next opens his eyes they are in heavy, slow-moving traffic. Lights flicker on the waters of the Seine and ahead, through rain, a dream image hovers—the splendour of Notre Dame, flood-lit against the night sky. The car turns away from the river and they drive under smoky street lights, past bars and restaurants, to his hotel in a quiet road.

There's no-one in Reception and he has to ring the bell. Soon he is installed in an almost triangular room with a thirties look to the decor. He has a bath in the gleaming bathroom and goes out in pouring rain, to find something to eat. It's quite early in the evening but the street is dark and deserted and after walking along and finding no restaurants, he turns back to the little cafe-bar he noticed next to the hotel. The proprietress is mopping the floor and tells him she's closed but when he asks her to suggest somewhere for him to find something light to eat, she relents and says she will look after him

She locks the door and sits him down with some bread and a bottle of wine. The last and only customer, he's placed behind a barricade of upturned chairs and with most of the lights off, he feels comfortably private. It occurs to him that, apart from ordering food and drink, he won't have to actually talk to anyone, if he doesn't want to, all the time he's in Paris.

The woman serves him with salad and a delicious omelette parmentière and leaves him in peace while she wipes the counter and puts away glasses. When he asks for coffee, she put a glass of Armagnac on the table beside it.

Back in his room, he thinks about ringing home but remembers that everybody will be at Don and Angela's. It's so quiet, he could be the only guest in the hotel. He gets into bed telling himself he probably won't be able to settle and falls at once into a deep sleep.

—

Faith's nose stops bleeding. She touches it gingerly, it's bruised and swollen, might be broken *for ages wanted to shock Alex into realising what he may be drawn into—shocked myself— didn't know I was going to say that about Verina—it just came*

113

out—*if I went too far, it may be no bad thing—certainly hit home judging by the wallop he gave me — must put some ice on my nose and change these sheets—covered in blood—not that Alex will come back tonight—don't want him to.*

Feeling hungry, she gets up out of bed carefully to make a cheese and pickle sandwich and a mug of hot chocolate. She doesn't feel much better *wonder if a bath would be a good idea?—could leave the bathroom door open in case Alex rings—in case Alex rings?—get real Faith!* In the bath, she splashes water over her stomach which usually causes a foot to poke out here or a fist there but the baby doesn't respond. She washes, then tries again to get the baby to move pressing her fingers into her abdomen, "Where are you baby dumpling?" More splashings nothing, he's quite still—*expect it's because I'm alone that I feel something's wrong—think back to earlier in the day, was he active then?—sure he was—expect he's resting—perhaps babies need to be still and quiet when they're near to getting born—build up their energy—any of my books mention that?—must practise my deep breathing—try to stay calm—is instinct warning me things not quite right?* She sits in her dressing-gown stroking her stomach and trying to discover with her finger tips, how the baby is lying. By eleven thirty, he still hasn't moved. Exhausted and desperately afraid she rings the hospital. Someone answers from the maternity suite and she blurts out "This is Faith Holland. Look I'm probably being hysterical but I'm on my own, I feel miserable and I've worked myself up into a state. I think there's something the matter with my baby. Could I please come in so that someone can reassure me, tell me I'm being silly and send me home?"

"That's not a problem at all. Why are you worried about the baby?"

"I can't get him to move. He's gone absolutely still. He didn't respond in the bath even." "Okay you come in and we'll put you on a monitor and do a tracing to make sure everything's okay. You say you're by yourself, how will you get here?"

"By mini-cab."

The driver is anxious "You are not in labour madam, are you? I am not clever in these things.

"No no, I'm not but just get me to the hospital please as quickly as you can."

He drives fast and Faith has to wind the window right down because of the smell of sweat and cheap air-freshener.

On the labour ward, she is received by Anne, a midwife she knows. "You're feeling worried?

"Yes. The baby seems to have stopped moving about. I expect it's all right. Just me fussing."

"Make yourself comfortable on the bed and we'll see what's happening."

Faith lies still, willing the baby to leap and stretch and cause her discomfort.

Anne leans over her "Let's have a listen. Try to relax a bit, you're very tense."

Faith closes her eyes and prays as she feels the monitor against her skin. The midwife probes her stomach gently and applies the machine here and there.

No sound. Faith opens her eyes. She's fearful. "Anything?"

"Not yet. I'm a bit concerned. We'll need to do a scan to determine that we have a foetal heart. Your husband's not here with you, is he?"

"No and I don't want him. Please do the scan."

Dazed with dread, Faith watches the screen. The image is fuzzy. "It seems as if there's nothing moving. What are we actually looking at?"

"The chambers of the heart, which should be pulsating."

"And they're not. That's it then. My baby's dead."

"There's no foetal heart there no. The scan confirms it. Your baby is dead. I'm sorry."

"Why?" Faith bursts into tears.

Anne sits beside her and lets her cry.

"So cut me open and get it out."

"Now hang on a minute" She holds her hand. "It's distressing to know you've a dead baby inside you and of course you want it out as soon as possible but you've just had a massive shock and naturally you're very, very upset. You need some time to think what's best to do. Is there any way we can get in touch with your husband so that he knows what's going on?"

"He's the last person I want near me right now. He couldn't help me with this. We've had an awful row." Tears flooded again.

Anne puts an arm around her, "Is there anyone else who could come and be with you, your mother perhaps or a friend?"

"My mother lives in the country, I wouldn't want to drag her up here. She'd only worry and there's not going to be a happy outcome. I think I must just get on with this by myself."

"You're quite sure you wouldn't like us to ring and see if your husband is back home or leave a message? The quarrel might not seem important compared with what's happening here."

"He might turn up anyway." She pictures Alex arriving exasperated. "I need to come to terms with this before he does. Alex never gives me any peace." She disentangles herself and stands up "You're very kind Anne, thank you but I need to be by myself for a while."

"Of course you do. I'll take you somewhere quiet." She leads Faith down the corridor and opens the door into a small pleasant room with armchairs, "Would you like a cup of tea?"

"Thank you."

"I'll leave you for a while then we'll talk things through."

Faith sinks into a chair *cruel, cruel, cruel—don't expect babies to die at the last minute these days—not prepared in any way for this—don't know what to do—I'd like to get out of this body myself—oh my poor little baby, why have you died?—you knew how much I loved you and wanted you.* She can't stop crying and doesn't hear the nurse come in with tea. *My poor mum's made all those sleeping gowns and knitted all those tiny woolies—dad's going to be miserable for me—I'm miserable for me—was so looking forward to having a new little person to love, who would love me—I'll be walking about with my arms empty.* Crying has taken the last of her energy, she rests her head against the back of the chair and drifts into a doze.

Panic wakes her, penetrating her sleep. She hurries out of the room, to try and find her way back to the labour ward. Anne finds her wandering in distress. "You looking for me?"

"Has it really happened? Has my baby really died?"

"Yes my love. I'm sorry, he has."

"What do I do now?"

"Let's go in here and sit down and I'll explain a few things. Nurse Robin, when you've a minute, some more tea would be good." She sits near Faith, and turns to look at her. "This is the way of it, if you want the baby taken out immediately, we would respect your wishes and give you the operation but actually we'd rather not put a scar on your uterus for a dead baby. It means an automatic caesarian with the next child. You're young and one day, when you've recovered from all the sadness, you might want to have another child. After this experience, we'd like to see you through a trouble-free pregnancy and birth which is why we would counsel you not to go for the section. Do you understand?"

"Yes. Thank you. So what would happen? Although the baby is dead, can the mother still be induced to give birth?"

"That's right. If you feel you can go through with it, it's what we would advise for the sake of the future. Take as much time as you need to make a decision, I don't want to rush you. It's hard to think clearly when you're distressed. What do you think your husband would want you to do?"

Alex would say 'For God's sake Faith, get on with it. Let them cut it out.'

"How long will it all take if you induce me?"

"That depends. This is your first child and you're only thirty eight weeks, so it could take a while. But we'll give you pain relief, you won't feel anything."

"I'm sorry, I know I'm dithering. I feel very shaky. You really think that's the best thing to do?"

"I do but no-one's going to bully you into going through what might be a long labour for a dead baby at the end of it."

"Well it's got to happen one way or the other—and soon. All right. Let's do it. When can we start?"

"If you don't want to wait for your husband, we can start as soon as you feel you're ready—really ready."

"I can't believe this is happening. All that joy and promise gone . . . What's the procedure?"

"We'll insert a gel to make your cervix dilate. It's a synthetic hormone that will stimulate contractions and persuade your body that it's time to give birth but it can take a while to get going."

"I need to be able to say, even if it takes a long time, it will definitely be over by . . . .?"

"Sometime tomorrow—well today, it's two-thirty now. Do you want to make a start?"

"Yes. Please."

"Right then, pop up here and lie back . . . Lift your knees for me . . . This won't hurt, it'll just feel cool . . . There, that's it. Now we have to wait. You could have a little rest." She pulls the covers over Faith and switches off the bright light leaving the room dim. Faith is overcome by the need to sleep. This is the worst day of her life but someone is taking care of her.

She becomes aware of the squeak of rubber shoes, backwards and forwards in the corridor and a voice somewhere in space, singing along to a tinny transistor radio. She opens her eyes, Anne is looking down at her.
"Hallo. Now you're awake, let's see how you're getting on."
"I've got tummy ache."
"I can give you some paracetomol."
What time is it?"
"Six-thirty." She examines Faith "Not much happening yet I'm afraid. We'll give it another couple of hours."
The tea-trolley appears and Faith's cup of tea brings her wide awake to the realisation of what she's doing. She strokes her stomach to caress the baby who won't now feel her fingers.
Anne goes off duty at eight o'clock and leaves Faith in the care of Denise. "You've had all this explained to you, haven't you? I'm sorry it's taking so long. We've decided to give you more of the protin gel to try and hurry things up. There's nothing stopping you from going downstairs for a wander round if you feel like it. We wouldn't expect much to happen before about mid-day. Come back if you get worried or too uncomfortable. We'll need to see you in a couple of hours anyway."
In the lift, a woman bumps into her. "Sorry!" Then she looks Faith up and down, "Still you're one of the lucky ones. I had four miscarriages, all before three months. I never managed to have a baby."
There's a WH Smith's on the ground floor and Faith browses among the books feeling like a ghost of herself. The pains in her stomach are becoming insistent but she knows she still has a long way to go and must somehow fill the waiting time. She buys a couple of books that look undemanding and to try and anchor herself in the real world, a newspaper
"Faith!"

Oh God, Alex. His sudden, physical presence frightens her and she wills him to stay the other side of the table but he's standing well back from her anyway as if he dare not come near. The skin on his face seems stretched tight and he's very pale. "I've been looking all over for you. Up in the maternity unit, they told me you'd gone walkabout. You all right?"

She can only shrug and bow her head, her eyes filling with tears.

"I know what's happened. They told me upstairs. It's awful. Why didn't you ring me? You should have rung me."

"I didn't want to." Keeping back tears is a struggle.

"I shouldn't have left you on your own but I was angry. What you doing down here?"

"I'm just having some coffee. You get yourself some. It's not very good mind." She breathes through clenched teeth and grips the table edge.

"Pain?"

She nods.

"They told me upstairs what's going on. Shall I get someone?"

"No."

"Why didn't you ask for a whatsit—a caesarian? It could have been all over by now. It's revolting hanging on to a dead baby. You're mad to put yourself through this. How long's it going to take?"

"I don't know."

"Can I get you some more coffee or tea? Or would you like some hot chocolate?"

"I don't want any more to drink, thank you."

"You all right if I leave you for a minute?"

"I'm okay."

They sit in silence when he brings his coffee. Faith is beginning to think it's time she went back upstairs.

"Was it my fault Faith?"

She makes him wait for an answer, giving in to the temptation to leave him in suspense.

"Faith?"

"Unlikely. Unless you wished it on me."

"You think I'm that bad?! . . . Look, it's strange seeing your unborn child moving about on the screen and at first, it makes you sort of proud. But once you start thinking, you realise that's macho rubbish and the truth is your life's going to be turned upside down. I didn't want it but I'm not a monster, I never wanted it to die . . . When they told me about the state you were in last night, I really thought clouting you might have given the baby a heart attack. D'you think that's possible?"

"No."

"I'm sorry I gave you a nose-bleed but you did provoke me."

"Oh Alex, none of that matters any more."

Lifting his cup with a shaking hand, he spills some coffee. Faith passes him a paper napkin. They sit in silence for some minutes.

"I suppose not letting me know was your revenge."

She sighs, "Oh God."

"You know I wouldn't have wanted you to go through all this on your own. You should have got one of the nurses to ring me. They must think I'm a right bastard."

She doesn't answer.

"The best thing you can do is go back to work as soon as possible and put all this right behind you. That'll keep you from moping and feeling sorry for yourself. Don't get me wrong, I do understand how upset you must be You wanted that baby but you'll have others."

"What time is it?"

"Ten-forty."

"I'd better go back up to the ward in a minute." "I'll come with you."

"No, it's all right Alex. It's going to be hours before things really happen. You won't want to mooch around the labour ward all day. You've done your duty. You go now, I'd rather be by myself."

"Oh don't be so frosty Faith. Let me keep you company at least. I should be here with you, I helped to make this baby. Let me stay."

Faith stands up. "I can't Alex. I really can't. I need to be on my own for this." He walks with her to the lift. "I don't know what to say. Good luck. I hope it won't be too ghastly."

At last Denise decides it's time to rupture the membrane so that Faith's waters break. This brings on severe contractions and she then administers an epidural and attaches a drip. During the long waiting hours, muffled in pain—relief, Faith feels alienated from her body *there's some meaning in all this though God knows what it is—are we being punished?—have we poisoned our environment—me with jealousy—Alex with indifference—and it's all somehow permeated through to the babe?— Alex will be relieved, he doesn't want to be a daddy yet—but me, I've dreamed so much about holding my child, I can't believe he isn't going to be here—wish they'd all stop talking to me about babies I'll have in the future—I want this one and I can't have him—I hate God!—nothing to stop Alex leaving me now and going off to live with Verina—what about Chris?—will he allow it?—what's going to happen?—losing my baby hasn't changed anything except me—this is all taking place in another country which I'm inhabiting by myself—I had to send Alex away—he can't comfort me—just makes everything worse—comes at life from a different angle—told him once, he's like a knight in a tournament, lance poised, charging furiously in the wrong direction!—he didn't know what I meant—how are we going to be with each other now?—'for better or worse'—couldn't even speak to him properly today.*

She's very tired. People talk to her at times, telling her things she doesn't understand. The medication sends her floating in and out of mauve rooms.

"Not long now Faith. You're a brave girl."

During the final stages, it's as if her body tightens its grip in protest at being made to give up the baby too soon, pushing him out becomes an agonising contest. "Come on Faith, push. Push hard. We can see the head. You're nearly there. Doing very well. Push!!!" Its as though she's tearing herself in half. One last heroic effort and the baby slides out.

"Oh look at this" a nurse leans over the bed. "Faith, this might be why your baby died, look."

She raises her head. Denise is holding up the coiled umbilical cord to show her that there's a knot in it. "Babies sometimes cause a knot in the cord if they are very active but I've never seen a true one before—one as tight as this."

Faith looks at the knot but avoids looking at the baby.

"Do you want to hold him Faith?"

"No, not yet," she whispers. Tears wet her pillow.

There's a tap at the door and Alex appears with flowers.

"I didn't know you were here."

"I've been here all the time. I've been so worried." He puts the flowers down near her feet and brings a chair over to sit beside the bed. "I kept walking past that ward and it was so quiet, I thought you had died too—that whatever had killed the baby had got you as well." He's holding her hand, there are tears in his eyes. "My poor little Faith. Bet you're glad that's over. You all right?"

His gentleness makes her cry. "I can't believe it."

"Of course you can't. It's such a shame. He's like a little statue, isn't he?"

"I haven't seen him."

"Didn't you see him when he was born? I suppose you couldn't bear to." She withdraws her hand. "I am sorry Faith. I don't know what to say or what to do. I seem to make you more miserable than you are already. I only wanted to make sure you're all right . . . Is this a private room? It's very nice."

"No, it's not private. It's for people like me whose babies don't survive. They think putting us in rooms with contented mothers and rosy babies would be too cruel and they're right."

"They're asking if we want a post-mortem."

"We don't."

"If there's been any negligence, we could sue."

"There hasn't been any negligence. He shut off his life-support system himself." She told him about the knot. "He didn't want to be our child."

"Well don't go putting it like that when you tell other people, just say there was a knot in the cord. Could that definitely be the reason? A post-mortem might give us more information."

"I'm satisfied that it was and I don't want him cut about."

"Although you haven't even bothered to see him? I don't understand you Faith. But you probably don't understand yourself at the moment."

"What I do want is to have him baptised, if that's all right with you? Do you want to be there?"

"What's the point?"

"The point is that it's the last thing—the only thing—that we can do for him."

"Well if you want to, go ahead but it's better to leave me out of it. You know I don't believe in all that stuff. I think it only drags out the misery."

This makes her cry again.

"Oh sweetie, don't be hurt. You know me. I'm blunt but I don't mean to upset you all the time. Look, you need to rest, you've had a horrible day. I should push off and let you sleep, I hope you'll be able to."

"You need some sleep yourself, you look very tired. Go home."

"I wish you were coming with me. It's like being in an earthquake. I expect the bed will split in half and crash through the floor. God knows how you feel."

"Bereft."

He stares helplessly at her.

"You need to do something normal Al. Take yourself to Giuseppe's, have a hearty supper and a bottle of Bardolino then you'll sleep like a log."

"I just might try that." He leans over to kiss her. "Goodnight. Try not to be too sad. I'll see you tomorrow."

She wakes from a vivid dream that the baby is in bed with her and presses her buzzer.

A nurse comes in.

"Would it be possible for me to see my baby now please?"

"Of course. I'll bring him to you."

He's wrapped in a soft shawl and looks exactly as if he's sleeping. Gazing at the perfect little face, she wants to memorise every feature to print his image on her heart. "Did you change your mind about coming?" she whispers. "I've loved you all these months and longed for you. I don't know if I can bear the disappointment, especially now I've seen you." His brow is smooth under her lips. She leans against the cold metal bars behind her, not bothering to adjust the pillows, as though moving might disturb him. She strokes the baby's cheeks with her finger and traces the faint, feathery lines of his eye-brows. "I wish I knew what your eyes are like. Where are you beautiful baby mine? Please try me again sometime." She feels she's receiving intimate messages from the peaceful child. "You come back. I'll be waiting. I'll never forget you. I'll love you always." She cradles him against her, overwhelmed by the surge of love and grief. "This is the only time we're going to have."

Someone has come in, it's Anne. "Hallo there. Father Pidoux is on the ward, would you like to speak to him about having the little one baptised?"

123

"Please." She clings to the baby, grateful for the privacy and calm of this tucked-away room. For the rest of her life, its details will stay with her sharp and clear like a close-up in a film: creamy waterlilies drifting down the curtains on a blue-green river, the pink cylamen in its shiny, grey bowl on the window-sill, that print of Bonnard's glorious garden.

"Is it all right for me to come in?" A big man is standing in the doorway.

She registers the dog-collar, "Yes of course Father."

The priest smiles kindly at her, puts his flat black case on her locker and pulls up a chair. "I always sit so that I don't tower over mothers and give them a fright. This is a dreadful, sad day for you my dear. I'm so sorry. It's Faith, isn't it?"

She nods. "Would you like communion Faith?"

"I'm not fit Father. I've been shouting at God all night."

"He'll be well used to that I'd say."

"I can't prepare myself today Father. It's the baby I'm concerned about. Can you please baptise him straight away? I must do something for him. I think I've failed him in some way."

"How could you have done that? I'm sure you wanted him?"

"With all my heart but he rejected me."

"That's the invention of a troubled mind Faith. Of course he didn't reject you. Why would he? That's grief talking."

"It's so hard to understand Father. I feel angry and resentful and cheated and miserable."

"Of course you do. When tragedies occur, we always want to know why and we ask ourselves why me? And no-one can give satisfactory answers. That's why we need prayer. Now, is anyone else going to be present? Is your husband here?"

"No father. He prefers to leave these things to me."

"Right. What name have we for the little fellow."

"Daniel."

"That's a great name." He has opened his case and puts a stole around his neck. Kneeling beside the bed, he gently takes the baby from her, making the sign of the cross "In Nomine Patris . . ."

Faith interrupts, "Please wait Father, I've just realised we haven't any god-parents." She falters as he gives her a long, solemn look. She gives a painful "Ah . . . I'm so sorry. I'm still muddled."

Father Pidoux places the wrapped up baby on the bed and loosens the shawl and the white gown. He touches the small chest with oil from one of his phials and prays quietly. Faith sees the delicate neck and the plump little shoulder and chokes. She watches through brimming eyes as the priest performs the ceremony slowly and reverently. He prays in English using some Latin phrases that Faith remembers.

"We've done the best we can now for your Daniel." He places him back in her arms.

"Thank you Father, very much. May I ask you something? Do you think souls can try again, I mean try to come back another time?"

"No-one's ever asked me that before Faith. That's another mystery I'd say. Everything is possible if God wills it. But remember, in any case, God loves you. He shares your sorrow like any loving father. Ask Him for the courage to bear this tragedy, He will help you. I'll come and see you again tomorrow." He rests his hands lightly on her head, blesses her and leaves. Holding the baby tight in her arms, she stares into the future.

—

It's bitingly cold as Chris leaves the hotel after breakfast. He turns up his collar and sets off with no particular direction in mind. Crossing the wide boulevard through heavy traffic he is at the gates of the Luxembourg Gardens and it seems as good a place as any to start. Setting off down a path, walking briskly to try and keep warm, he tells himself to keep his mind open to whatever he comes across. Verina's Christmas present is in his pocket. It's nothing like as good as any of the cameras he could have brought from work and he knows she gave no thought to its purchase, so why did he bring it? Marching along in a daze, he thinks he missed something and retraces his steps. Half hidden in laurels, a cracked marble urn on a pedestal guards the entrance to a narrow little path, a dead pigeon lies across its plinth like an offering. He takes a photograph and decides to investigate the little path which proves disappointing. Wandering along a wide avenue of trees, it's hard to work out what he's looking at *these patches of mist—I'm the only person here—the only idiot—this freezing cold is seeping into my*

brain—what am I doing?—no definite plan—messing about—
hoping something might trigger ideas—creative energies nil—that
statue has more life in its stone limbs than I have in mine—feel I'm
losing substance—could drift off, up among the trees.

Pushing on, his feet crunching on gravel, he wonders if the atmosphere is so profoundly bleak simply because it's winter or whether he's imbuing the place with his own mood. He discovers an arbour with a carved seat draped in ivy. On the low wall, stone cornucopias spill earth and a few straggly crysanthemum stems. It's like being in the desolate garden of a decayed country house. As he focuses his lens, another image superimposes itself for an instant—his shattered marriage. Putting away the camera and his notebook, longing for some hot coffee, he leaves the gardens by the next gate.

It's beginning to rain hard. Cold bars of sleet sting his face as he walks in the direction of Saint Germain where the streets are familiar and he remembers a little café-bar he likes off the Rue des Saints Pères. Hurrying down an alley, bright lights and brilliant colours glimmering through the downpour compel him to stop, immediately curious. The window of a small gallery is filled with a picture which opens up a world of sunlight and joyous life. Smiling young men, standing proudly in red and gold medieval robes, their hats trimmed with ermine, travel towards the viewer in a richly decorated gondola. Rainbow reflections in the water spread back towards the church of the Santa Maria della Salute floating against an airy sky. "Wow!" Chris speaks out loud. Oblivious to the icy drops on his face and neck, he stands smiling—unwilling to move—gazing into the painting.

In the gallery, he is greeted by the woman behind the desk "Bonjour m'sieur."

"Bonjour madame."

She smiles, "It's Kit, isn't it? How are you?"

He stares at her, astonished . . . "Yes it is but I'm called 'Chris' these days." Her name comes back to him, "Melanie? Good God!"

"I know I've changed a lot."

"No, it's not that. You're out of context. The last time I saw you was in a pub in Earl's Court. What are you doing here?"

"It's a long story. I knew it was you as soon as you came in." She gets up "I'm going to get you a towel, you're absolutely soaked. Where's your Englishman's umbrella?"

She fetches him a fluffy towel. "Thanks". There's no-one else in the gallery so he dries his face and hair.

"What are you doing in Paris? Are you here on holiday?"

"No, trying to do some work in fact. I'm in advertising. Only here for a couple of days. The idea is to mooch about, have a look at things and think. I've been having a depressing, unproductive morning but I've just been knocked sideways by that picture in the window."

"Glorious, isn't it?"

"I'm hoping it's not an original because I've got to have it."

"It's a lithograph, they all are. From a batch of pictures Bratby did in Venice—obviously. Have a look at the others. I don't know why everyone is in medieval dress unless there's some sort of festival going on."

"They're marvellous but the one in the window is my favourite. How much is it?"

She told him.

"It's well worth it. I've already justified buying it; it's guaranteed to cheer anyone up on a miserable day. Can I have it without the frame? Much easier to take home and I can sort something out in London."

"Of course but I'm afraid I can't let you have it until the exhibition ends but then I could post it to you in London. Is that all right?"

"Yes. It'll be something to look forward to." He gets out his credit card and watches her as she takes down all his details. "It's a hell of a surprise seeing you Mellie, after all this time. I suppose you can't shut up shop for half an hour and come and have coffee with me?"

"Not really. I've no staff. Are you by yourself then?"

"Yes. Verina, my wife, couldn't come because of the children."

"Oh that's a shame. Look, since you're here it would be lovely to catch up on things, why don't you let me cook dinner for you tonight? I don't like to think of an old friend stuck by himself in the evening."

"Er . . . you must have a husband or partner?"

"Not any more. I'm a widow Kit."

"Oh, I'm sorry."

"It's all right. I've been on my own for nearly ten years. You get used to it. Do come to dinner."

"It's very sweet of you but look you'll have been in here all day. Let me take you out instead, will you? You'll know the best places to go."

"All right then, thank you. That'll be nice. We have one of the best restaurants in Paris just round the corner. I'll book a table for eight, shall I?"

"Perfect. If you give me your address, I'll pick you up."

"That's easy, I live right here, upstairs." She smiles warmly at him.

They're sitting opposite each other in a snug alcove and Chris has just slipped off his tie.

"I didn't dress up Kit in case you thought I wanted to seduce you." She's wearing a shapeless, soft sweater and her hair is loose around her face.

"I'm not sure how to take that . . . You've become very outspoken and French."

"My husband was French."

"Ah." Chris looks at her. He would not have recognized her in the gallery if she hadn't spoken first and called him 'Kit', recalling student days. He remembers her as a smiling, dewy girl with lots of admirers, including himself. Now she wears loneliness about her like a fine veil. She's still attractive though, with her lovely, deep blue eyes shining in the glow from the fat candle on the table.

"So how has your day been Kit?"

"Miserable, mooching about in the pouring rain and freezing cold trying to get some ideas. Then this afternoon, I made the mistake of looking in at the 'Merci Warhol' exhibition which enraged me."

"Why did it enrage you?"

"For a start, there's none of Warhol's actual stuff and I was hoping to find the spirit of experiment, some pushing-out of the boundaries, instead it was all passionless—not even a sense of fun, though that could have been me. Warhol wouldn't have been flattered. It's like much of the stuff you see in London these days—pretentious rubbish. And you feel they're so pleased with themselves, 'Look what I made with my own faeces, bow down and worship my shit and pay thirty thousand pounds to take it home.'"

"Kit!" Melanie laughs, "I don't remember you as an angry young man."

"Well I wasn't but I'm jaundiced and middle-aged now. I can't appreciate what so many of today's so-called artists are doing. It makes me feel out of things and I resent that."

"Hasn't it always been like that in the art world? There have always been people, forgive me, slow to get it, grasp what's being attempted."

"Of course, you're right. You need to be constantly re-educating yourself if you want to keep up. I know I'm old-fashioned, I revere proper painting, work that's cost a painter some sweat and feeling. Which is why I bought that lithograph this morning, it's life-affirming. You can hear it and feel it—you know, little splashes in the water, the sun on your face, you can revel in all that sparkle and colour. I can't wait to get it home. It's just what I need at the moment. It's a reminder . . ."

"What do you mean, a reminder?"

"I'm not quite sure, my brain hasn't thawed out yet but I'll tell you this, tomorrow I'm taking myself off to the Musée D'Orsay to look at more pictures which celebrate beauty and humanity. Here endeth the lesson. He smiles.

"I'll come with you, if you like."

"Will you? What about the gallery?"

"I'm closed tomorrow."

The waiter comes to see if they need more wine and are perhaps ready to order.

"What do you suggest Mellie?"

"They do country cooking here and if you like rabbit, they do a superb casserole in wine."

"That sounds good. Let's have that then and another bottle of this." Chris sits back, enjoying a sense of well-being after his miserable day. He's pleased to have Mellie's company. He and Verina have not sat at a dinner table by themselves since the failed week-end in Suffolk.

"You don't show crap like the 'Merci Warhol' in your place, do you?" He grins at her teasingly.

"I have had one or two peculiar exhibitions which were not very successful. There was one of mechanical pieces made out of tin cans and lids and things that reminded me of Victorian toys. It was meant, apparently, to show the different speeds in the stages of one's life I must confess I couldn't see the point. Then there was another which interspersed still photographs between sections of videos. It was called 'Epiphanies' They often have high-falutin names."

"There you are, as I said 'pretentious'. Tell me how you got into the art business anyway, you were a ballet dancer when I knew you."

"I had given up dance and after I was widowed, I got a job looking after the gallery. The owner was a lovely old boy called Henri Poussin—no relation—he knew a great deal about art and took pains to try and educate me. I discovered why, when he died and left me the business. We were both alone in the world and had grown fond of each other. He regarded me as a daughter but I was astonished when he left me everything."

"He had no-one else though."

"True. I was nervous at first. I wasn't sure I could cope with the gallery on my own but then I thought I'd been doing it virtually alone for some years because Monsieur Henri was getting old and tired. Out of respect for him, and for my own sake, I've started to study art on a part-time basis and I love it more and more. With contemporary stuff, I try to keep an open mind and learn."

"So do I but I'm subject to panic attacks and apoplexy sometimes, especially when, as happened today, I'm made to be an unwilling participant in someone else's idea."

"How do you mean?"

"At one point, I realised I was watching myself on video and I looked ridiculous. I suppose it was funny the way rain was dripping off me but I was annoyed not amused. I can see that in a different mood, I might have learned something about myself and if that was the artist's intention, it's patronising. I've had to do a lot of self-examining lately in any case and I didn't go into the gallery to look at me. It was like an assault. An unknown artist getting some sort of capital out of making me look a fool. What I wanted was to be excited by the work on view and to come out with spirits uplifted."

"You should have gone to church then."

"Touché. Sorry to be boring, I can hear myself going on a bit. I'll blame the wine and shut up. Tell me about you. The last I heard, you were going for an audition in Paris."

"That's right. Fancy you remembering that. Well I was lucky, the people I was auditioning for had seen me dance in London and decided to take me on. I was absolutely thrilled and could hardly believe it."

"You deserved it. You were always very dedicated. I remember being at the stage door one night and an old chap asked me who I was waiting for. When I told him, he said 'Star quality. Star quality.'"

Their food has arrived and Chris is ravenous after tramping the streets all day. The casserole is hot and wonderfully flavoured.

"You like it?"

"It's scrumptious."

"It's years since I heard that word" she's beaming at him.

"Oh, that's my kid's vocabulary."

"Lucky you to have kids. Tell me about them."

"Two girls and a boy and they're wonderful. Have you any?"

"No." She gets on with her dinner.

They are too busy eating for a while to talk much. The waiter tops up their glasses. Both of them seem caught up in their own thoughts. Chris glances at her, she's looking sad again. "So tell me, what was it like being part of a French dance company?"

"Marvellous. We really had to work hard but I loved every minute of it. We danced all over the world. You won't have seen me, you were not interested in ballet."

"Not the classical stuff, no. Though I did think you were good. I remember you dancing—was it Titania?—you were radiant and so delicate, you gave the impression of being semi-transparent like a real fairy."

"You never said anything."

"I was too gauche in those days. Did you give it up when you got married?"

"Not straight away."

"And your husband, was he a dancer?"

"Alain? No, he was a doctor. He worked with Medecins Sans Frontières—unfortunately."

Their waiter is hovering. He clears the plates and they order cheese. The restaurant has filled up. There's a buzz of conversation and laughter all around them but Chris and Melanie, in their little recess, are cut off and private.

131

The camembert almost flows off its dish as they cut into it and for a while, they concentrate on eating and drinking. It amuses Chris to observe how much Melanie relishes her food. She's licking her fingers, "This cheese is good."

"So's this wine. Presumably your husband's work took him all over the world as yours did?"

"Mm."

"But at some point in time, you managed to arrive at the same spot on the globe for long enough to get married?"

"Yes, that's just about how it was. It was difficult but we did it."

"Must have been tricky trying to sustain a marriage if you were both away a lot?"

"You could say our marriage was a series of brief, glorious honeymoons. We didn't have time to experience the day-to-day hum-drum. Then after a while, I gave up the ballet because I wanted to have children."

"You said 'I', didn't you both want them?"

"Alain was half-hearted about it. I'd become a principal and he thought it was glamorous to have a wife who was becoming famous. I can boast a bit with you because I know I can't impress you." He shrugs. "Anyway, he finally agreed to go along with the idea, to keep me happy. He applied for a post in a local hospital and while he was waiting to start, he was asked to temporarily make up a team going to Africa—Ruanda. I begged him not to go, I had a sort of premonition. He persuaded me he'd only be away a few weeks. He was coming home as soon as the doctor whose place he was taking, could get out there. That was, when his wife had safely had their baby. So he went and one morning, crossing the road to get a sandwich, he was shot dead by a sniper."

"Oh God! You must have been devastated."

"Yes. And angry and bitter. I not only lost a husband I adored but also any children we might have had. I've never spoken those words out loud before but you're an old friend and I feel I can speak freely to you. It's taken me nearly ten years to come to terms with Alain's betrayal—as I saw it. I kick myself now for not having tried to get myself pregnant earlier. Like a fool, I waited for Alain's permission. Of course, we might never have succeeded anyway but now I'll never know . . . As you get older, you accept that there are things you'll probably never do again—hot air ballooning, even making love again

132

perhaps but if it's only ageing that makes you hesitate, there's always a very slight, trembly chance that a small miracle could happen if you don't lose courage. In the matter of children, of course, nature has the final say. It's too late for me now, that's something I have to live with."

"Oh Mel. There hasn't been anyone else in your life since Alain was killed?"

"No-one who mattered. No-one who could possibly matter. But listen I don't want you to think me the lonely, tragic widow and all that. I have a great life here in Paris—an interesting one—with some very good friends. I could even have lovers if I gave anyone a chance." She grins. "Now I want to hear all about you." He says nothing.

"Don't feel bad because yours is a happy story."

He sighs, "Well it was . . ."

"Oh I see . . . If you're not too tired, why don't we go back to my place for coffee and brandy and you can tell me about it. I've been bending your ear long enough."

A biting wind pushes them along the streets back to the gallery. Once there, Chris manages to tangle himself up in the heavy curtain just inside the front door which makes them both giggle. Melanie switches on the light and reveals a narrow, twisting staircase of polished wood. He follows her up past a small landing with two doors, a few more steps up and there's a well-lit kitchen, they continue up and round until they reach the top where she leads him into a large room, switching on lamps to guide him. One entire half of the sloping ceiling is glass. The moon hangs near and brilliant.

"What a marvellous window, it puts you right in the sky."

"This used to be a studio. I'll pull the blind across—make it more cosy."

"Please don't. I love the strangeness. People talk about the cold light of the moon but . . ."

"Lovers don't."

"When it seems so close, it's comforting, calming."

"Sit down Kit. Make yourself at home. I'll go and make some coffee." It's very warm in the flat. He sinks down into a deep, comfortable chair and looks around. It's an odd-shaped room stretching away to darkness in corners and furnished with a mixture of ethnic pieces and expensive-looking Italian furniture.

Melanie brings the coffee and pours brandy for them both. She kicks off her shoes and curls up on the sofa opposite. "Isn't this nice?" She's smiling at him like a child who's been given a treat.

"It's certainly not how I expected to end this wretched day. It was such a surprise walking in on you this morning. Here was the girl we'd all been in love with."

She laughs, delighted "Really? Even you?"

"What do you mean, even me?"

"You never showed that much interest."

"We were all in awe of you. You had already started your career while we were all still messing about in art school. We used to call you 'La Princesse Lointaine'. You were so lovely. Well you still are."

"Thank you." She's looking hard at him. "Although I knew you at once this morning, I see that you're no longer the gentle, dreamy boy. Unless you still are deep down. You've become a powerful, handsome man. Dangerous even."

Chis laughs. "If that's how you see me, it must be the brandy. I like your description but I don't have power over anything or anyone. My children only do as I ask out of affection and politeness."

"Have you got photos with you?"

"Yes." He gets out his wallet, "They're slightly out of date."

"Lovely children Kit. You are lucky."

"I know."

"And this is your wife?"

"Verina, yes."

"She's beautiful." She pours more brandy for them both. "So why are you not happy Kit? You don't have to tell me if you don't want to. I'm sure you have lots of friends but it's sometimes easier to talk to people outside your usual circle."

"How do you know I'm not happy?"

"When I told you in the restaurant, not to feel bad if yours was a happy story you said 'It was . . .' Something must have happened to make you use the past tense. I've told you my miseries so now you can tell me yours and we can feel sorry for ourselves together."

"I've been doing too much of that actually Mellie—feeling sorry for myself. I'm sure it's a way to lose friends, you can't maunder on to them day in, day out. You lose respect after a

134

while—theirs and your own. Everyone has problems. I don't want to off-load onto you. It wouldn't be fair."

She slips off the sofa and comes to crouch in front of him. "Don't worry about me. I think you were meant to walk into my shop today so you could tell me your troubles. If it makes it easier, I was always fonder of you than you ever guessed." She holds his face in her hands, kisses him on the forehead and goes back to curl up among the cushions.

He sips his drink and begins telling her the story in the third person. "There was this happy family, mother, father and three children . . ." Now that he has started, it's easy to keep going. She listens in silence until he finishes. "I feel I've got this cancerous lump in my head, poisoning my mind and it's not just drink talking. There's a shadow over everything all the time and I don't know if it will ever go away now."

"Oh Kit. It's awful. It's like a Greek tragedy. Thank you for telling me about it." She re-charges his glass. "Perhaps being away from it all, if only for a day or two, will give you a chance to think things through, get your breath back, make some sort of plan."

"Actually, I can't reason any more. I'm worn out. I operate like an automaton."

"I wish I could help but I don't know what to say, it's all so sad."

"You have helped by listening to me banging on. I've been like a wounded animal in a cave, licking my wounds in secret. Being with you this evening has made me feel human again. You are so sympatica."

"Thank you. I'm glad."

"You know you can get hemmed in by strange and deep experience. You can forget there are many other sufferers in the world who get on with it. Hearing your story, has reminded me of that. I needed reminding. I've got to get out of the 'poor me' syndrome and get some control over life. The kids are unsettled and I've watched Verina torn in different directions. You don't really understand the sort of person you are until something big hits you. I've discovered that I've got all kinds of nasty qualities hidden away. I'm choked up with anger, jealousy, resentment and malice."

"Malice? I don't believe that Kit. You can't be expected to have good feelings towards people who're wrecking your life.

135

Don't be so hard on yourself, jealousy and resentment are natural. May I ask do you two still share a bedroom at least?"

"We still sleep in the same bed but we no longer share anything. You could say we lead separate lives, privately. We don't communicate, it's become impossible. The kids are there so you keep up some sort of normality for them but . . ."

She gets up and goes to get more coffee. "Kit, you don't think your wife and the boy have ever—how shall I put this—gone too far? I know that's an awful question."

He blows out a long breath and takes a while to answer her. "The attraction between them is so strong it certainly could be sexual. When you're with them in the same room, you can feel the pull. It wouldn't surprise me if they have done things they shouldn't. I've imagined it often enough. Faith and I don't spell it out to each other but we both feel like intruders a lot of the time. You can understand the worry. Now is a particularly bad time for her of course, her baby's nearly due."

"When he sees his own child, that should distract him don't you think?"

"I hope so and I know Faith hopes so too." Chris is feeling sleepy, they've been drinking all evening.

"You may find things have changed when you get back home; perhaps the baby will have arrived. Babies are like magnets, they alter force fields."

This makes him smile. "I hope you're right. Quite the little wise woman, aren't you?"

"Do you often come to Paris Chris?"

"Not as a rule but I may be to-ing and fro-ing a bit over this account."

"Good. Now you know where I am, I hope you'll come and see me again."

"Of course I will."

"You might have Verina with you next time."

"Who knows? You might not be by yourself either. I hope you're not. I can't bear to see the waste of a good woman—a lovely woman."

"Thank you. What will you do if your Verina rides off into the sunset with your step-son?"

"Come back here and carry you off of course." They both laugh. Chris puts his hand over his glass to prevent her from pouring him another drink. "I've had more than enough." He manages to pull himself up out of his chair and is just about steady on his feet. "Thank you for listening to my tale of woe. Are you still on for the Musée D'Orsay tomorrow?"

"Yes but not too early please."

"I was thinking of getting there about 10.30."

"That's fine. And are you going to let me cook dinner for you tomorrow night? It would just finish the day off nicely. Don't worry, I've no hidden agendas—well, if I have, I promise to keep them hidden." She smiles disarmingly.

"You may be too tired after a late night and a trek round the museum. Let's play it by ear tomorrow. I'll push off now and let you get some sleep."

She has crossed her arms and is holding her shoulders as if hugging herself. "For me, seeing you has brought back all the innocence and sweetness of being young, if that doesn't sound too corny."

"It sounds nice. I really like this atticky place."

"You can stay if you like, that chair makes into a bed." The look she gives him shows how vulnerable she is. It would be easy to take advantage of her and he's tempted by the delicious thought of sinking into bed with this gentle, charming woman. "It's kind of you Mel but it probably wouldn't be a good idea. I'd better get back in case anyone has been trying to reach me. See you in the morning." He bends to kiss her cheek and she slips her arms around him to give him a gentle squeeze.

"You're sure you'll be all right? Not too mis. by yourself?"

"I'll be fine. Thank you for being so kind."

"Shall I call you a taxi?"

"No thanks, a walk will do me good, clear my head." She releases him.

"Goodnight little Mel. Thank you again. I'd better go backwards down these twisty stairs after drinking all your brandy.

In the hotel, he finds a note pushed under his door, 'Please telephone home.' He looks at his watch, it'll have to wait til morning.

He rings as soon as he wakes. Greg answers "Daddy. Oh daddy, something terrible's happened. Daniel died."

"Daniel? Who's Daniel?"

"Faith's little baby. Here's mum, she'll tell you."

"Chris? I tried to get you last night. You must have been out."

"I was. Is it true? About the baby?"

"Yes."

"Poor Faith. How is she?"

"In shock."

"Of course. Do we know why the baby died?"

"No. I haven't seen her yet. I waited for you. Can you come home?"

"I'll jump on the next flight I can. I'll let you know."

"Good. We all need you here."

He puts the phone down, his thoughts racing.`

—

Coming down the stairs in Gemma's house, Cassie hears her mother's name and pauses. Don is chatting to Angela in the kitchen, "She seems very cut-up over Faith losing the baby," "Yes. Well she may unconsciously have thought that if Faith had the baby, she could have Alex. There's probably an element of guilt mixed up in there too." "How many are we for lunch? I'll set the table."

Cassie rushes back upstairs to the bathroom and locks herself in. She plays back to herself what she's just overheard. Gemma is practising the same piece over and over on the piano making it difficult to think straight. *if only Sheldon was home — he often clears things up—makes you see when your response to things is out of whack—what did Angela mean?—mum has already got Alex—does she think mum wants to take him right away from Faith?—surely not—she must know mum wouldn't do that— couldn't do that—it doesn't make sense—mum cares about Faith— she's always telling Alex what he should be doing for her—she's not a possessive mother—loving, yes—possessive, no—why should she be possessive about Alex?—yuck!—okay, so she's his mother and he hasn't seen her for years but he's grown up now—if she's going to be possessive about anybody, it should be about Greg, Nan and me.*

She feels like a small child again, confused and unprotected. Also, the know-all way Angela talks about Verina irritates her *they're supposed to be friends—Mum's worried sick*

138

about grandpa at the moment—people should be supporting her not gossiping behind her back.

When Gemma calls her for lunch, she runs down and says sorry to Angela, telling her she's suddenly remembered she's supposed to be on an errand for her mother and hurriedly leaves. She's not hungry now anyway.

—

A nurse at the hospital tells Chris and Verina that Faith is in the day-room with her parents. They find her sitting on a sofa between two slight, grey-haired people who look alike. They are both neatly dressed, he in suit and tie, she in a dark jacket and skirt and a pastel blouse with a bow at the neck. Alex is there too and he gets up as Chris and Verina approach. They both bend down to kiss Faith and Alex introduces them to her parents, Beattie and Ben. Faith has been crying. "When did you get back from Paris Chris?"

"This afternoon."

"And you've come straight over to see me. Thank you."

"We're so sorry Faith."

She makes a helpless little gesture with her hands and her father takes one of them in his.

Alex brings up two chairs. "We're discussing the funeral for the baby."

"Already?"

Ben nods, "Faith's been encouraged to get on with it."

Beattie explains, "It's because, you see, you get everything ready for the baby before" she hesitates . . . "then if the baby's not going to be there . . . so they think planning what to do . . . instead . . . helps the mother to . . . work out how to say goodbye in her own way." Her voice betrays her and she searches in her bag for a handkerchief. Faith gives her a squeeze.

"We've been talking about burying the baby by the stream in our garden. It's Faith's idea. She always played there as a child and hoped her little chap would too. So did we." Ben chokes and turns it into a cough.

"I was saying won't they find that a bit morbid?"

"No Alex, not at all. I'm right, aren't I mother? If it's going to comfort our Faith to know her little lad is there and if you agree,

139

we'd like to arrange this for her. In any case, what better place for a child than near his grandparents?" He looks at Chris for support.

"A splendid idea. Is it allowed?"

"A friend of mine works for the council, he'll point me in the right direction if we need permission. I'm sure it'll be all right. And we'll have the mass in our local church."

"The children will want to come."

"Do you think so? You don't think they're too young?"

"I think they'd be hurt if you left them out. Which reminds me, they've all sent you cards, "Verina hands envelopes to Faith which she tucks in her dressing-gown pocket.

"We're taking Faith home with us for a while tomorrow" says Beattie.

"Just as well. I've got to go up to Birmingham for a few days anyway so I wouldn't be able to look after her."

Faith stares at Alex after this little speech. "Well do you mind us going ahead with the funeral arrangements?"

"No. It's up to you. Just do what you want and let me know the date and time and I'll be there."

With everybody gone, Faith is back in her room sitting down to read the children's cards. Nan and Greg have made theirs. Cassie's is shop bought. There's a vase of narcissus on the front. Inside, she has written:

Dear Faith,

We're all so sad for you. It must be about the worst thing that can happen to anyone. We all love you dearly and worry about you. So please come and stay with us and let our lovely mum take care of you, with our help of course.
Big hugs and love Cass. xx

Nan has written:

Dearest Faith,

I haven't got enough experience of life to understand why horrible cruel things happen to nice, good people. Mummy says we have to love each other through the awful times. I hope you are feeling better, though how can you? It makes me cry.

Lots of love, Nan xxxxxxxxxxxxx

Greg's words make her smile through her tears:

DEAR FAITH IM SORRY YOUR BABY DIED. I WON A COMPETITION. YOU HAD TO DRAW A CAR OF THE FUTURE. THIS GRATE PARCEL ARRIVED TODAY FULL OF MINICHER CARS. I CRIED ALL DAY WHEN MY GUINEA-PIG DIED SO I KNOW HOW YOU FEEL. HERE IS A DRAWING OF A PICNIC WE ARE GOING TO TAKE YOU ON SOON. LOTS AND LOTS AND LOTS OF LOVE. DON'T CRY ANY MORE. FROM GREGORY, YOUR BROTHER IN LAW. XXXXXXXXXX

Faith holds the messages against her. It's like having the three of them standing round her chair *dear Cass, thinking their mother could help me—heal me—if the children only knew . . . whatever happens between me and Alex in the future, these kids must go on being part of my life.*

—

The church smells faintly of incense. Small bunches of early spring flowers are fastened at the end of the first two pews and cover the top of the white shoe-box coffin in front of the altar. Only family is present: Faith and her parents, Alex with Lilian and Phil, Chris and the children.

The priest, Father Ryan, welcomes them with the reminder that he had married Alex and Faith. He tells them how sad he feels to be burying their first-born and invites them all to pray that God may grant the couple other children in the future.

Chris worrying about Verina and the state of her father, wonders how soon they might expect another funeral.

Cassie walks over to stand beside the coffin, facing them. She has written a poem for Daniel and Faith has asked her to read it during the mass. Her reading brings an ache to the back of his throat as Chris listens to her;

"For Daniel. 'Disappointment.'

When you long for someone to come
and preparations are made in the house
and preparations are made in the heart
but the expected person doesn't arrive
after all
and no-one can tell you why,
you have to put all the love
you had ready and waiting
into an envelope and post it into space."

Father Ryan takes up Cassie's words and incorporates them into his own message of comfort. As he talks about the difficulties of trying to understand God's part in our human tragedies, Chris switches off and pursues his thoughts about Verina—*loves her father so much—must dread losing him—the old girl's batty behaviour probably due to the same—hope she'll allow father and daughter some time together.*

They leave the church in pouring rain for the slow drive to the house. Alex and Ben carry the coffin, which does not need two of them, across the lawn and down to a secluded part of the garden where the small grave is open and ready. The others follow. Chris pictures Faith as a little girl, playing here with her friends. Willow twigs are yellowing at the tips and pink buds are pushing through on the camellias. This will be a lovely spot in a week or two.

The priest holds one hand over his book to keep the rain off and reads his prayers aloud, looking to them now and then to make their responses. They are standing very near the edge of the stream and Chris feels himself sliding slowly backwards down the muddy bank. Greg slips too and bumps into him and laughs. Immediately, he remembers it's a solemn occasion and whispers 'Sorry' to Faith. She reaches out a hand to haul him back up beside her and bends to kiss the top of his head.

As the coffin is gently lowered into the ground, a thrush bursts into passionate song. Father Ryan waits, while rain splashes down on his head, before pronouncing his final benedictions.

Beattie leads everyone into the house. Chris is walking beside Ben. "A sad day Ben." "The saddest of my life . . . Thank you for Daniel's tree. What did you say it is?" "An Acer Brilliantissima. It has colour all year round and is magnificent in autumn. We thought it would look lovely by the stream." "I'll get it in tomorrow. Somewhere near so that it grows over the . . ."

In the porch, Beattie is trying to persuade the priest to stay for lunch but he has work to do at the church.

Everyone files indoors and Beattie urges them all into the dining room "Come and have something to eat. Warm you all up."

Ben pours sherry for the adults. It goes straight to Lilian's head, she starts chattering, "I'm so sorry Verina couldn't be here, I was so looking forward to meeting her. Let's hope she'll be with us next time we're all together, perhaps it'll be for Alex and Faith's next little baby's christening."

Greg's bright, eager voice cuts across the uncomfortable silence "Are you pregnant again already Faith?"

"No."

"I'm starving."

Nan grins, "You always are Greg."

"We all get hungry at funerals" Beattie says soothingly, "it's the emotion. I hope you all like beef." She has cooked a magnificent roast which is very welcome since they all feel damp and chilled. A hush settles as they begin to eat.

Lilian asks "Why couldn't Verina come did you say Alex?"

"I told you. Her father is dying. Her mother rang to say she ought to go and see him before it's too late."

"Oh poor Verina. It's so awful to lose a parent."

"Well she hasn't lost him yet."

If Lilian feels snubbed by his tone, she doesn't show it. She turns to Chris, "I hope she wasn't offended by my letter?"

"What letter was that?"

"The one I sent with the photographs of Alex."

Chris looks at Alex "I don't think there was a letter with the photographs."

Alex feigns innocence "It must have dropped out of your bag Faith?"

Chris and Lilian both glance at her but her face is without expression.

"Oh dear. That's a pity. I wouldn't like her to think I'm thoughtless. I can imagine how it must have made her feel to see all those photos of him as a baby and a toddler and then growing up. She must have felt sad about all those years she missed."

Everyone at the table is listening and as Lilian catches the echo of her words, she looks in horror at Faith and bursts into tears.

Phil apologises for her "It's the sherry, she's not used to it and she feels things a lot."

Beattie gets up and comes to put an arm round Lilian's shoulders, "Come on into the kitchen, what you need is a nice cup of tea."

Ben is concerned for Faith "You all right my love?"

"Yes dad, thanks."

Chris has Nan on his other side, "You're very quiet sweetie."

"I've been stuffing my face, I was hungry. I hope mummy's all right. I didn't like leaving her to go down to grandpa's on her own."

"Neither did I but we'll all go with her next time."

They must have been having similar thoughts because Nan asks "Why are so many awful things happening at once dad?" Before he can answer her, Beattie reappears with apple-crumble and custard. Chris tries to imagine how life looks to Nan at present—*and to Cass and Greg—you can only protect them from so much—some things they have to endure—part of growing up, learning about life—it never stops.*

The sun breaks through as they file out after lunch to put flowers on the now filled-in grave. Greg holds tight to Chris's hand, his eyes brimming, "It's so small daddy."

Alex drives Lilian and Phil to the station to catch their train. Cassie helps Beattie to clear up. Ben takes Nan and Greg along the stream to give them a fishing lesson. Chris and Faith follow them.

"Is Alex staying over for the week-end?"

"No and I'm relieved he isn't. He's got to go to some conference thank goodness. He badgers me all the time. Keeps telling me I've got to pull myself together. I know that. I'm trying but he won't let me get on with it in my own way. He can't understand that my body is still as confused as my mind. He doesn't know what to say to me really or what he's supposed to do. I'm not going to ask him to just give me a quiet cuddle if he can't work it out for himself. Am I being unreasonable?"

"I don't think you are but then I'm biased."

They stroll in silence for a few minutes. "It's awkward Chris because the night I had to go into hospital, we'd had a fearful row earlier on. That's why I didn't let him know what was happening. We've got unfinished business to deal with and neither of us wants to face up to it at the moment."

"You don't think that's why you lost the baby?"

"No. Looking back, I realise things had gone wrong earlier in the day. I felt so strange and ill."

"You don't blame him then?"

"No. not for that." She explained the apparent cause of the baby's death. "What I do blame him for though, is leaving me when I needed him. As usual, he did what he wanted to do. He was determined not to miss Angela's party. At first I asked him to stay with me which he didn't want to do, so then I asked him to at least come home afterwards. We said some horrible things to each other, especially me—what I said was unforgivable — and he banged out of the flat."

"He must feel bad about that now. I was hoping losing the baby would give him a jolt and bring you close again, make him realise how much he loves you."

"I think it's confirmed how much he doesn't. And at the moment, I can't feel anything much for him either."

"Have you talked?"

"As I said, we're both avoiding it. He actually doesn't care about the baby. He's been going through the motions today. And I honestly think he's not in the least concerned about me."

"He might be one of those people who find it hard to show their feelings."

She thinks about this. "You may be right. My parents are rather reticent like that but I've always known they're devoted to each other and to me. My dad going to all that trouble with the council so that Daniel could be buried here and my little mum, cooking mountains of food. The table looked like Christmas. They've always been very supportive but even so, they've surprised me by being so wonderful, so sensitive, over this"

"They are both good, kind people and I'm so glad you've got them. As for the baby, I'm so sorry Faith."

"I know you are. I can still feel the weight of him in my arms you know." Her face is bleak.

Words and phrases come into his head but he rejects them, there's no comfort in words. "How long will you stay with your parents?"

"A few more days at least. I'm not ready to leave . . . yet . . . I want to be with mum and dad. Eventually, I'll have to go home to the flat and sort things out. I'm not looking forward to it. I'm in a strange country where I don't know the customs."

Greg has come to find them, he's lost interest in fishing, "When are we going home dad?"

"We should make a move now, go home and see what's happening to mummy. Go and find the girls please and tell them we're off in a minute." He hugs Faith. "I feel we're deserting you." "No you're not. I'm being thoroughly spoiled here. It was lovely of you all to come." "Come over to see us as soon as you can bear to. In any case, ring me when you get back home and let me know if you need anything, if there's anything we can do."

—

Verina is on the phone to Alex "I'm glad I've caught you."

"Hallo my beautiful."

"I tried you earlier on your mobile."

"Oh sorry. Faith rang me a couple of times and I got irritated and switched it off."

"I hope you're going to be kind to her."

"Look, I've only just got in—had to work late—and I'm dying for a beer."

146

"I won't keep you darling, it's just that I wanted you to know that I'm going down to spend the night and most of tomorrow with my parents again."

"I've hardly seen you the last few weeks."

"Alex, you have! It's just there's been such a lot going on."

"There always is."

She speaks gently "I know you're finding things hard at present." Greg calls out in the background, "Mum, mummy."

"You'd better go and see to your family."

"I'm on the phone Greg. Won't be a minute. You are my family."

"Doesn't seem like it."

"Look. I'm sorry you're feeling . . . a bit marginalised? at the moment but I must see my poor old dad when I can. In any case, Faith's coming home tomorrow, isn't she?"

"What if she is? What's that got to do with anything?"

"Are you driving down to collect her?"

"No. Her father's bringing her."

"She's going to need lots of T.L.C. You will look after her, won't you?"

"I'm not sure I've got your capacity for behaving appropriately in every situation."

"What's that supposed to mean?"

"Oh, I don't know."

"We're rather a sad house at the moment; the children love their grandfather and they realise he's dying."

"We all have to die sometime."

"Alex! God you're hurtful."

"You can't expect me to be interested. My grandparents haven't shown the slightest wish to know me."

"I've talked to you about all of that."

"I know, I know. I'm the inconvenient secret."

Greg calls her again, "Mum, I really need you to help me with this please."

She sighs "Oh God."

"I'd better ring off."

She rings back a few minutes later, "You put the phone down on me!"

"Yeah. I felt like it."

"Bit childish, isn't it?"

147

"Maybe."

"Alex, just let me get through this week-end, after that I may be able to . . ."

"Give me some attention? Allow me a little of your precious time? Don't worry about it. I'm not really part of your life."

There are tears in her voice which she tries to control, "I won't be able to talk to you while I'm away, I'll ring you as soon as I get back."

"I may not be here. I'm fed up. I may take myself off somewhere for the week-end."

"What about Faith?"

"What about her? Why do you keep nagging on about Faith?"

"Alex" she's pleading now, "have you forgotten we said we were going to look after the others? She's sobbing quietly and can't continue.

"Goodbye Vee." He puts the receiver down.

Faith is standing in the doorway.

"Didn't hear you come in. Where's your dad?"

"I got them tickets for 'Guys and Dolls' to cheer them up. They've been so wonderful. I thought if dad was bringing me anyway, they could both come. Traffic was awful, I made them go straight to the theatre."

She looks around at the dirty plates and mugs on the floor and on top of the television and goes to drop her suitcase in the bedroom. The window is closed and the room smells stale. The bed-clothes are on the floor, discarded socks and shirts have been thrown down anywhere, the sheet with the blood from her nose-bleed is bunched up by the laundry basket. Alex comes up behind her "I thought you were coming tomorrow. Sorry it's a bit of a mess. I've only just got in. It won't take long to clear, I'll give you a hand."

She stuffs the blood-stained sheet into the basket. "That's my mess tidied up. You can do the rest." She buttons up her coat.

"Where are you going?"

"Out." She closes the flat door with a bang.

She has to get out of the flat away from the squalor and Alex *I'm not ready for him—no speeches prepared—we'll have to talk about things—he'll avoid discussions if he can—first words I hear when I get home 'Goodbye Vee'—if only it was—does any of it matter any more?—don't know what to think about anything—can't think—all just a miserable blur—Al will find some way to blame me for Daniel.* Habit has taken her towards their wine bar, she pushes the door open.

It's early, there are few people. She climbs up on to one of the high stools at the bar. Dave, the owner, smiles at her "Hi Faith" then he remembers and looks solemn, "sorry about the news. Alex was in. What can I get you—on the house?"

"A glass of red please Dave."

"Coming up. Where's Alex?"

"Working late."

He has to attend to other customers and she's left to herself. Deep in thought, she doesn't notice that someone has come to sit on the stool beside her. She feels something against her hand and glances down to see a large plastic spider on the counter. She turns her head and meets the stare of a young man sitting so close their noses almost touch. She recoils.

"No scream?"

"What? Is that spider yours?"

"Yes. Do you like him? If you do, I'll give him to you."

"Aren't you a bit big to be playing with toys?"

"Not a toy, it's a ploy. You were supposed to be frightened. I would remove the spider and get to talk to you."

"That's how you try to pick up women, is it? By frightening them?"

"Actually, you're my first experiment."

"Thanks. Why choose me for the honour?"

"For the challenge. Because you're remote and mysterious."

"And you're crazy."

"It worked though. You are talking to me."

She can't help smiling.

"My name's Aidan, Aiden Melhuish. I've just moved round here. Don't tell me your name please. I want to name you myself." He examines her profile until she becomes disconcerted.

"All right?" Dave means 'Is this chap annoying you?'

"Yes fine thanks Dave. I think I'll have something to eat." He hands her the menu.

"Will you let me buy you dinner?" the young man asks.

"No thank you. I'd better tell you I'm an old married woman."

"Bride to Orpheus I hope."

"What?"

"Orpheus has to lose Eurydice. When he does, it means I can come and find you."

Faith slides down from her stool "I'll have chilli please Dave."

"Rice and salad?"

"Please. I'll go and sit over there." She says "Excuse me" to the young man but he follows her to the table and sits down. Dave appears with a bottle and two glasses and winks at Faith behind the young man's back.

"If I can't buy you dinner, I hope you'll accept some wine."

Faith looks wearily at him, "I don't want to be unfriendly but I have told you I'm married."

"Why are you by yourself then?" He pours wine into their glasses. "I wouldn't let a beautiful girl like you go out alone. There's a lot of riff-raff about these days."

"My husband will be joining me shortly."

"I'll look after you until he does."

"You'll find me poor company."

"Because you're sad? That's what makes you so appealing to me. Don't worry, I can see you're fragile. I won't intrude on your sorrows unless you want to talk about them."

Faith picks up her glass and drinks a little wine as she regards him; Mediterranean-looking, in his twenties. Distinctly odd but his large, gentle brown eyes persuade her he's harmless.

Her chilli arrives. "Aren't you going to eat something? I don't want you watching my every bite."

"I'll have some of your bread. You've got a lovely face you know. No wonder that bar-tender is in love with you. You should be dressed always in pale colours, cream, ivory. Ivory silk. I'd like to make robes for you."

"Are you a designer?" She's making conversation.

"No, I'm a medical student but I've always had this idea of how I would dress my ideal woman."

Faith glances towards the door, several people are coming in, among them she sees Alex. He sees her at the same time and realises she's with somebody. His face tightens. He pushes his way to the table.

"This is Alex, my husband. This . . ." She has forgotten his name.

"Melhuish, Aidan Melhuish. I've been taking care of your wife until you arrived. Glass of wine?" He signals to Dave for another glass.

Alex ignores him. "I guessed you might be in here. I was going to take you to dinner."

"As you see, I already have some food. Why don't you get some too?"

He sits down and absent-mindedly drinks the wine Aidan has pushed over to him. He's clearly put out, "You didn't mention you were meeting a friend."

Aidan corrects him "We have only just met. This wasn't planned. It was destiny."

"Oh," Faith says "is that your spider's name?" She and Aidan laugh.

"I don't know what all this is about." Alex gets up "I'll go and get some food."

Aidan watches him walk over to the bar, "How long have you been married?"

"Nearly three years."

"And you already don't love each other any more. I shan't have to wait long."

Faith can't stop herself from laughing again but it's mainly from nervousness.

Another bottle of wine comes with Alex's food and they share it. Aidan talks non-stop, presenting them with surreal images as snapshots of his life.

Faith is sure he's inventing it all. Neither she nor Alex are really listening. Faith is tired and the wine has made her sleepy. Alex suggests it's time they went home.

The three of them leave together but separate on the pavement. Aidan touches Faith's arm "I won't leave you long in the underworld Eurydice." He glides off along by the park.

"Nuts" Alex is scornful.

"Definitely, poor chap."

"Did you know he was going to be there?"

"Of course not. I've never seen him before in my life. He told you that himself. He's just moved here."

"You made a right fool of me in front of Dave."

"No I didn't. Dave saw the whole thing, he was keeping an eye on me all the time. I know what you're doing. You're trying to put me in the wrong so that I can't say anything about the state of the flat, or mention Verina or the awful row. Oh the weariness of it all."

They let themselves in and she sees he has cleared up a bit at least. "I think I'll go straight to bed."

"I'll just see the news and I'll follow you." His relief almost makes her laugh. *I can feel myself very near the edge.* She's grateful that he has changed the sheets and is slipping into sleep with the image of Daniel's face projected onto the screen in her mind when she feels Alex stoking her back. He slides his arms around her, pulls her close and holds her gently. This is comfort she has not dared to hope for. He draws his fingertips across her breasts while she lets herself stay half in sleep, wanting to trust this tenderness, waiting for him to speak. Chris's words come back to her *Alex probably doesn't know what to say—if I could tell him how much Daniel's still with me, it might help him to find words himself—might even bring us close again after all.*

He turns her round to face him. She tentatively strokes his face in the darkness but is jolted out of her dreamy state by the sudden roughness of his knee forcing her legs apart. A few seconds of confusion and anger "Alex. No!" she manages to push him away and get out of bed.

"What's the matter?"

"It would take half the night to tell you." She pulls her pillows off the bed, gets some blankets from the bathroom cupboard and makes herself comfortable on the sofa.

He comes into the living room "Come back to bed. You can't sleep here, you'll be cold. Come on, I won't bother you again, I expect it's too soon."

"Just leave me alone please Alex." Once she's sure he's back in bed, she is able to relax. Strange that mad Aidan said 'You don't love each other'. What made him say that? She calls up the memory of the summer evening when she and Alex walked down Hampstead High Street and people smiled at them and seemed to give their blessing. He was making her laugh and they must have looked happy. Did they love each other then? They must have thought they did. Surely they didn't marry on the strength of that moment?—a summer mirage?

She thought back over their time together. That shining evening was never repeated.

In the morning, she wakes to find him standing over her with a cup of tea—a 'let's make up' gesture? "Did you sleep all right on that thing?"

"Yes I did thanks."

"What do you want to do today?"

Not a lot. "Aren't you going over to the family?" She drank her tea.

"Vee's gone down to the country to see her father. Thought I might go to the gym for a while, then if you're up for it, we could go and see a film this afternoon."

"Why not?" *After all, nothing's happened—I've just given birth to a dead baby—you're in love with your mother—but you'd still screw me—I suppose I'm better than nothing.* She curls up under her blankets again and closes her eyes, aware of him walking in and out of the room.

He calls out "See you later."

He has to wake her when he gets back "Faith, are you going to lie there all day? It's nearly twelve. You haven't even put the washing in. I've got no shirts for Monday."

She sits up yawning. Like a sleepwalker she goes into the bedroom, rummages in the laundry basket to find some shirts and goes off to the kitchen to stuff them in the washing machine. He watches her do this and when she sits back down on the sofa, amid the disarray of blankets, he says "You're going to have to try and do better than this Faith." She looks at him, he doesn't seem real, he's got fuzzy lines round him, She feels herself dimming into nothingness.

Now he's banging about in the kitchen shouting "There's no food in this place. We'll have to do some shopping."

She makes herself get up and go to run a bath. He follows her "Look, I'll go and get things if you make a list."

He sits her down at the table with a pen and paper. Like someone in a trance producing automatic writing, she gets some items down. He snatches up the list and goes out.

Changes

Their Italian restaurant off St Martin's Lane, is buzzing with tourists, theatre people and would-be theatre people. Alex examines the photographs of actors along the walls. He sees Verina come in but he doesn't get up or wave, he simply watches her hesitate just inside the door looking for him with a harrassed air about her. She finds him and he stands up glancing at his watch.

"Sorry I'm late as usual." The waiter pulls out her chair.

"I was just checking to see how long we've got."

"Some client always seems to ring just as I'm ready to leave the house.

They are handed menus. "Anything to drink Sir, Madam?"

"Are we going to have some wine with our lunch?"

"Of course."

"Let's start with that then."

He orders Bardolino. "What do you want to eat?"

"Cannelloni and salad."

"I'll have the same."

Their bottle arrives, the waiter pours the wine and they clink glasses.

"You're very unsmiling Mummy-Vee. Your letter sounded as though you wanted to see me—couldn't wait to see me. Now we're together, you're trailing a grey cloud."

"Sorry."

"You look worn out, been doing too much for everybody as usual. If we weren't in a crowded restaurant, I'd massage your neck for you."

She's scanning the other tables.

"What is it? Afraid there might be someone you know in here? There never has been before. That's why we chose it, remember? Don't tell me you still worry about being seen with me."

"Of course not. Don't be always making dramas Alex, we're only having lunch."

"You're the one who feels guilty when we do."

Their food comes and Alex begins eating hungrily. Verina forks morsels into her mouth slowly.

"I miss our week-ends Vee. Are we going to be able to come over again soon?"

"It's impossible to plan ahead at the moment. I want to be with my father as much as I can; I'm conscious there's little time left."

"Couldn't you go down in the week?"

"No I couldn't, there's the family to look after and there's my work. How's Faith? I keep meaning to ring her but I'm afraid of disturbing her if she's resting."

"Resting is all she ever does these days."

"She's still recovering. It's bound to be psychological as well as physical. You must try to be kind."

"Women lose babies all the time. They get on with life. It's not as if Faith had time to build up any relationship with the kid."

"That's where you're wrong. When you carry a child in your stomach for months you form a bond."

"Really?"

She looks away from him. "Faith will eventually get on with life as you put it but she needs time. You judge people harshly you know."

"You going to eat any more of that?"

"No."

He swaps plates, reaches over for her fork and finishes her pasta. He pours more wine.

"I'm not sure I should drink any more, it makes me sleepy at lunch-time."

"You always say that. We'll have some strong coffee afterwards. The wine does you good, you look much better than when you arrived. Listen to Doctor Alex, he'll see you right."

She smiles for the first time since arriving.

"That was a lovely letter Vee. I keep everything you write to me. You come very close because you express your thoughts so freely."

"So indiscreetly you mean."

"Blackmail has crossed my mind." She hits him with a bread stick. "It takes us a while to get back on to our private wavelength sometimes; have you noticed?"

"Yes."

"I've been thinking . . . seeing that it's difficult for us to grab time together, why don't we go away one week-end—just the two of us?"

"We can't do that!"

"Why not? You could tell Chris you're going on a course or something."

"I don't lie to Chris."

"Never?"

"The odd little fib perhaps, covering up for the children or something but a big lie like that, no."

"So where does he think you are at this minute?"

"He won't be asking. He's at work."

"Listen, would it be so terrible? Wouldn't it be worth it? Imagine some little country pub. We could stroll through the woods and talk; have dinner by candle-light and just . . . be together. Where's the harm?"

She is silent, head lowered.

"We wouldn't have to keep looking at our watches. We wouldn't have to consider anyone else—just for a couple of days. Think about it."

"I don't know. It sounds lovely but I don't see how we could manage it and besides, I'd hate the subterfuge."

His voice is cold "I'm owed years, I'm only asking for a week-end."

All colour has left her face. "You made it sound so attractive, I was already trying to work out ways and means but now you start your bullying again."

"I have to battle to get a look in, you have to admit that." He puts on his wheedling voice, "I know I'm bad to you but it's only 'cos I want to be with my special Mummy all the time" he leans forward and lightly places a finger on her nose "she does have the prettiest nose."

"Can we be serious for a minute?" She outlines plans for the next couple of weeks and reminds him of her father's condition.

"So what you're saying is, everything's on hold until he croaks."

She winces "I'll never get used to the way you express things. This is my father you're talking about. You're hurting me as I'm sure you know. I love my father. You show some respect!"

"Sorry." He orders coffee and when it comes, he slides round beside her so that he can put an arm across her shoulders and murmur in her ear. "You know I don't mean to hurt you. I say bad things because I feel cheated all the time. You attend to the other children's needs, what about mine? All I want is to have you all to myself for a day or for two days, whatever. It's not impossible for us to get away—later on of course. People can always find ways to do what they want to do. You need a break. A porky is all right if it's not used to cover a crime. What the others don't know can't possibly harm them but think of how it would be for you and me. Just one short week-end. Please think about it Mummy-Vee. I'll be thinking of nothing else.

—

"That's a smashing picture dad!" Greg is watching Chris hang the lithograph in his work-room. "Did Joe make the frame?"

"It's an old one he had hanging around that he thought would be right for the picture; he's tarted it up a bit for me. Looks good, doesn't it?"

"Yeah."

Chris starts explaining what's going on in the painting and how he found it. Cassie looks in and interrupts "Some woman on the phone for you dad. Melanie something?"

"Melllie! You must be telepathic. You're not going to believe it, I've just this minute hung the picture and was telling Greg about you and the gallery."

"Oh really? How does it look now you've got it home?"

"What do you think Greg, now we've got it up?"

"Wicked."

"Greg says wicked which is high praise. I'm delighted with it."

"Good. It is okay for me to ring you?"

"Of course. How are you? Are you busy?"

"I'm fine thanks and I am busy. I'm organising an exhibition of paintings—actual paintings done with a paint-brush—by a young Hungarian. He's good."

"I hope it all goes well for him and for you."

"Did you get your camera back safely?"

"Yes. Didn't you get my email thanking you."

"No."

"I'm sorry, must have taken your email address down wrongly. Thank you so much. The camera was back here the day after you called me. Tell me what you had to pay the courier, the company will clear it. It was stupid of me to leave it behind. 'Sorry we couldn't manage our little outing. Perhaps next time. I'm almost certain to be back in Paris again soon."

"That'll be nice. Were you pleased with the pictures you took?"

"Very. I got a pleasant surprise, the awful weather must have concentrated the mind; I've got enough useful bits and pieces to give me a starting point for a new campaign. I'm very grateful to you."

Greg pulls at his sleeve, "Can we go now dad?"

"Excuse me Mel, Greg and I are going to football."

"I must go too. Take care Chris."

"And you. Send me the invoice and let me know how the exhibition goes."

—

Faith lets herself in with the shopping

Alex jumps up from his chair, grabs her arm and drags her into the bedroom. "What's all this Faith?" he points to the chest of drawers. On the top, arranged on a lace mat, is the photograph of Daniel, his framed hand-prints and a small vase of flowers.

"What's wrong?"

"You're what's wrong. You're turning this place into a shrine to a dead child. It's unhealthy."

"Let go my arm please."

"I have to sleep in here too you know. It'll be candles and incense and Christ knows what next!"

"Please stop shouting!"

He swings his arm and knocks everything down.

Ignoring him, she takes her bags to the kitchen and comes back to pick up the flowers, the vase and the frames. She knows Alex is watching her and commenting but she can't hear him through the wall she has created around herself. The flowers, back in their vase, go on the window-sill. She brings a cloth and dries the carpet. Collecting up the frames she can't decide where to put them. The box room of course. She opens the door and there is the cot, baby clothes and blankets piled up in it and perched on top, the Moses basket lined with rose-bud muslin, that Lilian sent them.

Alex is standing behind her "I'm going out to get drunk."

When he gets back, he switches the lamps on. She's been sitting in the dark. "Oh come on Faith, stop playing the martyr. I've got us Chinese."

"I thought you were going to get drunk."

"It's your favourite, lemon chicken and Singapore noodles. I'll warm up some plates." He runs them under the hot tap. "You set the table. Have we got any candles?"

She finds new ones, sticks them in holders and lights them.

"Come on then, let's eat."

"What's all this in aid of?"

"Giving you a break from having to cook." He pours her a glass of white wine, "Sparkling. Perk you up a bit. Why were you sitting in the dark?"

"I needed to think . . . You know Alex, you've completely misinterpreted the photos and the flowers. I'm not building a shrine to the baby. It's perfectly natural for me to want to keep his picture on view—it's all I have of him." Tears threaten. She drinks some wine and wills herself to stay calm. "The flowers are just a symbol of . . . love. That's all. I know I've got to let go of him in my mind but I can't yet . . . I'm very confused."

"I suppose it takes time. I'm confused as well. I don't know why but whatever I say or do seems to be wrong and I end up feeling a complete shit."

She senses Verina's influence and guesses he's been on the phone to her. Galling to have to be thankful to her for a change in the atmosphere. "I think the problem here is that I need to grieve Alex and you won't let me do it in peace. I'm not asking you to share it with me; you didn't want the baby but I did and I'm . . ." her voice drops to a whisper "heartbroken."

"Of course you are. This is the first time anything's happened to rock your little boat. But these things toughen you up Faith, help you cope with the knocks." He pours more wine. "I know it's sad for you but in fact it might turn out to be all for the best in the circumstances."

"What circumstances?"

"You and I might be moving to Singapore."

His words explode in her head. She has to clench her fists to keep from screaming 'No!'

"It's been on the cards for a year. Now I've been given a couple of months to decide."

"Do you want to go?"

"Yes I do."

"I don't think I want to."

"What happened to 'Wherever thou goest, I will go?'"

She can't answer him.

"I've just thrown it at you and I know it's not a very good time. But think about it, might stop you wallowing. Eat your supper."

Wallowing?—why do you want to take me with you?—you obviously think I'm dreary—is Verina going to let go of you?—I'd be glad to see the back of you for a while.

"Look, I can see you're depressed, why don't you buy yourself some new clothes? You wore that dress while you were pregnant."

"Perhaps I will, now I've got my figure back."

"You haven't got it back so much as lost it altogether."

Thanks.

—

Over a cup of tea, Verina is talking to Chloé about her father's death.

"At least you were with him, you must be glad about that."

"Oh I am. Though mum and I both missed the actual moment he slipped away, it happened so quietly. He was propped up in his battered old chair in the conservatory looking out at the garden. We put lots of cushions round and under him—he was just a bundle of bones—and we wrapped him up in a duvet. Mum was sewing and I was half-dozing. We were listening to dad's favourite Schubert quintet. At one point, he said 'I'm very happy'. We smiled at him and said 'Good'. Soon after that, I thought he'd fallen asleep. When the music finished, mum went over to him and I suddenly knew he was gone. There had been no . . . struggle. I only wish I'd been holding his hand."

Sounds a beautiful way to go Vee."

"I think it was."

"How's your mother?"

"Batty as ever but that's to be expected. They were married for sixty years."

"And they were very happy together, weren't they?"

"Yes they were. I'm back early because she wanted to be alone with him. Until his illness, she never had him all to herself. If you're a clergyman's wife you have to get used to sharing him with his parishioners. Dad was always at their beck and call. She colluded with him over the hospice because she wanted to take care of him herself. She loves me in her way but she would only let me make a couple of phone calls to the doctor and the funeral place then she couldn't get me out of the house quickly enough."

"Have you fixed a date for the funeral?"

"Tuesday week. Dad left instructions that the children are not to go. There's even money in an envelope to be used to take them out for a treat in memory of their grandad who loved them."

Cassie comes in while her mother is talking "That doesn't mean me though mum, does it?"

"I think he probably did mean you too."

"Well I expect he thought of me as a child but I'm nearly sixteen."

"That's true darling but you have all just been to a funeral, it seems hard on you to have to go to another."

"You'll need dad and me."

"So I'll be taking Nan and Greg out somewhere?"

"Yes please dear Chloé."

"What's your mother planning to do? Is she coming up here for a while?"

"No, she's worn out but she's determined to lock the house up and go away. She decided all this when she knew my father was not going to recover."

"Where's she going?"

"To Lindisfarne to grow holy vegetables or something. She's joining some sort of community there. She discussed it all with dad and he approved apparently."

Shouts are coming from the kitchen and Cassie goes to see what the trouble is. Nan and Greg are fighting over a dictionary. Greg insists that it's his and when Cassie shows him the inscription on the flyleaf—'To clever little Nan with love from Grandad'—he storms off into the garden banging the door.

Chloé is surprised "It's not like those two to fight. I expect they're upset about their grandfather. Joe and I will think of something nice and different to do with them on the day of the funeral. Is there anything we can do for you today?"

"Chloé you're always doing something. Here you are, holding everyone's hand as usual. Angela's brought us round a casserole in case I was held up. See how lucky we are Cass, to have such wonderful friends."

—

Chris mentions to Verina that he has spoken to Faith today and that she still seems very down. "I suppose she will be for quite a while poor kid."

"She and Alex could do with some time apart from the sound of things. She's obviously suffering from post-natal depression and I don't think Alex can handle it."

"She's also grieving remember. Your son doesn't strike me as a particularly sensitive individual."

"You've hardly taken the trouble to get to know him. He's vulnerable too and he's also lost the baby. Besides. being too sympathetic to people isn't always a good idea, it can prolong the period of feeling sorry for themselves."

That's not how you used to talk. Chris is disinclined to pursue this any further. "I've sorted out next Tuesday by-the-way."

"Thank you. That's good of you."

"Good of me?"

"I feel I've forfeited your support."

These words bring a rush of fears and images to his brain. He's afraid of what she might say next, what she might confess."

"And I'm so ratty these days."

"You've had a difficult time. You'll never lose my support."

The telephone is ringing. Verina goes to answer it. "It's that Melanie woman again. Is she 'the other woman'?"

"Of course. Hallo Mel. How are you?"

"Very well. Was that your wife again? She sounded a bit cool. I don't want to land you in it."

"I'm already in it. What can I do for you?"

"Well, it's the other way round really. I'm ringing because I've got a sort of proposal to make. You might think it crazy."

"Try me."

"Well, first of all, how's the little lass who lost her baby?"

"Not good. Very low in spirits."

"So she could do with a holiday?"

"I imagine she could, why?"

"Well, a very dear friend of mine Françoise has just had a major operation and is going to convalesce at her villa in Italy. She's got staff there during the day but no-one stays at night. Her husband wants her to find a temporary companion. He can't get away until later in the year and neither can I. I happened to say the other evening that it was a pity she and your daughter-in-law didn't know each other because they could have recovered together. I've told her about you and your family. Nothing private. Anyway, she's very sympathetic about your young woman, What's her name?" "Faith." "She's had problems along those lines all her life and never managed to have any children, to her sorrow. She said 'You know, that might be an idea, for that poor girl to come and stay with me. At first I didn't think she was being serious but she was. She said 'I realise we don't know each other but it might be of mutual benefit. The girl could come for a few weeks on the understanding that she could go home at once if she wasn't happy.' Françoise would like to invite her and she asked me to ring and talk to you about it. I'm to tell you that Faith would be doing her a favour. In return, she wouldn't have to lift a finger. The villa is beautiful, it's on a lake. All Faith would have to do is rest and eat delicious food. Françoise is a professor at the

Sorbonne, she speaks perfect English and is very charming. You are fond of Faith so I'm sure she is charming too"

"She's a lovely, gentle girl."

"So what do you think?"

"You've taken me completely by surprise but I'll talk to Faith, She's with her parents this week-end and could discuss it with them."

"She won't be going off into the unknown Françoise and I have been friends since I first came to Paris. She has always been very kind to me. You trust my judgement?"

"Implicitly."

"Let me know then what Faith thinks. If she decides to consider this, Françoise will talk to her by phone."

"Leave it with me Mellie. Thank you. I'll get back to you." He puts the phone down and goes to tell Verina and the children about the call.

Cassie volunteers to go if Faith is not interested. "It would be an adventure."

"What do you think Vee?"

"I think it's extraordinary, seeing that Faith and this woman have never met. It could be a disaster."

"Faith could come straight back."

"Who is this person who keeps ringing you? Is she reliable?"

"I did tell you. We knew each other as students. She's not a former girl-friend, She runs the gallery where I bought my lithograph."

"You didn't wander in just by chance?"

"That's exactly what I did. I've already told you, it was a pure co-incidence. I was drawn in by the painting. And since you ask, I would say yes I do think she's reliable."

"Even though you only saw her that one time, after all these years?"

"People don't change fundamentally, she was always good-hearted."

"Well on your head be it. You going to talk to Faith?"

"Why not? It sounds as though it could be an experience for her. And not half an hour ago you were saying Faith and Alex could do with time apart."

"I was thinking of the odd long week-end. How does this friend of yours know about Faith?"

"I told you, we had dinner together and she wanted to hear all about the family. We had a pleasant evening."

"Did you?"

"Yes. Well it could have been you, you turned me down, remember?"

"Because of dad."

"I know. Anyway, it's very sweet of her to have thought of suggesting Faith to her friend."

"Very astute of her too."

"Why do you say that?"

"Surely it's a way of keeping in touch with you?"

They're discussing Faith's invitation to Italy—or rather Chris, Verina and Alex are; Faith is saying little.

Chris asks her what Madame Auteil sounded like on the phone. "Very nice. Did I tell you she's also written to me?"

No."

"She's very understanding about . . ." she glances at Alex, "everything. I'll read you a bit of her letter." She pulls it from her bag and scans the pages, reading to herself *'When a person has been wounded emotionally, it is necessary to feel absolutely safe in order to get better.'* She reads the next bit aloud; *"My suggestion is that you come to my house in Paris for a little visit with Melanie. We can talk and then Melanie can take you back to the gallery to give you time to think about it. You must feel quite free to decide and if you are not comfortable, please do not worry, I will find a temporary companion from an agency.* She has sent me a return ticket."

"So, you're going?"

"Part of me would like to but I don't know if I've got the stamina for the journey."

Alex sighs "Oh Faith . . ."

Chris cuts across him, "I've just been thinking, let me get my diary. When would you travel if you go?"

"Next Thursday. Why?"

"Well I've got to go back to Paris myself, perhaps we could go together? Would it make any difference to you Vee if I brought my trip forward?"

"No."

"So why don't I accompany Faith then I can introduce her to Melanie? "He explains to Faith, "I'd be there for a couple of days if you needed me. Then if you weren't happy about going on to Italy, we could travel back together. What do you think?"

"Have you really got to go anyway?"

"Yes. I've already discussed it with Vee. I tried to persuade her to come with me this time."

"His French lady-friend wouldn't be pleased."

"She's not French and she's not my lady-friend. If you came with me, you'd see for yourself."

I've got too much work on. I got behind while dad was ill. In any case, you'll be traipsing round all day drawing and taking photographs"

"You could go to exhibitions."

"I'm not in the mood for exhibitions. Anyway, I can't go at present. I do think it's a good idea for you to go with Faith though, you know Paris so well."

"Okay then Faith?"

"Yes, if Alex is all right about it."

"Yeah well, it might stop you . . ."

"Stop me what?"

Alex waggles his hands about, "Wallowing."

—

The doorbell rings.

"That's the taxi." Faith starts gathering up her smaller pieces of luggage.

"It's not too late to change your mind you know."

"I'm not going to change my mind."

The doorbell rings again. Alex shouts through the entry-phone "We're just coming. You shouldn't go, you know."

"You said you couldn't wait to see the back of me."

"I didn't really believe you had the guts to do something like this. I'm not letting you out of the house!"

"Don't start shouting Alex."

"You're enough to make anyone shout. You should be here supporting me. I've got to make that presentation on Monday. You're not going!" but she's already at the front door.

"Please bring my big case for me Alex."

"You're mad! Going off to stay with someone you've never even met. She'll probably turn out to be a raving dyke."

As Faith gets into the taxi, a voice calls out "Eurydice, Eurydice mon amour." Faith sees the young man from the wine bar a few feet away. He's in a sweater and jeans and looks very thin. He stretches out both hands to her "Aide-moi, sauve-moi." A woman with him is apparently trying to persuade him into what looks like some sort of local government office Alex gives Faith a push, jumps in and slams the door. The cab draws away. "Was that who I think it was, the nutter from Dave's?"

"Yes."

"I hope you haven't been encouraging him with any more little secret meetings."

She thinks of Aidan's gentle brown eyes and feels sad. "I wonder what's happening to him? Another victim of 'Care in the Community' I suppose."

"People like that create havoc. They're better left to the professionals. Look, when we meet Chris at the airport, I'm not going to hang around okay?"

"Of course."

"Now you take this opportunity to sort yourself out and get back to being how you used to be." He pulls her to him, grabs her chin and grinds his mouth savagely against hers.

—

Cassie can't sleep. Worrying about her exams sends thoughts swirling round and round in her head. So as not to wake anyone, she creeps down the stairs to make a hot drink. A door opens upstairs, she hears footsteps behind her and instinctively slips into the dark sitting-room. In the dim light of the hall, she sees Alex hurrying into the kitchen pulling his dressing-gown up over his bare shoulders. The fridge door thumps closed and there's a clink of glasses *he's taking wine up to mum in her bedroom—why aren't they asleep?—they wouldn't be drinking in the middle of the night if dad was here.* She makes herself a mug of hot chocolate and decides to sleep in her father's downstairs bed *what's going on in this house?—God I'm tired—life doesn't seem safe when you're not here dad—please come home soon.*

—

167

The two girls have spent the afternoon revising together and Angela suggests that Cassie stays for supper. Because her father is away and she feels lost in the house without him, she's pleased to be invited.

Across the table, Don asks her kindly "How's your mother Cass? Is she sleeping better?"

She crosses her fingers under the table "Yes I think so."

"Even when you know it's coming and you've tried to prepare yourself, these things are always a terrible blow and it takes a while to recover."

For a moment, Cassie doesn't realise what Angela's talking about, then remembers her grandfather's death and feels ashamed. Both she and Verina cried and cried at his funeral and now, just a few weeks later, they hardly mention him. *If mum or dad died I'd never get over it.*

Sheldon is talking to her. "You're very quiet Cass."

"Lot on my mind." She smiles wanly at him.

"Exams I suppose?"

"And other things."

"Is it true that Alex and Faith are going to Singapore?"

"According to Alex."

Nobody notices that Gemma' face has gone flaming red.

"None too soon if you ask me. Otherwise somebody's going to have a breakdown."

"Angela!" Don protests but she's busy serving the food and pays no attention.

Cassie is instantly afraid "Who do you think's going to have a breakdown?"

"Chris or Verina—one or the other. I'm sorry to say this but that young man has put a great strain on the family. I can see it in you Cass, you haven't been your bubbly self for ages."

Don tries again "That's enough now darling."

"Oh Don, we're old family friends. I've known Cass since she was born. She's used to me speaking my mind, aren't you love? I'm glad he's going. Verina will miss him at first. He seemed a blessing when he first came but I've watched him over the months and I've decided he's more of a . . . well . . . he isn't a blessing."

Don apologises to Cassie "It's because she loves you all. She hates to see anyone causing an upset in your family. But you mustn't let anything Angie says affect your feelings for your brother."

Cassie says nothing but she's thinking *he's not my brother— he doesn't want to be—he just wants to push dad out of the way so that he can take over and boss us about.*

"You mustn't say any more about Alex darling. It's none of our business and he is Cassie's brother."

"Actually, I hate him." *Didn't know I was going to say that.*

"You've stirred up a hornet's nest" Don tells his wife.

"It was already stirred up."

Sheldon and Cassie are with Gemma in her room listening to a new CD. Gemma is lying across the duvet on her stomach, snuggling into the pillows. The other two are sitting on the floor, backs against the bed. Cassie has her knees pulled up and is resting her head against them, hiding her face.

Sheldon gently tugs at her hair "You're fed up aren't you?"

"You could say that."

"What you doing on your birthday?"

"Dunno yet—depends on dad and mum. But I can't have a party can I? Not with Mr Gorgeous in residence. He'd make sure he's the centre of attention. You'd think having mum, Nan and Greg adoring him non-stop would be enough but he never stops showing off. If Gem calls for me to go to the library, he starts preening and giving her the treatment, doesn't he Gem?"

No answer.

"She's asleep."

"Is that why you hate him?"

"I know I shouldn't say I hate him but I do hate the effect he has on our family. Since he arrived on the scene, everything seems to revolve around him. My mum and dad never used to row, they do now."

"Well he'll be gone soon."

"Thank God."

"I'll take you out somewhere on your birthday if you like?"

"What?"

"Try and cheer you up. We could go to a film and have some supper."

She turns to face him "Let me get this straight. You're asking me out on a sort of date?"

169

"Only in a brotherly way of course. You'll be quite safe. You know I don't fancy you or anything." He's half smiling at her but she can see he's nervous.

"You're asking me out because you feel sorry for me then?"

"Something like that, yeah."

"Thank you Shel. Just to punish you, I'll come."

He relaxes and grins widely. "What if your parents want to do something?" "Well . . . we could go out another night?"

"Yeah. Good."

They lean back and close their eyes to listen to the music. Sheldon strokes the back of Cassie's hand very delicately with a finger. She opens her eyes and looks at him. "You've got nothing to worry about with your exams."

"Thanks."

"You're all right, you know Cass."

"You're not so bad yourself *in fact you're quite cool.*"

They hold each other's gaze for a second.

—

Cassie always makes tea for everybody on Sunday morning. While the kettle's boiling, she runs upstairs to see if Nan is awake and to explain that she slept in their father's bed again.

"It's funny waking up and finding you not there. I was deciding what I would pinch if you ran away."

Laughter is coming from their parents' bedroom. "Dad must be back." Cassie hurries off to see. What she finds, is her mother and Alex engaged in some sort of struggle and giggling.

"What's he doing in your bed?"

"You all get in our bed occasionally, what's the problem?" Verina is flushed and smiling.

"Has he got pajamas on?"

"Oh Cassie, what does it matter?" she turns the covers back on her side, "You can come in too, come on."

"No thank you."

"Are you making tea darling?"

"No. It's Alex's turn." She leaves them, desperately wanting to be by herself. Nan calls out to her "Is daddy back?" "No." She tries the bathroom door but Greg's in there. She longs for her father to put his strong arms round her and tell her everything's all right. The house has great empty areas without him. Mum is only interested in Alex these days. She collapses on the stairs wondering whether to go down and make tea after all. Nan calls her plaintively. "Could you come here please Cass?"

"What's the matter?"

Nan's face is tragic, "I think I've started . . . you know, that disgusting blood business."

"I'll go and get mum."

The door is closed and she doesn't feel like going in. She knocks and Verina opens the door in her Japanese wrap. "I suppose you want breakfast?"

"Mum, I can get my own breakfast and everybody else's. It's not that, it's Nan. Could you come out here for a minute please?" She can see Alex lolling against the pillows.

"What is it?"

She whispers "Nan's got her period."

"Well you can deal with that, can't you?"

"Mum, she's upset. Please come and comfort her."

"Oh, all right."

Nan sulks all day. She won't play with Greg. She won't talk to Cassie, "Leave me alone. I hate life."

—

In the restaurant, Chris and Melanie are in their little private alcove again. Her eyes are shining. "I'm really enjoying this."

"So am I. It's beginning to feel sinful."

"Oh come on! We're only having dinner. Verina couldn't be jealous, could she?"

"She could be if she saw you."

"Is that a compliment?"

"Don't start fishing."

She laughs. "I will if I feel like it. I'm going to make the most of this evening."

"That's what I want you to do. The marvellous way you've fixed things up for Faith! I want you to have the best of everything. I've only ever seen her that relaxed with my children; she's generally rather reserved."

"She and Françoise have obviously got a lot in common— look how they immediately started talking about books. It made Lucien laugh and I think he's very relieved."

171

"So am I. Françoise is a nice woman. I was expecting Faith to come away with us last night and then make up her mind but by the time Lucien suggested we all stayed for supper, she'd already moved in."

"I knew she would. Have you spoken to her today?"

"Yes. I'm not worried about her at all. She's comfortable and happy with Françoise. She likes Lucien too and she's looking forward to Italy. Now I've seen photographs of the house and the lake, so would I. And it's all down to you Mel. Thank you very much" He pours her more wine.

"This is very good Chris, You don't expect Englishmen to know about wine."

"You've lived in France too long you little chauvinist. Remind me not to drink too much of it. I want a clear head tomorrow." He nods to her plate, "Is that nice?"

"Delicious. How's yours? It must be a treat for you to eat as well as this."

"What do you mean? London has become the gastronomic centre of the world. Come and see for yourself sometime."

"I rarely go to London now. I fly to Manchester when I visit my parents . . . I suppose it's not likely we'll be seeing each other again for a long while, if ever."

"You never know . . ."

"Must you go home tomorrow?"

"Yes I must. I've actually stayed longer than I needed to this time. I could have gone home this afternoon."

"You can use Faith as an excuse . . . You know, it's a shame, just when we're getting to know each other all over again, Fate snatches you away again. It's too cruel. I'm going to miss you."

"I'm going to miss you too."

"Really?"

"Of course. It's been great finding you and realising you're just the same. You've been so sweet listening to my moans."

"How are things, any better?"

"Rather worse if anything. It looks as if Alex is going to remain billeted with us while Faith is away. He doesn't seem to be able to manage his own socks."

"So you'll have him around all the time?"

"Looks like it."

"Well perhaps he'll leave a ring round the bath or drop his dirty laundry on the floor and get himself in the bad with Verina."

"He won't do any of that. On the contrary, he'll find more ways to dig himself in so that he can manipulate her— manipulate all of us. He's brilliant at doing things which annoy me but which he knows I can't say anything about."

"Like what?"

"You'll think this is stupid but he'll help the children with their homework and make it look as though he is all wisdom and patience whereas dad is tired and really rather past it. It's all quite subtle. Of course he never leaves Vee and me alone together, he barges in to pour us drinks or put on a CD for Verina and so on and so on."

"At least he can't invade your bedroom."

"He almost has. He sleeps in the room above ours and clatters about. It gets on my nerves and keeps me awake. Doesn't seem to bother Verina, she sleeps through anything. I might as well not be there anyway, as far as she's concerned, so for the time being, I've moved downstairs to sleep in my study."

"Oh Chris, that can't be a good move."

"When you're suffocating Mel, you get out for air. I made some excuse about needing to work late some nights."

"I'm so sorry you're going back to all that. You know, you could occasionally come over just for the day. It only takes a couple of hours now. I could meet you off the train and we could have lunch and talk."

"That's something to consider, I suppose."

"You won't though. Please give me some more wine. I can't imagine how all this is going to end."

"Neither can I."

"You'd better make a contingency plan."

"Such as . . .?"

"We . . . ell"

He remembers her words the last time they had dinner here *'I'm not trying to seduce you'*. Tonight she's changed her hairstyle and it suits her. She's wearing a clinging dress with a low neck line and she's looking boldly into his eyes.

"You, you mean?" he says gently.

"You could do worse."

173

"Indeed I could. I'm honoured Mel, but meeting like this, comforting as it is, doesn't have much to do with our real lives. It's pleasant make-believe. I'm grateful for it but I suspect that I get more out of it than you do. What you need, what you deserve is a good man of your own. It's all wrong for someone like you to be by yourself,"

"Now you're being patronising."

"Oh God, don't say that." He puts his hand over hers. "That's the last thing I mean to be. Mel, if I were free I'd be getting through this meal as quickly as possible so that we could go somewhere and make love."

This startles both of them. They stare at each other.

"I shouldn't have said that. I'm sorry. I've been trying not to sound like a stuffy bastard and then I go and . . . I'd better stop drinking."

"Don't be sorry, You've restored my morale." Her eyes suddenly brim with tears.

"Oh Mel. Oh Christ!" He takes her hand in his.

The waiter comes to remove their plates.

Chris keeps her hand in his and they sit quietly for a few minutes.

"I'm sorry Chris. I'm upset because I don't know if I'll ever see you again. I didn't mean to make a fuss."

"You haven't made a fuss."

She withdraws her hand. "I know you won't want to hang around late tonight but can we at least, spin things out here for a while? Could we have some cheese or would you rather we left?"

"Let's have cheese and we'd better have more wine."

"You want a clear head tomorrow."

"Yes but we need a drink now."

The waiter brings more wine and pours a glass for each of them.

Melanie gulps hers down fast. "I feel marooned in time and space."

She helps herself to more wine. "You know what I'm thinking? You can live a different life in different places—be a different person even. That doesn't mean an experience is 'make-believe'. It can still be valid."

"Won't the rules of the game be the same though?"

"Not necessarily, in a different world. I think the brave thing to do is to accept the possibility of living parallel lives."

"Like sailors you mean? A wife in every port? I imagine it could only work for sailors."

"I don't really know what I'm trying to say but some people seem to have their cake and eat it."

"Do they though? I doubt it. People who boast about their 'open' marriage for example, are seldom happy."

"Were you happy? Before the young man arrived?"

"Yes we were. Very happy. That's why it's all so hard."

The cheese arrives and they give it their attention, choosing and eating it slowly as if to avoid talking.

"Part of me wishes you happiness again in your marriage and part of me wants to plead with you to remember I'm here if ever you need me."

"You're very generous."

"No I'm not. When you first appeared, I was so pleased to see you again and I persuaded myself that it was because I always liked you when we were young. Then being able to speak English with someone of the same background is a relief—you know, same sense of humour and so on. But it's more than that . . . You'll think it's because I'm lonely . . ."

She holds out her glass for more wine. "I don't want to embarrass you but there are things I want to say while I still have the opportunity. I think you're a special kind of man . . . but I've discovered some bad things about myself; I realise I'm quite capable of trying to lure you away from your wife and would justify it easily by telling myself she deserves to lose you. That's the unpleasant truth about me. I thought it only fair to warn you. Aren't you glad you'll be escaping me tomorrow?"

"How can I be glad? I feel cheated too. You're a kind and beautiful woman who likes me and I'm going home to a wife who won't see or hear me."

"We . . . could have a night Chris."

He looked into her eyes, "No we couldn't. We'd spoil what we have."

—

Chris goes into his work-room to deposit his luggage and Nan comes running in, "Daddy, I'm so glad you're home. I've started my periods. It's horrible. I don't want to be a woman."

175

Chris looks down at her agonised little face "At least when you grow up, you can have babies. Chaps can't. I've known men who are quite jealous about that."

"Really daddy?"

Cassie clings to him as if he's been away for months. Greg is delighted he's home and gives him a squeeze before going off to the garden. Verina offers him her cheek and doesn't ask him about his week-end. Alex, on the other hand, wants to hear all about it and asks about Faith. "I've got a present for you, by-the-way"

It's 'The Concise Wisden'. "That's very good of you Alex."

"It's a little thank-you for letting me stay. I was in Waterstone's Friday lunch-time and I saw it and thought you'd like it."

"Exactly my sort of book . . ."

Verina, passing the door, calls out "Why don't you two have a drink. Dinner isn't quite ready."

Do you want any help?" Alex shouts back.

"No, give your tired, old step-father a drink."

"Your usual?"

"Please."

Handing him the glass Alex asks "Do you think we can lick the Aussies this summer?"

He's making efforts so Chris tries to respond. "God knows. We need to do better than we have the last few seasons."

They drink in silence for a while.

"How was the week-end?"

"A lot of fun. I always wanted brothers and sisters, I never enjoyed being an only child."

"I imagine Lilian and Phil were very good to you though?"

"Oh God yes. They're two of the best but they are a bit, how shall I say, staid in their attitude. You and Verina are so much more easy-going."

Chris represses an hysterical laugh. "Have you heard from Faith? How's she getting on?"

"She's enjoying Paris and is excited about going on to Italy. She needed this time on her own, apart from anything else, she's never gone off and done anything solo before. She went from home to university straight into Hall, safe and protected. Then she moved in with me and soon after that we got married, so she's never had to cope with anything by herself."

"Until recently."

"The baby you mean? Well I tried to help her with all that but she turned against me for a while. Apparently it's quite common."

"Vee tells me Faith doesn't want to go to Singapore."

"She'll change her mind when she's home again. You're not in the real world when you're on holiday. I'll get her to Singapore and once she's had a taste of the good life, she'll get back to normal and we'll have another baby."

Verina has come in and is waiting for him to finish what he's saying.

"Come and eat."

As usual, the younger children take over the kitchen table after supper to finish their homework. Cassie goes off to read in her room. Alex is in the sitting-room watching television. A fight breaks out between Nan and Greg, over felt pens. Verina shrieks at them. They're astonished and immediately fall silent and heads down, get on with their work.

Chris mutters "What's the matter with you?"

"They get on my nerves."

"Are you upset about something? Has Alex been getting at you?"

"In what way?"

"In his emotionally—blackmailing-way. You spend a lot of time keeping him sweet about something or other."

"You're the one I have to keep sweet all the time."

He gives up. "Do either of you need any help?"

Greg shakes his head and Nan says "No thanks daddy, Alex has lent me his project to look at. He did one on the Aztecs too when he was at school and won a prize. He got Lilian to send it."

"You're not to copy it Nan."

"Of course not mum, I'm only going to get some ideas on how to set mine out and a bit more information. Look daddy, isn't it good?"

Chris picks up the folder. 'Alexander Holland.' An inscription on the front cover, 'Summer Project—First Prize.' It's beautifully presented. The eleven year old Alex went to a lot of trouble. There's a neatly-labelled diagram of an Aztec city. The text is written in firm, well-shaped handwriting. Chris turns to the last page to read the summing-up: 'The Aztecs were mysterious even to themselves because where they had come from was lost in the mists of time. Some people think they may have come from Atlantis because the Aztecs could remember an island with lots of fishes and birds. They were happy there and longed to return but they could never remember where it was or find their way back to it. They called it the place of the herons.' *Precocious little bugger!*

As usual, Joe has a pint waiting for him when he pushes his way into the pub.

"Watcha mate. How's things?"

"There's something rotten in the state of Denmark and I think it's me."

"Yeah I'm a shit too but what's brought this on? Or need I ask—the lad? When Chloé and I looked in, it all seemed serene."

"Because I wasn't there, the fly in the ointment."

"Haven't you got that the wrong way round?"

"I hardly know any more. According to Verina, I'm the one who spoils everything. Back in the beginning, she almost had me persuaded that if she and Alex were happy, we'd all be happy. Try telling that to Faith, let alone me! I tell myself it's all in my mind but when they're going over the top and I'm there, I feel a mug; it's as if I'm sanctioning their behaviour."

"What do you mean 'over the top', pawing each other around still and all that?"

"That sort of thing. On the face of it, it could all be innocent—must be innocent. Maybe I see more in it than there is because she ignores me most of the time. I've become the 'tired old step-father'. You were right you know. Remember calling him a cuckoo? Well he's won, the little bastard. And somehow, I've allowed it to happen. He's chased me out of my own bedroom. I can't look myself in the eye when I'm shaving."

"Christ! You're not saying he's moved into it?"

"Not quite. He sleeps above our room and I'm reminded of his presence all the time. It got so bad I was tempted to ask you to rent me your basement."

"Any time mate. Sod the rent but you don't want to let him chase you out of your own house."

"I've solved it for the time being, I made some excuse and I'm sleeping in my study. Never mind, the good news is, he's going to Singapore. And I can't wait!"

"Is he? When?"

"In the next few weeks."

"Well Faith will be back before then, won't she? And he'll go home."

"Even that's not certain, especially since Faith doesn't want to go abroad with him."

"Blimey. And what about Vee? She's not going to want him to go, she's only just got him back."

"She doesn't talk to me anymore but I suspect she might partly be relieved—once she gets over the separation—he gets her down a lot. He's brilliant at keeping her on an emotional see-saw."

"Because of the adoption and all that?"

"Perhaps." Chris goes up to the bar for another pint for them both.

"Thanks mate. When Alex does go, you'll have to pick up the pieces, I suppose."

"I know. When I was away over the week-end, I was thinking back to how things were last summer—before all this."

"It's a bloody tragedy. Chlo and I were talking some time back and I said it was just a matter of adjustment, that nothing and nobody could ever come between you and Vee and she said Alex would. She called him the destroying angel. Whatever that means. She's been unhappy about all this from the beginning. We've both been worried Chris."

"Thanks. I had a couple of drinks before I came out and I'm getting pissed and probably maudlin, right now it seems to me my marriage is disintegrating like wet tissue paper."

"What you gonna do?"

"Take care of her and the kids. Alex is an illness, there's no cure and she'll need a lot of nursing."

All this hasn't turned you off? You still feel for her then?"

"I married her didn't I?"

—

From her window seat, Faith looks down and watches the baggage handlers throwing luggage onto the plane's conveyor

179

belt. A powerful smell of perspiration comes from the seat in front of them; someone's fear of flying is not being soothed by the calming waltzes lilting through the sound system. She glances at Françoise who turns the corners of her mouth down. "Not too cold for you if I turn on the air conditioning?"

"Not at all. Good idea."

The plane lifts off. Alex's image haunts her but it's beginning to blur *good to have a break from him for a while—good for both of us—that bruising kiss he forced on me at Waterloo, not love—a branding!—did he think I was escaping him?—well I am, for a time anyway—telling me to get back to what I used to be!—how can he not understand that's not possible?!—it's as if Daniel's existence has not touched him at all—oh hell—done enough thinking about him— thinking about him means thinking about Verina—shut them both out—must use this opportunity to try and accept losing Daniel and to face the uncertain future—try and decide how I want it to be.* She concentrates on the view from the window. At this altitude, the plane seems to be scarcely moving; the clouds beneath are like patches of snow on a wide blue lake and she's dreaming about what she'll see and experience in Italy.

They are met at Malpensa by a young couple, Paulo and Gabriela. They help Françoise into the front passenger seat and Faith slides into the back with Gabriela. Paulo, clearly wanting to practice his English, talks to Faith as he drives. "You live in London Faith?"

"In the outskirts."

"We like very much London. If many tourists come this year and we make big money, I want take Gabriela to London for holiday"

Gabriela explains "We get marry in October."

"Yes? I hope you'll be very happy."

"We will be!" Gabriela is slim and pretty with masses of reddish dark hair, loosely pinned up on top of her head and laughing brown eyes. Paulo is thin, full, of eagerness and energy. His eyes are a vivid blue and Faith thinks he's like a bird because of the darting movement he makes with his head to emphasise what he's saying.

They're driving through Arona. Gabriela waves a hand towards the window "This is my town". Splendid white hotels with palm trees and beds of red and yellow begonias, overlook the dazzling expanse of Lake Maggiore. Blue hills glimmer in the distance.

"Lucky you. It's wonderful, like driving through a holiday brochure." *Looks a bit hot and Hollywood—hope it's not like this where we're going.* "Where did you two learn English? Have you studied in England?"

Paulo answers for them both "We learn in London. We meet in class. Gabriela lives few kilometres from me in Italy and I find her in London."

"Destiny!"

"Si, il destino. It's mean, now I have to marry her. Is terrible."

Gabriela gently cuffs the back of his neck

Their happiness is infectious. The conversation in a mixture of languages becomes more and more hilarious. Faith is frequently called upon to supply English names for things. At the same time, she tries to work out meanings of words on advertising posters that she sees from the car. Just when she's beginning to feel she's had enough of teaching and travelling, they reach a sign for Orta S. Giulio and Françoise tells her "We're nearly there."

"I expect you're tired."

"I am. Thank you Paulo for getting us here so quickly and comfortably."

"Prego, Signora."

Gabriela asks, "Is possible we see you sometimes while you stay Faith? I no work every day."

"Oh yes Faith. Do spend some time with Gabriela."

"Thank you. When Françoise doesn't need me, it would be lovely to see you."

"Bene. We telephone you."

"Anyway, tomorrow you come to my father's place for coffee."

"Good idea Paulo. Pepina can take her when she goes shopping."

They turn in at wide gates and go crunching slowly down a steep gravel drive edged with blue and scarlet anenomes. Magnificent cedars tower over terraced lawns.

They climb out of the car, into sweet-smelling air. Although Faith has not managed yet to see the house properly, she senses that it's very big.

The door opens as Paulo is depositing luggage in the wide entrance porch.

A stout, black-clothed woman with graying hair in a bun, welcomes them in. She puts an arm around Françoise to draw her gently inside and turns to Faith "Prego Signora. Si accomodi."

Faith follows them in to the cool, shadowy hall—mosaic floor—spectacular lilies—marble fire-place. Everybody talks at once, rather loudly. Gabriela kisses her cheek "Ciao Faith" and she and Paulo are gone.

"Would you like tea Faith or shall we have a little rest first?"

"A little rest would be good I think."

"So, Pepina will show you up to your room and I'll see you in—what shall we say, about an hour? You might fall asleep and so might I."

"Thank you. That would be lovely."

Pepina leads her up a hidden staircase away to the left of the hall and opens a door. Faith stands surprised and delighted, just inside, taking it all in: high-arched white ceiling, pale green walls painted all over with birds, butterflies and flowers. Watching Pepina closing the shutters, Faith glimpses a little balcony outside the window. The four-poster bed has white muslin curtains looped up and held in place by gold cherubs. "Lei piace Signora?" "Si molto. Gratie." "Il bagno e qui. Ecco!" Green and white marble bathroom, big, fluffy white towels and bottles of bath oils. "Va bene Signora?" "Si, va molto bene. Gratie." Pepina closes the door quietly.

Faith slips off her dress and shoes and slides under the light the bed-cover. She tells herself that when she gets up she will check to see if the birds and butterflies have been hand-painted.

It's only when she hears a whispered "Signora, Signora Faith" that she realizes she has actually been asleep. Pepina is at the foot of her bed. Faith mimes washing her face and goes to the bathroom.

Pepina takes her downstairs and then across the hall to the main staircase.

"La Signora e nello salotto piccolo." The landing is a small picture gallery. Pepina knocks on a door and stands aside for Faith.

Françoise is lying on a sofa at the far end of the room. She pulls herself up, "Did you have a nice little rest?"

"I fell fast asleep. How about you?"

"I dozed a bit. It does me so much good just to be here. I hope it will do the same for you. Pepina is bringing us some tea."

Flickers of sunlight pattern the wall, Faith looks out from the French windows and realizes the house must be right on the border of the lake. "Oh Françoise, from here, it looks as though the water is part of your garden, you even get reflections on your walls."

"One of the reasons why I love this room. How do you like your room by-the-way?"

"It's fairy-tale."

"Paulo did that for me last summer. You're the first person to stay in it."

"I'm privileged. It's so pretty. He's very clever."

"He's a very good artist but he doesn't make enough money from his paintings yet. Local galleries take his work and one or two restaurants let him hang things which tourists buy but he has to supplement his income by taking on things like your room."

"Can they afford to get married then?"

"During the season he helps his father in the café and he has just been offered an autumn exhibition in Milan. Gabriela makes a lot of money. She's a professional photographer and does fashion shoots for magazines like Vogue. I often let her use the house and garden. We've got some rather grand rooms we hardly ever use, they make perfect settings. Ah, here comes tea."

Pepina carries in a large tray which she deposits on the low table by Françoise.

"Why don't you sit there Faith and you can be mother. Pepina has made these little cakes in your honour; she thinks they're 'English'." Faith smiles at Pepina "Molto gentile, gratie."

Faith pours tea and they try the little cakes which are delicious.

"This is a beautiful room."

The walls are hung with aquamarine silk and the sofas and chairs are covered in a soft, ivory fabric. Subtle colours glow from pictures, oriental lamps and a Chinese silk carpet.

"I'm glad you like it, it's my favourite room in the house. I spend most of my time in here. The light is lovely, isn't it?"

"Yes. It makes the room so tranquil."

"You'll find it a perfect place to sit and read and, as you see," she indicates the long book-cases, "we have plenty of books for you. You shouldn't get bored."

"I'm quite sure I shan't get bored. More tea?"

"Yes please. I know you only met them for a short time but did you like Paulo and Gabriela?"

"Very much."

"That's good. I could tell they liked you. I would be happy if you spend some time with them, it would be more like a proper holiday with people your own age. You musn't feel you've got to stay and keep me company all the time."

"I promised Lucien that I would look after you."

"Well Pepina is here with me in the day so I'm not going to keep you prisoner. Really, I would be all right by myself at night but Lucien wasn't happy about that. Anyway, it's a pleasure for me to have you here and you and I will go out and do things when I feel stronger. What would you like to do now? Have you unpacked?"

"Not yet but if it's all right with you, I'd love to explore the garden."

"Then do. There's plenty of time. We'll be having dinner about seven if that's not too early?"

"No that's fine. Is there anything I can help with?"

"Pepina wouldn't allow it."

"What about you? Do you need me for anything?"

She smiles "Faith, go and see the garden. Just out there, you'll find steps down on the right."

A green alleyway between high box hedges slopes down to a rose garden. The fragrances are wonderful. The scents follow her. She wanders through a carved stone archway and discovers a secluded courtyard with a pool.

The statue of a hesitant girl with flowing hair, dips a marble toe among the lily-pads.

Faith sinks down on a low wall to absorb the stillness. *Even when you can't see the lake, you're aware of it all the time—occasional little splashings—dad would love it here—he'd say 'got history, a garden like this'—wish he could see it—beautiful—makes me cry—everything makes me cry these days.*

Someone is calling her. She wipes her eyes and hurries to the house.

"Il telefono Signora." Pepina shows her where the telephone is.

"Hallo?"

"It's me. I'm ringing early because I won't be around tonight. You okay?"

"Yes thank you."

"What about Madam Whatsername? Not collapsed on you?"

"No. She's fine."

"Only you don't want to be treated like a skivvy. What's the house like? Got a decent room, not some cupboard under the stairs?"

"Think Monte Cristo."

"What?"

"The Count of Monte Cristo. Have you never read it?"

"Faith! I didn't ring up to talk about books. How long do you think you'll be staying?"

"I don't know. I've only just got here. Why're you asking? Don't tell me you're missing me."

"It's just that if you need to get hold of me, I shan't be at the flat—Chris and Vee have invited me to stay with them while you're away.

"Oh I see."

"You're not the only one who needs a change of scene, you know. Besides Vee needs a lot of support getting over her father's death."

"She's got Chris."

"I'd better go, this is their phone. I'll ring again in a few days, see how you are."

"You needn't Alex, I'll be fine. Give my love to the children, Goodbye."

'Chris and Vee have invited me' you mean Verina couldn't wait for me to get on the plane before she kidnapped you. The image of Verina clearing up after him and sorting his dirty clothes gives her a moment's spiteful pleasure. However, just these few words with Alex have tired her.

She goes up to her room to lie down and is immediately assailed by a wave of homesickness *this lovely place—how can I want to go home?—Verina has won—she's got Alex now—robbed me of my say—my future—how did I let that happen?—can't ever go back to the way things were—weren't as I assumed anyway—not*

185

all her fault—hope Al gives her trouble—poor Chris in the thick of it—really on my own now—so tired—could sleep for a week—better wash my face again—the last thing Françoise needs is a gloomy guest.

They chat as easily as old friends.

"One of the things we'll do, when we're both feeling better, is go to Milan and buy some clothes. Talking of which, that's a pretty dress Faith."

"My mother made it for me and a couple of others to bring here. Nothing fits me at the moment, I seem to have shrunk."

"Well Pepina will build you up. She's a marvellous cook."

"She certainly is. Dinner was delicious."

"She's so enjoying having us here to look after. What with her and her husband, Luigi, who does the garden, we're very lucky."

"The garden's magical. I haven't seen it all yet. There's been so much to try and take-in today. I had no pre-conceptions about what I was coming to and I can't believe this is all real."

"We still feel like that and we've had this house for years." She smiles. "Shall we have some music?"

"Yes."

"Do you want to choose?"

"Mm. You have a wonderful selection, beautifully organised. Is that your doing?"

"Yes. I like to be able to put my hand on something straight away. What are we going to have?"

"Well I was vaguely looking for something classical but I've found this—if you're in the mood for it. Piaf? My parents introduced me to her. They spent their honeymoon in Paris and she brings it all back to them."

"Yes. Let's have that. A good start to our holiday."

The CD begins with "La Vie En Rose" and Faith has to go and look out over the lake and practise deep breathing to ward off tears. She hears Françoise saying "This must be the most romantic love song ever written."

"Life's not really like that though, or not for long."

"Oh Faith. It can be. Not for you at the moment perhaps, you're too sad."

Faith is listening to the words *'bonheur' has no meaning for me—no happiness in my life—deep down inside—can't believe there ever will be again—life's relentless—have to go on smiling somehow—hiding—can I do it?*

Françoise interrupts her reverie, "Tell me about your parents, who spent their honeymoon in Paris."

"Oh they're absolute dears. They're both reserved and gentle but I think they're privately romantic. Dad buys mum flowers and takes her off on surprise trips and when you're with them, you just know that they adore each other. They are the best, most loving parents you could have and yet I sometimes feel slightly in the way."

"Do you?"

"Yes. I've never said this to anyone before or even spelled it out to myself. It isn't ever anything they say or do. They love me dearly but they don't need me—for their ultimate happiness I think I mean. But then, why on earth should they? Their world is each other. When I got married I had the distinct impression that there was a sense of relief, that they would now be able to do what they wanted to do. I know they've always put me and my needs first. They rushed to me when Daniel died. They were devastated and took me home and looked after me. Dad organised for him to be buried in the garden near the stream, right where I used to play as a child. Then I found out, just before I came here, that they cancelled a cruise they'd been looking forward to, so they could be with me. I love them dearly."

"Do ring them whenever you want to. They will be anxious about you."

They're now listening to 'Johnnny, Tu N'est Pas un Ange' and the telephone rings. Faith gets up to leave but Françoise motions her to stay. Even though she can't understand all the rapid French, she knows by the warmth in her voice that Françoise is talking to her husband.

After putting the receiver down she smiles shyly at Faith. "The heart does not cool with age you see. We've been married for twenty five years and we don't like to be apart. Perhaps we're a bit like your parents? Lucien is lonely. He said it sounds as if we're in a night-club and he wishes he could join us."

"Twenty five years? Excuse me but looking at you, that doesn't seem possible."

"Even with my white hair?"

"You have a very young face."

187

"When I met Lucien, I was brunette but I went grey at twenty six and was quite white by twenty eight. It's a family thing. He has always teased me saying that with my white hair and my slanting eyes, I look like the result of a liaison between Marie Antoinette and a Tartar prince."

"You're certainly exotic if I may say so. Melanie prepared me for that but she didn't tell me you were beautiful."

"Perhaps she doesn't think I am but thank you Faith. I forgot to ask you if you take coffee after dinner?"

"I don't, thank you. It keeps me awake. And Françoise I don't know what time you usually go to bed and you are convalescing. Please don't think you have to stay up and entertain me."

"In fact, I was just thinking it was nearly time for me to go to bed. Don't feel you have to. You can play more music, or watch television. But I expect you're tired too?"

"I am, very."

"I'll say goodnight then." She kisses Faith's cheek. "It's lovely to have you here. Sleep well and don't get up until you feel like it. Breakfast is whenever you choose. Pepina will be delighted to look after you."

—

Meandering along beside the lake, Faith and Pepina stroll under ancient oaks and loiter to examine bronze-coloured lizards dozing on a wall. Pepina points across the water to where she was born, a village half-hidden in the thickly-wooded hillside. Birds sing them on their way as if they're glorying in the morning. Where the path diverges, someone has scratched on a rock 'Elena, ti amo. Giorgio.'

They turn into a narrow, sunless street where shopkeepers are sweeping the pavements down with water. In a shop with pungent salamis hanging in rows, they buy eggs, handed to them across a counter stacked high with mouth-watering cheeses. Pepina is constantly greeted and has to stop each time for a chat. Faith dawdles contentedly beside her. Jewellery gleams from the windows of small, mysterious boutiques and dim courtyards with fountains entice behind wrought iron gates. *What must it be like to live in one of those places?—do they have back gardens which look over the lake?—fun to do-up and furnish— Françoise would know where to find the right things.*

Just at the end of the shady street Faith steps straight out into blinding sunshine and a whirl of reflections and colours. The yellow-paved piazza is open to blue sky, the sparkling lake and hazy, mauve hills in the distance. "Oh! . . ."

She lets Pepina propel her into a seat at a table by one of the cafes facing the water and tries to adjust her eyes and her mind to all that's going on around her. Children are playing in the shade of chestnut trees along the little promenade; lovers saunter hand-in-hand; a boat steers slowly past a nearby island.

"Buon giorno!" it's Paulo. "How are you Faith?"

"Very well thank you. What about you?"

"Bright eye, bushy tail."

Faith bursts out laughing.

"Is not right?"

"Yes it is right, just unexpected."

"You not expect so good English." He's smiling, playing the fool. "I understand. I bring you coffee."

Pepina gathers up her purchases talking all the time. Faith understands that she's to be back for lunch at one o'clock. "Capito Signora?" "Si Pepina. Gratie."

"Ciao Pepina." Paulo takes the chair she has vacated.

"What you think of Palazzo Giallo?"

Faith is puzzled.

"The house where you stay?"

"It's lovely. Oh and Paulo, I'm sleeping in the room you painted. You are clever. It's beautiful."

"I hope it makes beautiful dreams for you."

"That's a charming thought. Thank you. This coffee's good."

"I bring you more?"

"Not just yet thanks. How's Gabriela?"

"She is well. She working in Rome for two days. On Thursday, she will come to lunch. You will join us?"

"Wouldn't you rather be by yourselves?"

He laughs, "We are not English. We like to make party. Gabriela asks you to come."

"In that case, thank you. If it's all right with Françoise I will."

"Good!"

189

He goes off to look after some customers and Faith gives herself up to the view. The island is like an ornament on the lake, its huddle of medieval buildings shining silver in the sunlight. What goes on over there?—something else unexpected?

Over lunch, she asks Françoise about the island "It looks the sort of place where you might find a religious community"

"There was one there for centuries. There is still a Benedictine monastery but whether there are any monks there now, I can't tell you. I haven't seen any about for ages. Perhaps today, young men prefer to choose practical ways to serve God rather than contemplative. San Giulio has a special atmosphere. You might even call it holy. All that praying over the years must have sunk into the walls. You should visit."

—

On Thurday, Gabriela has brought her brother, Eduardo, to lunch and introduces him to Faith, "He is on holiday from America."

"You work in America?"

"Yes, I'm in research at the Johns Hopkins in Baltimore. I expect you've heard of it?"

Faith shakes her head "Sorry, I'm afraid I haven't."

"Are you Irish?"

"English"

"Faith is from London" Gabriela explains.

"Three of my colleagues are Brits. They got frustrated in the UK not being able to develop their research through lack of funds."

"That's a shame. What's your field?"

"We're working with stem cells."

"How interesting. I've read a little about that."

"Ugh! Don't ask him about his work please Faith."

"I'm not allowed to say much. It frightens these two."

Gabriela agrees with her brother, "Is true. I frighten that scientists will make a cloning soon just to see if they experiments work."

"They won't Gabriela. Scientists work within tight ethical boundaries."

Paulo snorts "Someone will!"

Faith asks "Won't the ethical boundaries be different from country to country?"

"To some extent."

"And what about religious beliefs?"

"They can also be different; you're right. You come up against problems all the time and all we can do is try to balance progress with respect for life."

"Well presumably, your work is all about respect for life? Much of what you do must be an attempt to improve people's health?"

He beams at her "Of course and to help couples have healthy babies."

The embarrassed silence after this remark, signals to Faith that the three of them know about Daniel. She actually would like to hear more about Eduardo's work but Gabriela is looking particularly upset. "That's reason enough for what you do."

"I love the way you talk." Eduardo looks at the others "Hasn't she got a charming voice?"

"Eduardo!" Gabriela is glaring at him.

He smiles at Faith. *Good-looking like his sister. Eager penetrating dark eyes.* "American girls have awful voices, very loud and they either drawl or whine through their noses." He glances at Gabriela "I'm not talking about Livia. Livia is my girl-friend in America" he explains. "Her family is Sicilian and my sister thinks that if I only smile at another girl, I'll be shot by the Cosa Nostra. Difficult not to smile at <u>you</u> though."

Smoothy Joe?—no, too nice—just a confident young man having a bit of fun—Gabriela is marrying someone like her brother. "It's all right Gabriela, I'm an old married woman. He's quite safe."

"Are we going to eat anything? I'm hungry." Paulo pushes menus at everybody.

After rowdy disagreements about what to choose, the conversation changes to discussion about weddings. Like his sister, Eduardo is also getting married this year. Gabriela and Paulo have not yet met Livia and a lively argument breaks out about where the four of them might meet up, vaguely half-way between America and Italy. They settle on London, possibly at Christmas and Faith is invited to join them—with Alex—on Westminster Bridge and while they're all laughing, a letter from him menaces from her bag. She couldn't bring herself to open

191

it when it arrived this morning; he might be asking her to go home—not likely while he's with Verina—he's an intrusion on the peace here. She pushes him away in her mind. The other three manage to eat, talk and laugh all at the same time, leaving Faith to her own thoughts *holding this moment so that it stays with me—this place, these three, don't want to be anywhere else—thankful—want time to stretch out—happy just being.* Eduardo is staring at her. She can't look away from him and she smiles.

"La signora, Faith, how is she?"

"She' fine I think. Getting stronger by the day."

"That's good because we hope you can come out with us on Saturday night. We want to go to a restaurant in the mountains, good food, live bands and dancing. But we will be late back. Would the signora be all right, you think? She won't mind?"

"I don't know. I'll have to ask her and let you know."

"Will I be allowed to dance with Faith, Gabriela?"

"If she want dance with you."

"I'm not a very good dancer."

"You will be with me."

Gabriela growls at her brother and everyone laughs.

The lunch party breaks up with Paulo telling Faith they will pick her up at seven on Saturday, ignoring her reminders about asking Françoise.

The Ortensia, one of the big white boats that carry people round the lake is at the jetty. Knowing that Françoise will be taking her afternoon rest, Faith decides to visit St.Giulio. The crossing takes a matter of minutes and the island appears deserted. A few tourists linger uncertainly on the steps of the church. Faith takes a look in and is repelled by the gloom and the ugly statues. She wants, anyway, to get away from people and sets off along a narrow walkway, 'La via del silenzio'. The high walls carry encouragements which she tries to translate: 'Listen to the water, the wind, your footsteps to learn who you are', 'In the silence, accept and understand.' *That's addressed to me.* Turning a corner, she comes across a family sitting on a wide stone slab. The husband, a small girl on his knee, is shielding his wife as she suckles her baby. A pang shoots through her. Hurrying past, she finds a passage leading to the lake's edge and walks down to sit in a hollow cut into the stone wall, her feet almost in the water *should be feeding my baby—'accept and understand'—I'm a long way from that—wish I had Daniel's photo here—dying to look at him—so afraid his image will fade—Al shouldn't have taken his picture from me—hope he's put it somewhere safe—might even have thought to enclose it—did say in the taxi 'you've been through a lot lately'—was touched— perhaps misjudge him sometimes—maybe he's written something kind.* She draws the envelope from her bag and holds it against her, closing her eyes. Taking a deep breath, she tears it open—only a post-card inside *of course no photograph— why am I always imagining Alex saying and doing things out of character?*

The card says :

Faith, I've said yes definitely to the
Singapore job. Too good an opportunity
to pass up, Thought I'd better tell you
a.s.a.p. You get a house——staff easy to
find. Great shopping. Shan't be sorry
to leave our little shit-hole. Hope
you're feeling better. Love Alex.

She sees herself drifting out on a sea of grief in an unsafe boat. Not a word connects with her, it's like reading someone else's correspondence. She turns over the envelope to read her name on it. Tears spill down her face *at least I can cry here without disturbing anybody—I've lost my baby and to all intents, my husband and he writes to me about shopping and staff—'love Alex'— what acquaintances write on cards—doesn't know the meaning of the word—God, I'm so tired I could just walk into that lake and lie down and stay there.*
Something bangs her sharply on her head. She looks back up the alley, there's no-one in sight, no windows, yet there's a ball rolling towards the water. Mystified she picks it up and examines it as if it were a globe of the world. *Singapore? No thank you—how did Al and I ever get together?—we never will again that's for sure.*

—

193

It's very quiet in the room. They are both reading. "Faith, do ring home whenever you want to. Have you spoken to Alex lately?"

"Actually, I had a post-card from him today. He's accepted a job in Singapore."

"Is this out of the blue or . . ."

"I knew it was on the cards."

"How do you feel about it?"

"I don't want to go. I've already told him so."

"You don't think a new experience, a new start might help you both come to terms with losing the baby?"

"No, I'm afraid I don't."

"I don't want to intrude and please stop me if I distress you but has losing the baby caused problems between you?"

"Losing the baby added to problems we already had. Communications for a start. Alex hasn't a lot of patience and doesn't really listen. When I talk to him I have to try to be brief and clear but it's as if my words change colour in the air and mean something different by the time they reach him . . . When we're together, he can so quickly and easily shrivel my spirit. We were not close at the time the baby died and I didn't manage things very well."

"Did Alex manage things well?"

Faith sighs and shrugs.

"Men aren't always very good at coping with family tragedy. Were you disappointed perhaps, at his reaction? You say you'd already had problems before, did you feel he couldn't or didn't support you?"

"All that I suppose."

"And it's changed your affections? Do you feel you no longer love him?"

"I honestly don't know. I'm confused. I love bits of him—his almost innocent conceit, sometimes his playfulness, his looks."

"You sound like his mother."

"Oh he's got several mothers and they all spoil him."

"Now I'm confused."

Faith is uncertain about what to say and has to think for a few minutes "I've been wanting to explain things to you but I didn't want to burden you and I didn't want to be disloyal to Alex,"

"You won't burden me."

Faith tells her about Verina, the evening of the row and the discovery that Daniel had died in the womb."

"You poor girl and then you went through all that to give birth to a dead child. I'm so sorry."

"Please don't be sympathetic Françoise, I cry at the drop of a hat."

"I'm not surprised. You've had a very difficult time. After hearing all this, I'm so glad I asked you to come and stay; if there's one place on earth to find comfort for the spirit, it's here. I hope this place will work its magic on you."

"It already has. I'm beginning to see things more clearly—some things. It's a strange situation we're in. There's poor Chris, who I'm sure you could see, is a very nice man, having to watch his wife become obsessed with her son. Verina is not a monster, she must be torn between her children, Chris and Alex. Alex, I'm sure is in a turmoil too and I can't help him, though I've tried . . . I can't quite fathom this Singapore business. I can't believe he is prepared to leave his mother. She's been the centre of his existence since he found her. He may be trying to break away because he can't cope with the intensity of it all. Well he's not going to use me as a substitute. If I did go, he'd be missing her all the time and resenting me. He's always comparing us and I never match up. I'm not going and I shall write and tell him in the morning."

"You don't want to leave it a little while longer? You might feel differently in a week or two? Perhaps going right away together might give you both a chance to find each other again, have a new beginning."

"Not after today's post-card. Alex thought I might change my mind after my visit here but I'm more determined than ever."

"I think you've caught the 'bastian contraria' Faith."

"What's that?"

"It's supposed to be something in the air around here. The locals use the expressson to describe somebody who is determined to go their own way—often against majority opinion. Lucien and I were affected by it according to Pepina. On our second visit to Orta, we were thinking of looking for a little holiday apartment. An agent showed us this house—far too grand—not what we were looking for—we fell in love with it and against all advice, bought it. 'Bastian contraria'! Now you've caught it."

195

"Well it didn't cause you to make a mistake, did it?"

"No indeed."

"Why would 'bastian contraria' be something in the air here, where it's so tranquil?"

"Maybe to balance things out or maybe it's a legacy from St. Giulio. He was determined to stake his claim to the island because he wanted to build a basilica there with his brother. The locals believed it was inhabited by monsters and they tried to prevent him from going. The legend says that he threw his cloak down on the water and floated on it to the island. Whatever happened, the truth is he did get there and he did build his church."

"Good for him and good for 'bastian contraria' if that's what has given me the determination to say no to Alex."

Resolutions

She writes her letter to him up in her room with the balcony doors open onto the view of the luxuriant garden.

Dear Alex,

Of course you must take up the offer of the post in Singapore. It's what you've always hoped would come up and you told me it's an important career move.

However, I am not going with you. The implications of this statement will be clear to you. Please don't think of trying to make me change my mind, it won't be possible. You already knew that I didn't want to go and you don't need me to spell out the reasons.

It's no bad thing to be forced into making a decision. Events this past year have not only shown up profound differences between us but have also left us both convalescent, me from the loss of Daniel and you from your encounter (collision?) with Verina. That situation would not have arisen if you and I had really been right for each other.

If I did go with you to Singapore, it would be under false pretences because I don't want to live with you any more. These days, for the most part, we get on each other's nerves. I think that is because we made a mistake getting married and should now let each other go without bitterness.

Part of me feels sad for you going off so far away on your own but you will be all right.

Wishing you well, Faith.

—

Salvatore's is a large, airy restaurant on a plateau in the mountains. It is crowded but they have booked a table and are led right through to the back and out on to a glass-roofed terrace. The garden slopes down to a hollow which forms a perfect, natural amphitheatre in front of a breath-taking view of the Alps.

"It's like a film set," Faith is entranced.

"And you're the star of the movie."

"Eduardo. Cattivo!" Gabriela wags a finger at him.

Their wine comes with bread and olives. There's a buzz of expectancy as the musicians make their way down to the stage. This group is rapidly climbing the charts and it is clear why, the moment they start to play; they instantly create a wild, happy mood. People spring up to dance on the small dance-floor near the band. Paulo and Gabriela hurry down to join them.

Eduardo asks Faith if she would like to dance.

"Perhaps later when I've had some wine. It's ages since I've danced. Look at your sister." Gabriela is moving to the music so enthusiastically that her hair has come unpinned and is sweeping round her shoulders. "She's such a beautiful girl."

"So are you."

Faith folds her arms on the table and looks at him "I expect you've been told to make sure I have a good evening but you don't have to flatter me."

"I was asked to make up the number and of course I was told to look after you but it's a great pleasure. I'm not bull-shitting, I can't take my eyes off you, you're a real, delicate English rose."

He's smiling into her eyes and she's disconcerted. "Thank you. Tell me about Livia."

This makes him laugh. "Now you're scared of the Mafia. Livia is dark haired."

"And dark-eyed because she's Sicilian."

"Yes. She's very attractive and very clever—much cleverer than I am. We met in the laboratory and became friends at once. We've been seeing each other for over two happy years. Her parents approve of me so now we're getting married."

"I hope you live happily ever after." They clink glasses.

"Thank you. Now as two people off the leash, do you think it's okay for us to dance or not?"

"Of course." As she stands up, Faith feels light-headed. She trips and Eduardo catches her by the arm. "It's the wine."

"No, it's the altitude."

Laughing, they go down to dance, moving with the others through the growing dusk, the floor lit only from the tiny stage. She relaxes with him, lulled by the rhythms in the music.

When the band takes a break, Paulo and Gabriela go to talk to friends at another table. Eduardo and Faith sit down again.

"Faith, when we met the other day, I felt as if we already knew each other. This is not a line, we seem to have an affinity. Do you feel that?"

"I think perhaps I do a bit," she touches the bottle "it could be this of course. Also I've . . . fallen out of my box and . . . you're a long way from Livia."

"There are all sorts of things in my mind that I would like to say to you if you were not married and if I were free. Why are we here together tonight? Why am I being made to endure this painful pleasure?"

"Perhaps to confirm that you really do want to marry which I'm sure is the case. It's about 'forsaking all others' and all that."

"Well yes but I also really like you and want to know you."

"I think I'd like that too but we can't have everything."

"Why not?" He bangs his fist on the table "I want everything!"

She smiles at him. "In literature, when people meet who can't become friends, it's usually for a special purpose in the plot. Oops! Sorry. You can tell I'm a teacher—I'm boring."

"You're dangerous."

This makes her laugh "Me?"

"Yes you. There's something special about you. Do you know how graceful you are?"

She doesn't know how to reply to this.

"And you have this repose which makes you mysterious. That's madly attractive. Don't look so surprised, I can't be the first man who has said these things to you. But perhaps you haven't discovered your powers yet. I've got to take a magic photograph of you."

"What's that?"

"Well, I look hard at your face—really study it—now I close my eyes, and fix your image in here" he taps his forehead then opens his eyes again and smiles tenderly at her, "My hidden secret."

A magnificent full moon has risen over the mountains, shining like aluminium. Candles are being lit all over the terraces. The band is back and as an introduction is being played, a stocky girl walks over to the microphone and begins to sing the blues in a husky voice. She sings with such aching melancholy that although Faith can't make out the words, her eyes well up and a lump rises in her throat. The singer holds the evening, the gardens and the people completely under her spell. Much later, after responding to many requests and singing her heart out, she tries to say goodnight but the audience keeps applauding and begging her for more. Finally she turns and says something to the band and as they start to play, she urges everyone up on their feet and sings a slow and tender song to finish the evening.

Eduardo holds Faith gently as they dance. "Will you have lunch with me, spend my last day with me before I go back to the States? . . . Please?"

She shakes her head.

"Why not?"

He's holding her close and she speaks quietly into his neck "What's the point?"

"The point is that we seem to be soul-mates who need to talk to each other.

May I ring you? . . . Faith?" He squeezes her to him "Please."

". . . All right."

"You're a sweetie." He kisses the top of her head.

Gabriela drives because she only drank one glass of wine. Eduardo insists on sitting in the back with Faith and they hold hands. Paulo, Gabriela and her brother sing current Italian pop songs for Faith and then grow quiet because it's late and they're all sleepy.

At the house, they all get out to whisper 'good night' and give Faith lots of hugs. "I've had a wonderful time. Thank you very much."

Eduardo taps his forehead, "You're my favourite blind date."

They wait for her to let herself in and close the door. She creeps across the hall and up the stairs feeling like a fifteen year old, back much later than allowed from a party.

—

Verina has bought a pin-striped trouser suit and is parading in it for the family's approval. Chris looks over his paper but before he has a chance to say anything, Alex has jumped up "You look amazing. We'll 'ave ter take yer up west dearie." He links arms with her and sings "Any evenin', any day, when yer git darn Lamberf Way . . ." and he makes Verina dance the Lambeth Walk with him around the kitchen table. Nan and Greg clap delightedly.

After she has changed, Chris covertly watches her teach Alex how to make a salad dressing. To get her to test it, Alex dips pieces of lettuce into the mixture and feeds them into her laughing mouth, mopping her with kitchen roll when she gets oil on her lips. He reaches over to pick at the salad and she smacks his hand so he pulls her hair. She washes her fingers under the running tap and flicks water at him. He grabs both her hands and with lots of shouting and laughter a struggle ensues. Verina pleads to be released "I've got to get supper Alex". Still holding on to her, he says "Forfeit then, forfeit" and she stretches up to kiss him lightly on the lips.

Chris shoots a glance at the children; Nan's copying a poem into her book, Greg's drawing a space-ship and Cassie, ignoring the pantomime by the sink, is gazing out of the window.

He finds a moment later in the evening to say "In your pleasure at having Alex here, you won't forget about the children, will you?"

"I don't! What are you talking about?"

"I think you should try not to give him all your attention, let them join in the fun sometimes."

"It wouldn't hurt you to try and join in the fun sometimes. I think you're forgetting how to enjoy life. "She looks properly at him "Don't you think you're working too hard at present?"

"I'm trying to turn things round. Dean's breakdown has left us in a bit of a mess, then losing those two accounts . . ." he's already lost her interest. "I'd better go and do some work, got things to prepare for tomorrow." As he leaves the room, Alex enters.

—

A tired Verina, carrying heavy bags, is just turning the corner when she sees Gemma run down the steps and hurry off. The door opens as she's getting her key out and Alex grins at her and takes her bags.

"What are you doing here so early?"

"Been to the dentist, remember?"

"What did Gemma want? I saw her leaving the house." They have come through to the kitchen and Verina is unpacking the shopping.

"She was looking for Cassie."

"Cassie's at school, why isn't <u>she</u>?"

"They've got a study day or something." He's putting the kettle on.

"Is Cass home then?"

"No. Don't think so."

"She must be at the library." Clearing some space on the counter, she finds a scrunchie for a pony-tail. Gemma has gone home with her hair dishevelled. "How long was Gemma here?"

"Not long. Why?"

She holds out the scrunchie "I see she was here long enough to take this off her hair. Did you make her take anything else off?"

"What a question." He's unperturbed.

She's deadly earnest "I hope you haven't been up to anything with that child Alex."

"I believe she's the age of consent actually."

She collapses into a chair "Stop tormenting me, tell me you haven't."

He gives her a maddening smile "Nothing serious. Look, I had no-one to play with this afternoon; Gemma's been coming on to me for ages so when she turned up and obviously wanted to hang around, I put her through a little initiation ceremony."

"You what?! Oh God!"

"It's all right Vee. Absolutely nothing to worry about."

"Don and Angela might not agree."

202

"They're not gonna know. I haven't deflowered her if that's what's worrying you. I haven't harmed her at all, she enjoyed herself."

"Enough to come back for more?" She's icy.

"I can't help my fatal attraction mummy-Vee. I never pretended to be an angel."

"Gemma will probably tell Cass all about it, she's her best friend, so prepare yourself for some fireworks. Make the tea please Alex, your complicated games are very wearing."

"Well I'm not going to be around much longer to tire you out,"

"Don't remind me" she groans and rests her head on her hands.

He hands her a cup of tea "Don't forget, you still have the ultimate mandate."

—

They're breakfasting out on the terrace.

"That call was from Gabriela's brother. He's asked me to spend the day with him tomorrow. I told him I would check with you first and call him back."

"You don't have to check with me Faith, you know I want you to enjoy yourself. Eduardo is a delightful young man. I believe he's also getting married this year."

"Yes he is." Faith grins at her "Having lunch with me won't alter anything."

"Forgive me, I didn't mean to imply . . . Although you are coming into your beauty now that you've had some rest. And the sun has blonded your hair and given you some colour. You look wonderful."

"Thank you. Eduardo started telling me a bit about his work in stem-cell research and I'd like to know more. Paulo and Gabriela are frightened of it. I'm not, although I have some reservations about plundering embryos, if that's what they do. I certainly wouldn't want to have to consider the ethical decisions doctors and scientists have to make. I'll be asking Eduardo some awkward questions; it will be interesting to hear what he thinks."

"Ah well, if your outing is for research purposes, I'll have to excuse you."

Françoise is smiling broadly.

"You're surely not shocked that an engaged man and a still-married woman should have a day out together? I thought the French had a wider view of things."

"Oh we do, we do. We Frenchwomen have a saying: 'un ami pour le chic, un amant pour le choc, un mari pour le chèque.'"

They both laugh. "I like that. I'll have to remember it."

"In these times of course, 'l'ami' tends to be a beautiful homosexual. I don't think Eduardo is homosexual."

"He's going back to the States the day after tomorrow."

"I'm only teasing you Faith. I think it will be very good for you to go out with him."

He's sitting on the wall by the jetty and when he sees her, he jumps and comes to meet her. "Good morning. We'll go straight onto the boat. They waited for you."

"Am I late?"

"Not at all. I got our tickets and told them I was expecting a friend. I was afraid you might decide not to come." He puts an arm around her and gives her a little squeeze.

On the boat, they stand looking out over the water watching the little piazza moving backwards away from them. Neither of them has anything to say.

The first stop is St. Giulio. "Would you like to get off and see the island?"

"I already have. It's a bit claustrophobic."

"You think so?"

"Yes, the cramped path and the high walls hem you in."

"It's peaceful though. I would have thought it was just your sort of place."

Faith is uncomfortable, she's disappointed him. "It is really but I don't think I was in the right frame of mind. Also I couldn't understand the philosophic writings, my Italian is too basic but I did love the quiet."

They relapse into silence again as though they've had a quarrel.

The boat is pulling away from the island now and moving slowly across to the other side of the lake. A sudden flock of small birds fans out ahead as if leading the way. "What are those birds?"

"I don't know about birds but Pepina has been telling everybody that having you to stay is like having a dove in the house." He looks into her face "And I've got you in my bird-catcher all day."

"You don't look very happy about it."

"That's just because I'm anxious not to spoil things. I want us to have one special day before life carries us off in different directions."

"We're having that, aren't we?"

"You seem withdrawn."

"I'm a bit nervous."

"I'm on edge too. It was so easy the other evening. Today, I don't know how to behave towards you. It's making me restless."

The boat is pulling in to Pella and people come clattering down from the upper deck.

"Let's just treat each other gently. Shall we go upstairs?"

Changing places on the boat alters their mood. They have the whole upper space to themselves. Faith closes her eyes and lifts her face to the sun. "What a heavenly day. I'm so glad you suggested the boat it's lovely to be on the water and we can see so much. Look at the hills and the sky."

"All spread out just for you."

"For both of us."

They sit close, holding hands, occasionally tightening their fingers. Their silence is different now, companionable. He slips an arm around her and she relaxes against him, her head against his shoulder. It's as if the boat is moving at it's unhurried pace to prolong the morning especially for them. He whispers into her hair "This is a dream." "It's an indulgence."

At Omegna, they disembark at a busy street market permeated with a strong smell of leather from stalls selling bags and belts. Among some bric-a-brac, Faith spots a tiny dark blue bottle, decorated with gold filigree. "I must buy this for Françoise, she collects scent bottles." Eduardo bargains with the stall-holder and gets the price down for her. "Thank you. I'm delighted to have found a present for her, she's so kind to me."

"And now I'm going to buy one for you. Come over here."

"Please don't buy me anything." He's holding out a scarf, pale mauve silk edged with silver embroidery. He drapes it round her neck and the stall owner claps her hands. "When you wear this and feel a tug—it'll be me. Now we must find a taxi."

The taxi takes them out of the town and up a very steep hill on to a road that curves around it like a girdle. They are driving fast and Faith grips Eduardo's hand as she looks out of the window and sees they are very high up and the camber slopes towards the edge and the drop. Turning into the woods they travel down again, this time on a bumpy, narrow track, down and down to a clearing and there is the restaurant, raised up from the road.

The very small village sits at the foot of towering hills. A smiling man is welcoming them and talking very fast to Eduardo.

"This is Antonio. Would you like to sit outside or go in?"

"Outside please."

Red and white covered tables under an awning are screened from the pavement by a carved wooden balustrade. They are the only customers. Choosing a corner table, they sit at right angles to each other. "Are you hungry?"

"Yes."

"Well they have marvellous food here that you won't find anywhere else—all local dishes."

Faith is studying the menu

"Would you prefer to leave it to me?"

"Yes please."

Eduardo orders a bottle of Erbaluce and some water. Faith looks up at the hills which imprison the village and thinks of landslides. "This place is very isolated."

"That's why I brought you here."

"How on earth did you find it?"

"I used to have a motor-bike."

Antonio, comes with the wine and takes their order.

Eduardo raises his glass to Faith, "Well here we are lovely girl where no-one can find us. And we've got it all to ourselves. Let's talk absolutely freely, we haven't got time to waste. Agreed?"

"Agreed."

"There are so many things I want to say to you. I've rehearsed them in my mind but I'm not sure they're appropriate. Since I met you, I've begun to feel that I'm rushing along a motorway; the road is all marked out; there's nowhere to make a u-turn."

"But you have a plan at least. You do know the direction you've chosen."

"Well yes . . . but . . ."

"I haven't the faintest idea where I'm going. I've only recently realised, I'm in the process of separating from my husband."

"Bit soon, isn't it? You've only just met me."

She laughs and throws a punch at him.

"Are you really separating?"

"Yes."

"Why?"

"It's a long story."

"We've got all the afternoon and I want to know as much about you as possible."

She thinks for a moment or two, takes a few sips of her wine and gives him a summary.

"It sounds as if he's trying to get away from her."

"If that's true, he must have suffered a massive change of heart. It's so unlikely. I can't understand it at all."

"Well he wants you to go with him."

"He assumed I would go with him—I'm his wife, his property."

Some little starter dishes have arrived with freshly baked bread.

"Alex is someone who wants to have his cake and eat it."

"I'm like that. I'm thinking of becoming a Mormon then I could marry you and Livia."

She's too deep in thought to respond to this. "He's devious. Part of me thinks he's made it impossible for me to even consider going with him so that he can be free to do what he likes. He and Verina have even talked in front of us all about her going to Singapore for a holiday. It's surreal, all of it."

"What will you do with yourself?"

"Get another job. Find a flat. Turn right", she flips her hands to the right "and start again."

"Will you get divorced?"

"I won't need to. Alex will be there before me 'If you're not for me, you're against me. Get out of my life'."

"I don't know how he can let you go. He must be mad."

"He is, since he fell in love with his mother. So is she poor woman."

"He may come to his senses."

"Even if he does . . . when the lamp is shattered . . . ." she makes a despairing little gesture with her hands,

"When you got married, did you assume it would last?"

"I certainly intended it to but the Verina business made everything so fragile and then losing Daniel woke me right up—I'd just been dreaming through life up 'til then. I began to see things very sharply and a kind of guilt set in."

"Guilt? What for? You explained how the baby died."

"Not to do with the baby, to do with marrying . . . almost, shall I say?, casually, irresponsibly."

"Didn't you love Alex?"

"I thought I did—he told me I did. Now even that seems to have been in my imagination. Our parents approved so I thought we were doing the right thing. I'm honestly not sure of anything now . . . I'm sure you're not marrying irresponsibly?"

"No but not without a backward glance." He strokes her cheek.

"Well I've already said I'm here to remind you about 'forsaking all others'."

"And what am I here to remind you about?"

"Possibilities perhaps, in the dim and distant future."

"When I won't be around."

"When you won't be around, no."

Forgetting the food, they sit looking looking at each other.

"If life had placed us both in Europe, we'd have got together, wouldn't we?"

"Surely we have?"

He sighs, "Cara mia. We have so short a time."

"Just as well since it's not appropriate."

"That's going to be our phrase for this day, is it?"

"'Fraid so."

"Oh Faith, being here with you is . . ." he sighs, "indescribable."

The main course arrives and with it, sudden violent rain. Although they are under a canopy they are getting splashed and Antonio hurries them inside and when they are settled again, he leans against the wall, folding his arms, watching them.

"We'd better show more interest in the food. It's been specially prepared for us."

Faith smiles at Antonio.

"I tried to plan a perfect day and what happens?!" Eduardo waves his hand at the windows.

"Doesn't matter about the weather."

They're sitting very close together. "You're right of course."

"Look at the hills through the rain, they seem to be shivering."

"You could write a haiku about that."

Faith is delighted, "You interested in haiku?"

"Yes. A colleague and I write them on e-mail to each other, mostly about the workings and non—workings of our computers."

"Can you remember any?"

He thinks . . . "Not from the top of my head . . . but I have been trying to write a poem about you". He pulls a note-book out of his pocket.

"Are you going to show me?"

"It's not good enough yet. I'm too ambitious."

"Give me a piece of paper please and I'll try and turn this moment into a haiku."

"I'll try and do the same with these notes. Look at me . . . thank you, that helps."

They write as they eat. Faith puts her pen down first "It's very rough but here it is, I hope you can read my writing" she passes it to him.

Downpourings of rain
batter the wooded mountains,
shifting the landscape.

"It's a Japanese painting. I can see the streaks of the wet brush-strokes down the scroll."

"You're making more of it than it deserves. I haven't quite succeeded. I love trying to write Haiku but I find it difficult. Now let me see yours."

"Give me a couple more minutes."

Faith likes watching him concentrate. He tries out different phrases, crossing them out impatiently when they don't work. "I'm never going to be satisfied in the time. Here you are."

Gentle stir of air,
a window left open, now
a dove in the house.

"I'm jealous. That's lovely."

"It's about you."

"Thank you. I like yours much better than mine. You're a poet Eduardo."

"I don't know about that. I try for a pure distillation of an idea and hope what's hinted at gives a satisfying puzzle for the reader to solve."

Antonio comes to clear their plates and is pleased when he sees they've eaten everything and they tell him the food was delicious. He examines the wine bottle, it still holds a couple of glasses. He offers them the menu again but Eduardo tells him they'll be happy with just the wine for a while.

Faith is re-reading Eduardo's haiku. "You have to be imaginative to be a scientist, don't you? You must always be saying to yourself 'I wonder what would happen if? How does this work? Where does this fit in? 'etc. Then you have to think through and write your findings clearly. Perhaps that's why you and your colleague enjoy writing in this form and are probably good at it."

"Maybe."

"Tell me about your work."

"Now?"

"What other time do we have?"

"You're just causing a distraction."

"Maybe . . . tell me anyway."

"Well, I told you, our team works with stem cells. The point about stem cells is that they can renew themselves and they can divide and change into a varied range of specialised cell types such as those in muscle or nerves or other tissue."

"So you can use them to patch up damage?"

"Yes. That's one thing. But it's early days, if we can successfully grow them and transform them for use in counteracting injury or disease, the potential is mind-boggling"

"Where do you get stem cells from?"

"The umbilical cord. It's not the only source but it's the one we're concerned with."

"I've read a bit about that. Some midwives don't like interruptions so soon after birth when mother and child should be tranquil."

"We do our best not to intrude and to be sensitive. The mothers have given permission in advance."

"What do you think about helping to create a baby, free of an illness—let's say leukaemia—in order to provide a healthy transplant match for a sibling?"

"What do you think?"

"Well there are people who say a child brought about like that, for that reason, will resent it and feel not loved for himself. I think it could equally be a source of pride that he's been able to save the life of a brother or sister and feels he's even more cherished because of it."

"You wouldn't be against it then?"

"I don't think I would. Presumably, such a procedure would only be considered anyway for people who want more children and a proper family life?"

"I believe so. In any case, matters as delicate as this are never lightly undertaken."

"No of course not. I'm sure that's true. I was saying to Françoise that I would not like to have to make the ethical decisions that scientists have to make, especially when you consider the different views other cultures might have. I think we need a world-wide set of rules, if we could all agree on them. Couldn't the W.H.O. draw up something?"

"A sort of ten commandments you mean?"

"If you like."

"Actually, there's more accord among the world's scientists than you might suppose. We are already agreed about the necessity for respect and responsibilty for the material we handle such as eggs and foetuses. In fact, the list of rules you would like to see drawn up is actually likely to come into being in the very near future and rumour has it that it will come from the UK."

"I get impatient with some of the religious arguments. Jews and Catholics say that the soul doesn't enter the body until forty days after conception. I think I've got that right. Do they mean by 'soul' the persona? And who told them that? Do they have a direct line to God? Forty day gives scientists a long time to experiment on a foetus that is alive but considered not—quite—human yet. Oh, please forgive me Eduardo. I can see by your face, you don't really want to talk about these things—especially with someone so ill-informed but it's work that interests me, fascinates me and scares me. I don't know anyone else I can talk to about these things."

"Couldn't you talk about them with Alex?"

"No. He's not interested."

"What is he interested in?"

"Cinema mainly, films. Mind you, I love films too."

"Excuse me a moment, Antonio is making signs at me."

Faith watches with a smile as the two men talk and emphasise what they're saying with many hand gestures.

"Does he want us to go?"

"On the contrary, he's offered us a room. Don't look so shocked. He knows I'm getting married and thought it was to you. I told him you're my very special friend." He gives her a smile of such tenderness and sadness that Faith has to look away. "Shall we have some coffee?"

"Good idea."

Eduardo signals to Antonio. "Then perhaps we should be thinking of leaving, it's going to take us a while to get back. My mother will have been preparing all day for my parting dinner. Paulo is coming over of course. I only wish I could invite you but my mother has hawk's eyes."

With the coffee and almond biscuits on the tray are two small liqueur glasses. Antonio sets light to them. "Sambuca! Do you know this drink?"

"No. Is it to shut me up?"

"Not at all, it's to celebrate our day. The flames are symbolic."

Waiting nearly an hour for their taxi, they talk about their childhood and plot the twisting and turning paths that have brought them to this place at this time. Antonio turns on some lights and they ask him to turn them off again. "I can just about see you "Eduardo whispers. "it's like being a child again in some hideout we've made."

"Drinking liqueurs? More like a clandestine rendezvous."

"Does that bother you?"

"Makes me feel a bit more interesting."

Faith has not been looking forward to the drive back to Omegna. She thinks the road will be slippery after the rain and their car might slide over the edge but their driver is careful and the road already dry. He stops at a high point so that they can enjoy the view of the valley in the evening glow but Faith keeps her eyes tight shut. Eduardo explains to their driver that she is terrified and he begins the slow descent.

"I haven't said the things I meant to Faith. You got me talking about work."

"Which told me a lot about you. In any case, you and I don't need much in the way of words to understand each other."

He lifts the hand he is holding tightly and kisses it.

Although the boat chug-chugs its way back at the same gentle pace as the morning, the journey passes all too quickly. When Eduardo points out the yellow palace where Faith is staying, she realises they are almost back where they started and are approaching the jetty. They decide to say goodbye on the boat and turn to each other resting cheek against cheek in a long sweet hug.

"Thank you for today. Goodbye Lovely Faith. See you in another life perhaps. Meanwhile, have a good time in this one."

"Thank you for a wonderful day. Enjoy your wedding. Have a really happy marriage. And win the Nobel Prize."

The boat bumps against its moorings. They have arrived. Time to move apart and stand up.

Off the boat now, where others may see them, they shake hands and give each other a lingering smile. Eduardo taps his forehead. They untangle their fingers and walk off in different directions.

—

Without the children it's an empty house. You realise how much space they fill, physical and psychological. Chris wonders if they pick up on the constant tension he can hear almost crackling between Verina, Alex and himself. Can't stand another evening with the three of us, I'll take Vee out if she'll come on her own. He hears her on the stairs and goes out to her. She's dressed for a disco.

"Why're you dolled up like that?"

"I told you, I'm going with Alex to his firm's 'do'."

213

"Not like that you're not!"

Alex is waiting for her by the front door. "We take our mother to works parties now, do we?" He's furious with Verina, "You didn't tell me anything about this. Give us a moment please Alex."

No-one moves.

"You don't have to go Alex."

"Look, the pair of you, this is not on." He's shouting now.

"Well Faith isn't here."

"Faith is your wife! You can't take your mother instead of your wife to a company party, you'll look ridiculous both of you."

"My MD knows, he said it would be okay."

"What else could he say? Everyone will laugh at you secretly for bringing 'mum' along. I don't care if they laugh at you but I won't have Verina ridiculed. As for you Vee, have you lost your mind? Look at the way you're dressed! You're not twenty-five any more."

"I think she looks great."

"You look as if you're going out on the pull. I won't let you do this Vee. Where's your dignity?"

She stands, hesitant, on the stairs.

Alex comes towards her but Chris bars the way. "She's not going out with you. I've had enough of this."

As if he hopes to force him to back down, Alex concentrates all his will in a ferocious glare but Chris is so full of bottled-up violence that he feels himself growing taller and bigger and he glares right back *in another minute, my young friend, I'm going to pick you up by your collar and throw you down the steps into the street.*

Alex backs off. "Fuck you Chris!" He bangs the front door behind him. Verina slips away, back upstairs.

Now I need a drink. I was ready to bash him. Calm down.

He goes in search of Verina and finds her changed into jeans and a sweater, sitting on the bed with her head bowed over clasped hands.

"I was thinking that since nobody else is in, we might go round the corner for some supper."

"I don't want any supper. You go."

"I'd like you to come with me please."

"After that 'High Noon' scene?"

214

"It was good, wasn't it? You should have enjoyed being fought over."

"I didn't enjoy being told I looked like a tart!"

"You should be thanking me."

"I feel like thumping you," she speaks wearily.

"Well at least I seem to be getting through for once. I didn't set out to make you feel bad, you gave me a shock in that short skirt and not much blouse."

"Oh God!" she sighs.

"Listen, for the moment, we're stuck with each other. Let's go out and have something to eat like a normal couple for once. I promise not to say anything about anything." He sees she has no fight left in her. "Come on, put your jacket on."

He chooses the little Thai place with dim lighting so that Vee's troubled face won't be noticed and there will be something light and delicious on the menu to comfort her. He orders a Rioja that he knows she will drink.

During the near-silent meal, he tells himself that a good marriage builds a fortress that can withstand siege, pestilence and storms. You just have to hang on in there. No point wondering how you're going to view things in the future, you can never have any idea beforehand. In spite of all that's happened, looking across at Verina—who refuses to look at him—he knows he'll never want to be married to anyone else.

When they get back home and part for the night, Verina, her face still averted, says "Thank you Chris."

She makes two telephone calls in the morning; the first is to Alex.

"You didn't come home last night."

"No."

"Where were you?"

"That'd be telling."

"Oh stop being aggravating! How did you manage? What about a clean shirt and all that?"

"It's cool to show up in a dinner-jacket."

"Are you coming back this evening?"

"I don't know. That rather depends on the domestic hero."

"I'll talk to him and call you back."

She rings Chris. "Do you want Alex to move back to his flat?"

"It's a matter of supreme indifference to me."

"So if he comes back tonight will you be all right with him? Let him be one of the children?"

Chris wants to shout 'Are you mad?' but of course, she is. "Well he needn't expect any pocket-money."

"Thank you Chris."

I'd rather have you where I can keep an eye on you both.

—

Faith has been telling Françoise about her day with Eduardo. "It was special but we're never going to meet again and I've already let go of him in my mind. What I need is to start planning what I'm going to do when I get back to England. I shan't stay on in our flat. It's furnished in horrible taste, not by us, and is depressing. Alex and I have not been happy there, it's time to move on. I'll find somewhere near where I am going to work."

"Are you going back to your old job?"

"They will all expect me to show off my baby. Couldn't face that. In any case, I need a complete change I think."

"I'm sure you're right."

The French doors are open and they wander out to look at the lake. A mist has settled over it and around the hillside opposite, lights are just beginning to gleam through the ghostly trees. The evening is absolutely quiet and still.

"I don't know how you manage to tear yourself away from here."

"It's always hard but I know I can come back. Besides, I also adore Paris and I enjoy what I do so I'm happy there too. And Lucien is at home. I miss him and he can't often join me here. Have you heard any more from Alex since you wrote to tell him you're not going with him to Singapore?"

"No. Either he doesn't care or he thinks he can persuade me when I go home."

"Will he be able to?"

"Definitely not. Thanks to you, I've had the peace and time to think things through and my mind is made up."

"All the same, perhaps you shouldn't put yourself at risk. Once you've escaped from the dragon's cave, why go back?"

"You don't realize Françoise, I have turned into the dragon myself. Shall we go in? It's getting a bit cool out here."

They settle in their usual places. "I shall have to see him. I'll want to say goodbye. I just mustn't be feeble that's all. I don't think I will be, I feel so good physically and mentally. It's funny you should mention the dragon's cave, I've had the same image. I do feel I've escaped and I won't be tempted back. Alex is going off to pursue his career, it's time I gave some thought to mine. Would you like some music?"

"You choose."

Faith puts on 'Claire de Lune' and they pick up their books.

Françoise tosses her book aside. "Perhaps it's true, the novel is a dying form."

"They've been saying that for a hundred years."

"You don't agree?"

"No. I think it's far from dying. I think it's evolving, changing shape. The more we're surrounded by machines and technology the more we need to look for ourselves in novels, to share experiences and to be reassured that we're still human . . . and important. What's wrong with your book?"

"It's written in rap so I find it difficult to understand. I think the author—he's from the Côte d'Ivoire—must have been on drugs when he wrote it. It reads like a long incantation. It doesn't work for me, although I'm interested in experiment. Perhaps it's a generational thing."

"Have you read any Afro-American writers?"

"No."

"I've read mostly women. People like Alice Walker and Toni Morrison. Their work is extraordinary. The novels read like heart-breaking poems or song but they have to sing extra piercingly to be heard among the white male literary giants."

"Who do you consider are the giants?"

"We're talking about Americans?"

"Yes."

"Well, I suppose Steinbeck, Bellow and more recently Roth. Have you read him?"

"I must confess, I haven't. I'm sure I should."

"You'd probably enjoy his trilogy."

"You'd better make me a list."

"I will of course and you must make one for me. I've no idea who I should be reading among French contemporaries."

Françoise points to Faith's book "What are you reading now?"

"This is 'A River Sutra' by an Indian writer, Gita Mehta. Beautiful prose. She strings stories connected to the river like beads on a necklace. I tell you what fascinates me Françoise, it's how a language that originates in one part of the world gets transplanted into another and takes on new colours. Do you know what I mean? I'm not talking about politics here, though they inevitably come into it."

Françoise is smiling and nodding."

"I'm talking about a sort of alchemy. It must have happened with your French colonies. Gradually the imposed language becomes subtly changed by being used in a different environment—alien landscapes, exotic vegetation. You've got the Academie Française to monitor everything so perhaps I'm talking rubbish when it comes to French but it's certainly true of English. I'm thinking of Indian writers who live in Europe or the States who, while writing in English, draw on an Indian background to enrich their work. They have long perspectives of history behind them, smells and sounds we don't know about, living religions and a different conception of beauty, all of which they find interesting ways to describe. They use English but it's their English. Oops! Sorry, I'm on my soap-box again but you know how much I enjoy talking books with you."

"And I with you. You have some interesting ideas."

"Thank you. I need to develop them further. Read more, research more, think more."

"Excuse me for changing the subject for a moment, do you know exactly when Alex will be leaving for Singapore?"

"No. Why?"

"I've got something in mind, if dates work out. I know you want to see him before he goes. I'm going to be unwilling to part with you."

Faith expects her to go on to say 'but of course you must go'. What she actually says takes a few seconds to register. "Do you think you would like to come to Paris and work with me? I would like to offer you a job in my department if you'd like it."

Faith is astounded. "But you don't know much about me."

"You've lived in my house for a while and we've discussed literature every evening and I'm convinced that you would be a useful member of my staff."

"What have you got in mind?"

"Well, it so happens that we are in the process of reorganising our programmes to bring things up to date. You could be involved in that. I see you planning modules in say, world novels in English or contemporary American writing. You've got lots of ideas. If you think you might be interested, the thing would be for you to make suggestions and plan a draft syllabus for us to discuss. You said something about the novel changing shape, you could run a seminar on that."

"I can't believe this. You've completely thrown me. It's the last thing I would have expected you to suggest."

"You think you'd like to do it?"

"Would I?! Françoise! I don't know what to say. I would simply love it. I'd only be afraid I might disappoint you."

"I'll take that risk. Let's have some champagne to celebrate. There's a bottle down in the fridge, if you wouldn't mind getting it."

They clink glasses and Françoise says "It's going to be good to have you on my staff, we need a fresh face. You'll like the others. And Faith, when you see Alex, if you change your mind, you are not to worry about it. I wouldn't want my plan to influence you or cause you any distress, You've had enough of that."

"I won't change my mind. Thank you. I'm on cloud nine, all I can say is 'hooray!'.

—

When she comes through the barrier she looks straight at Alex but he doesn't recognise her.

"Hallo Alex."

"Hey! Look at you! Where'd you get that outfit?"

"Milan of course."

"It suits you. Are you hungry or did you eat on the plane?"

"I didn't bother, it looked awful—not what I'm used to now. I've brought some cheese and parma ham and wine, we can eat at the flat."

"I don't fancy an evening in that hole. I haven't been there while you've been away. I thought I'd take you to dinner now I've got you back."

Got me back? "Fine, if that's what you'd like to do."

"This is a new place that's opened while you've been away. Let's get the luggage back home and then go straight out. Okay?" She nods.

The restaurant is all glass, stainless steel and bright lights. It's packed with young people who've been drinking for hours and are now loudly having a good time. However, the service is good and when it arrives, so is the food. Because he's asked her about it, she starts to tell him about her holiday but can see he's not listening, he wants to be elsewhere. It was probably Verina who told him he must meet her. Discomfort settles over them like a heavy blanket

Strolling home afterwards, Faith dreads arriving back at the flat so when Alex suggests a brandy at Dave's she agrees. She suspects he isn't eager to get home either. They find seats at a table near the window and the discreet lighting made it easier to relax. They sip their brandy. Alex grins at her "You're looking so much better. Are you feeling really well now?"

Instantly she knows he's wondering if he's going to get any sex tonight.

"You didn't really mean all that nonsense about not coming abroad with me, did you?"

Maybe he thinks the brandy, on top of the wine they had at dinner, will have made her tipsy and docile. Instead, it's bolstered her courage. "It's not nonsense. I've thought about it and I've made up my mind. I'm not coming." She waits for his outburst but he just stares at her. He's not going to help. She takes a deep breath and forces herself to meet his gaze directly "We haven't been getting on well for ages. It seems to me now is a good time for us to separate while life is changing anyway."

"Oh really. That's your decision is it? I'm supposed to accept it?"

"You made a decision you assumed I would accept."

"Of course I did, 'wither thou goest, I will go' and all that." He leans across the table at her, his expression hard. "Listen you, remember the tra-la-la you made about our wedding? You insisted on the full church carnival because 'marriage is important.' I didn't want any of that, I went along with it to please you and now you're the one who wants out!"

"Don't raise your voice please Alex. We should continue this conversation at home."

"It doesn't seem to have occurred to you that I might need your support. I'm going out to a strange country and a demanding job. You've picked a fine time to reneague on your promises."

She clutches her glass and gulps down some brandy. "I don't quite understand why you're so angry, I rarely seem to measure up. Most of the time you give the impression that you'd be glad to be rid of me."

"I know what this is all about, you've met someone and you haven't got the guts to admit it. Been picking up men in wine bars again? Some Italian gigolo?"

Instinct tells her there's an element of play-acting in all this. He's up to something but she can't work out what. "Think what you like. I thought I'd explained it all in my letter."

"Oh you did. Very cool your letter was and as usual, very negative."

He goes off to get more drinks then they both sit looking out of the window without talking. When he next speaks to her, his mood has changed again, he says gently "You say this is a good time to make a break but couldn't it be equally a good time to start again? This is not a good moment for you to be making emotional decisions, it's not long since you lost the baby. Why not come out to Singapore and see how it goes? I think you owe it to me to give it a try. I promise I'll look after you, give you a good time."

Does he believe what he's saying? "I'm sorry Alex, it's too late. You talk about needing support, did you support me when I needed you?"

"Here we go. Yes, I did support you, I spent hours at that bloody hospital. But you've got to justify yourself for your own selfishness so what can we fling in Alex's face?"

"Well, for a start, the night you left me on my own to go to a dinner party when you knew I was frightened that something was wrong. You should have been with me, in the flat, in the taxi, in the hospital holding my hand and showing me some kindness for once. The only time I get a warm word from you is when you want to take me to bed."

221

"Shall I tell you something Faith? You're the kind of woman who drains a man, you expect too much."

"Fine. So go to Singapore and leave me in peace."

"You won't survive on your own you know. You've got no idea."

"Well that won't be your concern."

"You're not expecting me to support you financially, are you?"

"Why should I? I've always supported myself."

"You're going to have to get back to work then. By the way, the lease on the flat is up next Friday, I haven't renewed it. I've also let the deposit go on the house."

"That's all right, I'll be living in Paris."

"What?" He laughed "Cloud-cuckoo-land more like. Poor Faith, do you know it takes a woman two years to get her brain functioning again after childbirth."

"Françoise Auteuil has offered me a job."

"As what? Lady's companion? Cook? Lesbian friend?"

"I'm going to teach literature in her University department."

"Got a proper contract have you? Going to live with her?"

"Oh Alex what do you care? Leave me alone."

"Why would she offer you a job? She hardly knows you. Seems fishy to me. I'd be careful if I were you, the French education system is miles better than ours. It won't be like teaching your semi-literate ethnics. If Madame whats-her-name's offer is genuine, you're going to have to really know your stuff and how to put it over. The French are very chauvinist, they'll be only too pleased to see an English woman fall flat on her face."

"Thank you for your vote of confidence."

He gave her a sneering grin "You'll have to smarten up too if you really do go to Paris. You look all right today but usually your hair's a mess and you've never had much dress sense."

Getting ready for bed, when they finally get home, Faith begins to put covers on the sofa.

"Have I become a leper or are you frightened I might persuade you to change your mind?"

"My father's picking me up early. I can slide off without disturbing you in the morning."

222

"You've changed you know Faith, you've become cold. I don't recognize you anymore. I don't think I like you anymore." She's putting on clean pillow cases.

"What do you want from life Faith?"

"I'd like you to be happy."

He snorted "To salve your conscience."

"Goodnight Alex."

As she tries to get comfortable on the sofa, she returns to the questions that have puzzled her all evening *what about Verina?—has the infatuation burned itself out?—have Chris and Alex had a showdown?—it's clear that Alex is definitely going—can't believe he's going to take himself off to the other side of the world from Verina.*

—

Verina has asked friends round for drinks to say farewell to Alex. Angela is talking quietly to Chloé "Vee's putting on a brave face."

"She's very proud of him, it's a marvellous job he's landed. She doesn't want to spoil things but it will hit her hard on Monday when she knows he's finally gone. It's been an odd time."

"It certainly has. Don's keeping an eye, he thinks Vee is very near the edge."

"Chris doesn't look so hot either."

"No he doesn't. We'll just have to rally."

"In some ways I think this is almost worse for Vee than her father going."

"Especially since she's only had Alex back in her life for a few months. What's happened to Faith by the way, an inevitable casualty of all this I suppose?"

"She's feeling much better after her holiday. She was invited tonight but I think she and Alex are separating. Her hostess, in Italy, who is a French academic, has offered her a job in Paris."

"Well I'm very glad for her. I like Faith."

"She's with her parents at the moment. Cassie's going up there to stay with her next week-end."

Alex has found an old conical hat in the cloakroom and he is clowning around like an excited school-boy as he moves through the room pouring wine for everybody and speaking

223

in a comic Chinese accent, "You want bly post-cards? I show peectures ob lubbly laydees—lubbly Singapore laydees." If he's unhappy at leaving Verina, there's no sign.

Angela whispers to Chloé, "Poor Vee's trying so hard to laugh. We must keep her busy in the next few weeks."

"That's why I suggested going to the jazz in the park Monday evening. The children love a picnic supper."

Joe asked Alex why he wasn't leaving his luggage in London so that he could just pick it up on Monday.

"I haven't properly packed yet. I've just thrown everything from the flat into the boot to sort out when I get to Phil and Lilian's."

"When do you actually start your new job?"

"Not for three weeks. I'm going early to give myself time to look for somewhere to live and find my way around."

"I suppose you won't get back to the UK for some time?"

"Not for at least two years."

Wonderful smells are permeating from the kitchen and people are starting to leave. Verina is like an automaton, holding herself in so tightly that although she's managing to say the right things, Chris fears something might happen to cause her to snap. She has cooked two ducks and a chicken.

"What a superb meal" Alex croons.

"In your honour Alex."

"You spoil me mummy-Vee."

"Mum, I don't like duck."

"I know Greg, you can have chicken."

"You're very lucky" Alex told him, "think of poor me, I expect I'll be living on rice and noodles forever. I'm going to miss mum's cooking and I'm going to miss my mum." He caught her hand as she passed and bestowed on her his most seductive grin.

Chris wants to yell "Stop flirting with her, you callous bastard. You must see what's she's going through."

Nan touches Alex's hand "I wish you weren't going away."

Chris jumps in fast "A man has to go where his work is" as though he believes Alex could be dissuaded at this late hour.

Greg waves his knife in the air "I would never leave you mum and dad."

Verina gives him a twisted smile, "You will one day, when you get married perhaps."

"Mummy, can we take time off school on Monday so we can see him off?"

"No thank you Lobby-lou. I hate people seeing me off." He sees she is hurt and adds "You can come and welcome me home again though."

"That won't be for ages and ages."

"But think of the presents" Greg reminds her. "You always get presents when people have been away a long time, don't you mum? That's some consolation."

Verina is stony quiet *she must be wretched inside, coming to terms with it all.* As if he's reading Chris's thoughts, Alex says to her, "You must come out for that holiday when I'm settled." To Chris, the gleaming smile that accompanies these words expresses pure malice.

In the dress that Chris likes, the brown one which leaves part of her shoulders bare, she looks beautiful and slightly crazed. Her head is bent to hide her face which has gone red and hot as if she's suddenly running a temperature.

"That would be nice."

Cassie has scarcely spoken during dinner. Now and then she gets up to clear plates or bring a dish to the table. She seems aware of what her mother is feeling and is supporting her unobtrusively.

Chris thinks she has every reason to resent Alex for taking her place—as it must seem to her—this may have contributed to her growing up so quickly. She senses him observing her and gives him a shy smile. It's going to be good to have a week-end on their own, even with a distracted Verina.

They sit late round the table over pudding but eventually the children have to go to bed because of school next day. Greg hugs Alex "Goodbye, good luck."

Nan, trying not to cry, says "You will write to me, won't you?"

"Of course."

Cassie is giving an assembly in the morning, "I must go and practise my reading."

Before going to bed, Chris thinks he'd better shake hands with Alex, if only to please Verina. "Shan't see you in the morning so goodbye," *don't come back* "hope it all goes well."

"Thanks for everything."

Sleep eludes him. He tries to imagine what Verina and Alex are saying to each other now—*a drama has been going on here and we've all tried to carry on with our lives as though it wasn't happening—nearly all over—he'll be gone tomorrow and in another couple of days he'll be flying out of our lives and we can begin to salvage some of our former peace—I'll be holding my breath until I know the plane has taken off.*

It's two o'clock when he goes through to the kitchen for some water. Verina and Alex are still sitting at the table. Alex looks up at the clock "Is that the time? Sorry Vee I'd better let you get to bed. We've said all our goodbyes. Goodnight" he bends to kiss her cheek and presses his hand onto her shoulder.

She doesn't answer him and when he's gone, she lifts a face full of anguish. It's as if she can't see Chris, her eyes are clouded with pain. He feels his stomach contract *poor Vee, one jarring word will shatter her—I'll have to go carefully.* "I know this is awful for you Vee but you should go to bed and try to get some sleep. Getting over-tired makes everything worse. You were wonderful this evening. Shall I make you a hot drink?"

She shakes her head "No thanks Chris. Yes please, a cup of tea." He makes tea for them both. "Do you want to take this up to bed?"

"What? No, I'll have it here." She wraps her fingers round her cup. "I'm at a cross-roads."

He isn't sure what was going on in her mind but he wants to steer her away from panic and sorrow and help her back into safe old routines.

"I've learned a lot about myself lately Chris and it's been painful."

"I know you're not happy but this isn't the moment for analysing. I'm not shutting you up but you're going to need all your courage to get through the next few days. Dwelling on things will undermine you. There'll be plenty of time to talk and I promise I'll listen. Right now I want you to go to bed."

As soon as she's finished her tea, she obeys him and pulls herself wearily up the stairs like an old woman

—

On Sunday night she seems to be finding excuses to potter around as late as possible.

226

Chris watches her "Don't you think you should go up now Vee? Tomorrow's going to be a hard day for you. Would you have preferred to go and see Alex off?"

"No. I couldn't bear that."

"Would you like me to stay home—give you moral support."

"No. Don't do any such thing!" she almost screams at him.

Resolutions

Cassie is reading an essay to her mother and Chloé while they prepare the picnic. Greg is listening carefully, trying to understand and Nan too is giving her full, admiring attention.

There's a sudden crash as the kitchen door is flung open.

Alex is standing there like a madman, eyes glittering with rage. He roars at Verina "You fucking bitch! You lying, selfish cow. What the hell are you playing at? I've been out of my mind with worry. I thought you'd walked under a bus or something."

The knife Verina is using falls from her hand to the floor. No-one moves to pick it up. She stares at him, mute with terror, her face grey, fear in every line of her body.

He can't keep still, he's pacing backwards and forwards "This is my life you're buggering about with. I trusted you. I adored you. I trusted you completely. I can't believe you've let me down." His shoulders droop and for a second, he sways as if he might fall. Then he straightens up again and bellows at her "You never had any intention of coming with me, did you? Now I see what you really are."

Her voice comes out in a croak "I couldn't leave the family."

"But you could leave me at the airport like a spare dick at a wedding and go on acting out your earth-mother bit here as though nothing else matters. Who the fuck do you think you are?! I suppose you timed it for your sniveling little message to get through just as we were being asked to board so that I'd have to get on the plane and out of your life and you could carry on as though nothing had happened. As if you hadn't completely destroyed me! Well your ploy didn't work. 'I'll follow you later' "he sneers at her, "what's that supposed to mean? When these kids are eighteen? Well don't fucking bother. I can't

228

get far enough away from you." He slams his fist on the table so hard that the sandwiches lift off into the air and land round the feet of the transfixed family.

Chris appears "What's going on? What are you doing here Alex?"

"I came to kill Verina but I don't think I'll bother. She's not worth it."

"Aren't you supposed to be on a plane?"

"Yes and so is she."

"What?"

Alex pulls an air-line ticket from his jacket and flings it at Verina. "I curse the day I found you. Can you see what you've done to me?" An ugly sound between a laugh and a howl comes out of his mouth and tears spurt from his eyes. "You've destroyed me. I worshipped you. And all the time there's nothing there. You're hollow. There's just this precious image you like to project. Nothing behind it." He appeals to the children "Why couldn't she have told me the truth? Your mother's full of lies and deceit." He collapses into a chair, drops his head in his arms and sobs.

No-one stirs. They all watch in horror. Chris puts his hand on Alex's shoulder and gives him a piece of kitchen roll. After a few minutes, Alex becomes calmer. He blows his nose and gets up, his eyes red and his face blotchy from weeping. A taxi can be heard ticking away outside.

Verina remains stricken and wordless.

He speaks quietly to her now "I never want to see you or hear from you again as long as I live. Stay right out of my life. I was wrong about you. Now I detest you and I hope you rot." He pushes past Chris and is gone.

Cassie says "Good riddance."

Nan and Greg have their arms around Verina who has dropped into a chair and sits frozen, staring in front of her.

The air-line ticket has fallen in the butter. Chloé picks it out, wipes it clean and puts it on the window-sill to dry.

Chris, helping Cassie pick up the knife and sandwiches from the floor, wonders how much the children have understood of the scene. How much has he understood himself?"

Chloé looks uncertain whether to stay or go. He catches her eye, indicates the children and she nods.

Cassie has salvaged what she can of the picnic, "You three go off. I'll ring you on your mobile Chloé. We'll join you later if we can."

As Chloé, Nan and Greg slip quietly away, Chris fetches brandy for the silent Verina. He and Cassie sit on either side of her not daring to touch her or speak to her.

There's a ring at the door-bell. Cassie goes to see who it is and hurries back

"It's the taxi-driver dad. He wants to know how long he's got to wait."

Chris goes out to him. "The young man you brought has left. Didn't you see him?"

"No, I aint seen 'im. The only one I seen coming out your 'ouse was a blonde lady wiv two kids."

Chris looks at the meter, "Hang on. I'll go and get some money." He pays the driver and looks up and down the street. No sign of Alex. He has a horrible thought and rushes back into the house. The downstairs cloakroom is empty. He throws himself up the stairs and looks in the children's bath-room. Nothing.

Surely he wouldn't go into our bathroom? When he tries the door, he finds it locked. "Alex. Alex are you in there?" No answer. He stands well back, takes a run at the door and kicks it in. "Oh Christ! Oh sainted Christ Alex! What have you done?" He runs to the landing and calls Cassie. "Ring for an ambulance. Now! Tell them it's an emergency. A man is unconscious and bleeding heavily. He's cut his wrists."

Travelling with him in the ambulance, Chris is afraid Alex has lost too much blood and will die. On the other hand, if he drank the contents of the two empty vodka bottles, that would make anyone pass out.

At the hospital, Alex is whisked up to theatre straight away. Chris tells the nurses he's Alex's step-father and they show him into a waiting room. He rings home and gets Cassie. "I've cleaned up the bathroom and put mum to bed. I hope it's all right but I rang Chloé and told her. She's keeping Nan and Greg for the night. How is Alex? How are you daddy? When are you coming home?"

"Can't answer any of those questions yet. I'll ring you when I'm coming home. Thank you darling for looking after mummy. See you soon I hope."

A nurse finally agrees to let Chris see Alex. "Only a few minutes mind, he's very distressed and in shock."
"Is he going to be all right?"
"Eventually. If he doesn't do anything like this again."
The small room looks like a torture-chamber. Alex is being given a blood transfusion, he's on a drip and he's wired-up to various monitors. Lying there, his face puffy and shiny, he looks like a schoolboy. *You poor young sod* Chris thinks.
Alex opens his eyes, "Have you come to finish me off Chris?"
"You've had a go at that yourself it seems."
"Don't tell Lilian and Phil."
"Not if you don't want me to. What about Faith?"
"Don't bother."
"You must be feeling rotten."
"My own stupid fault."
"Is there anything you need? Anything you'd like me to do?"
"No thanks Chris. They're looking after me as if it matters whether I'm alive or dead. I wish I had succeeded in finishing it." He closes his eyes.
"Nurse told me not to stay long. I'll come back tomorrow."
Alex seems to be asleep. Chris regards him from the foot of the bed. The words of Paul Valery come into his mind 'un home seul est dans la compagnie mauvaise'. The words might equally apply to himself.

—

Alex is out of bed, sitting in a chair reading the paper.
Faith walks in.
"What are you doing here? Come to gloat?"
"I wanted to see how you are."
"I suppose Chris told you I was here?"
"Yes."
"What did he tell you exactly?"
"Not much. He told me about this" she pointed to his wrists "he couldn't tell me why you did it. He said he didn't know. I'm

sorry you felt bad enough to do such a thing. I don't suppose it was anything to do with me? I hope it wasn't."

"Don't flatter yourself. I got drunk, that's all. The flight was delayed so I went on drinking and in my drunken stupor, I persuaded myself that life wasn't worth living. It was only the alcohol and the crappy people around me. I don't remember much about it, apparently I drank two bottles of Vodka, had some sort of collapse and woke up here with a king-sized hangover. End of story."

"Are you all right now?"

"What do you care?"

"I was worried that I might have contributed to your state of mind."

"You didn't seriously think that I might have tried to top myself over you? You don't even figure any more. I've blanked you out. I don't actually want you hanging around here now."

"All right. I'll go away. What will you do?"

"You know what I'm going to do, I'm going to get on the next flight I can."

"Are you well enough to go?"

He picks up his paper again and behaves as though she's not here.

"When they discharge you, would you like me to come with you . . ." she falters, "wherever you're going?"

"Why, have you changed your mind?"

"I only meant to your hotel or . . ."

"That's a shame, I thought you meant Singapore. I would have enjoyed telling you you're not wanted on the voyage."

"There's nothing I can do for you then?"

"Yes there is, you can fuck off Faith. Oh I like that, it's very satisfying. Fuck off Faith." He laughs spitefully at her and makes dismissive gestures with his bandaged hands. "Go on. Fuck off Faith."

She's tempted to say 'and fuck you too' only she can see through the bravado. Inside, he's shattered and she can't help him. "Goodbye Alex. Good luck."'

—

Alex makes a phone call: "Chris, hallo. I've discharged myself and I'm back at the hotel making my apologies and all

232

that. I didn't want you schlepping up there again tonight, you've done more than enough."

"Are you all right?"

"I'm fine. The thing is, they sent round this little rat-faced runt to talk to me about counselling and all that crap. I told him I was Plymouth Brethren and was out of there before they could stick me in a nut-house. I've been on to the air-line and they can get me on a flight late tonight, they think I've been in a car crash."

"Tonight? Isn't that a bit soon?"

"It's not soon enough for me, I can't wait to get right away."

"Did the hospital tell you it's okay to travel?"

"I've convinced them I'm urgently needed in Singapore. I'm all right now. One wrist will have a permanent bump and I've lost a bit of sensitivity in the finger-tips but that's all. You saved my life. Wish I could thank you. Got to go Chris. Goodbye.'"

In Departures, Chris has given up hope of finding Alex when he catches sight of him across on the other side of the bar, bending to pick up his bag. He turns round and sees Chris.

The two men approach each other.

"Is this 'High Noon' again Chris, got a gun?"

"Fortunately, no."

He looks past Chris "Are you by yourself?"

"Yes."

"I thought you might try and stop me boarding the plane."

"I'm here to make sure you get on it."

"Don't blame you. Actually, I'm just going through to the gates now."

"There's time for a drink, isn't there?"

"Er . . ." He looks at his watch, "I suppose there is. But would you mind getting them please? I'm still bandaged."

"Sure. Pint of lager?"

"Fine."

He comes back with the drinks and sits.

"I wasn't expecting you to come to the airport Chris, I thought I'd managed to escape."

"Why the fuck should you? I haven't escaped. Faith hasn't escaped. You and Vee between you, have buggered up both our marriages.

"I know, I know. Why didn't you stop us?"

233

"How do you stop a cataclysm?"

"I don't know what to say. If it's vengeance you want, you've got it. I'm as far down in this pit of hell as I can be."

They drink mechanically.

Alex starts again, "I can't pretend anything with you, you saw what happened, you were there. I couldn't explain to that shrink in the hospital but you know it all. This whole business has driven me crazy, turned me schizo. I really believed I could have Verina and when she left me standing there the other day, I just wanted to kill her and when I couldn't, I got in a frenzy. If I couldn't kill her, I was determined to kill myself. I was full of violent anger. I had to get rid of it somehow. By the time I woke up in hospital, the madness had gone—flowed out of me with my blood. It was like an exorcism. I'm beached now, calm. Washed-out and messed up big time. There's nothing I can do to put any of it right . . . I'm going."

Chris walks with him to the exit, "Goodbye Alex."

"Goodbye Chris. I don't understand you but I envy you your core of steel."

With his key in the front door, Chris is looking forward to his peaceful room, a drink and his bed but Verina is waiting for him in the hall.

"He's gone?"

"I saw him through departures."

"Did he say anything?"

"No."

She pulls her dressing-gown tight across her front and stands gazing round.

"Go to bed Vee. Take one of your tablets and try and get some sleep."

On the stairs, she pauses, "Chris."

"Yes?"

The hall light shows up silver threads in her hair, her face is haggard. "I can't sleep properly without you there beside me."

Her words hang in the air.

"All right. I'll just lock up."

Standing in his study, he downs a large brandy, switches off the lights and follows her up in the dark.

234

Lightning Source UK Ltd.
Milton Keynes UK
UKOW04f0208240615

254023UK00002B/106/P

9 781481 787246